The Dying Thief

The *Dying Thief*

CHOVWE INISIAGHO

Copyright © 2015 by CHOVWE INISIAGHO.

ISBN: Softcover   978-1-4990-9637-8
           eBook   978-1-4990-9636-1

All rights reserved. No part of this book may be reproduced or transmitted in any form or by any means, electronic or mechanical, including photocopying, recording, or by any information storage and retrieval system, without permission in writing from the copyright owner.

Any people depicted in stock imagery provided by Thinkstock are models, and such images are being used for illustrative purposes only.
Certain stock imagery © Thinkstock.

Print information available on the last page.

Rev. date: 06/16/2015

To order additional copies of this book, contact:
Xlibris
800-056-3182
www.Xlibrispublishing.co.uk
Orders@Xlibrispublishing.co.uk
517191

CONTENTS

Dedication.. vii

PART I
Love and Marriage... 1

The Dying Thief.. 9
Unbelievable Marriage 29
The Witness 63
A Basket of Fortune 86

PART II
Life 117

Cyber Lover 125
Raped! 161
Bitter Experience 188
The Escape 208

Author's Note..241
Index..243

DEDICATION

To my sweet mother, Rose Inisiagho

PART I

Love and Marriage

CHOVWE INISIAGHO

Marriage . . .

Marriage,
The union that consummates love
And legally binds two
Making them
One body,
One flesh.
Profession of love
Exchange of vows
Witnessed by many
Sealed with a ring.

Onome

Onome,
When I look into your eyes
I adore you.
Onome,
You are the flower
That beautifies life.
Onome,
You are the shining star
You are love personified.

A Lover's Dream

Like a seal upon my heart,
So the slash on my flesh.
Incision of love.
An indelible mark
That leads,
To rivulets of blood.
Flowing on its course
Mingled with tears.
Those drops of hope,
Invisible
But audible.
With a rhythm
Played by cupid alone.
Familiar sounds
Now an emblem.
For it is
The cut that never heals

Courtroom Love

She stepped into the room
In graceful strides.
Lustrous hair,
Luminous eyes,
And luscious lips.
Before the judge
Did she stand
In the dock
To make her plea.
When she did speak,
The legal counsel
Was mesmerised.
He stuttered and stammered
For lack of words.
His defence evaporated
In the heat of amour.
With heart captivated
By alien beauty.
'My lord,' he blurted
'I pray this case for another date'
Clear like crystal.
Physician not needed.
He had blind sight
Or love at first sight.
The gavel came down
Adjournment decreed.

Hold Me

Hold me in your hands,
And lead me
In the allies of love.
I know not the paths.
Hold me in your hands,
And teach me
In the classroom of love.
I know not the rules.
Hold me in your hands,
And feel me.
In the arteries of love.
I know not the flow.

Shadow of Love

In my mind
A picture not erasable
In my heart
A beat inexplicable
In my steps
A road invisible
In my dreams
Someone I cherish
In my eye
A tear not flowing
In my life
A shadow of love.

Euphoric Love

Let me sing your eulogy.
My love and my all.
For I bask in the euphoria
Of our union.
I breathe you,
I sing you,
I celebrate you,
I dream you.
Your love refreshes me
And quenches my thirst.
It gives,
Respite to my soul.

THE DYING THIEF

Tare flung herself on her bed without changing her clothes. She hadn't the patience for that. She desperately needed to rest. The students of Excellence Academy, where she taught health science and biology, just had their final exams. As one of the invigilators, it had been a busy day for her. Preparations started as early as 7 a.m. and lasted till late in the afternoon. Tare was forced to leave home an hour early in order to get to school on time.

Her home was quite a distance from her school. Now she was back home completely exhausted and worn out.

Tare hated teaching. She had only accepted the job as a last resort after years of unemployment. It was her father's idea. He said it was better to accept a teaching offer than idle away at home always. In spite of the fact that she was a graduate in business administration, getting a job was tough. The job-hunting experience was a harrowing one for her. She had had series of rejections, and in some cases, the managers wanted to lure her to bed before offering her a job. Tare could not understand why everything happening around her appeared to be negative. Sometimes she thought she was jinxed. At thirty-nine, she was yet to find a suitor. Her mother had always assured her that she would marry one day. But for her, it was a forlorn hope.

There was a gentle knock on the door. She was just not in the mood to see anyone, so she pretended not to have heard the knock. Then, the knock came a second time. She reluctantly enquired who it was.

'It's me Vero.'

'Oh, Vero, I hope you're all right?' she asked wearily.

'Some people are asking after you,' Vero replied.

Tare wasn't expecting anyone. She wondered who the 'people' must be.

'OK, tell them I'm coming,' she said as she got up lazily.

She adjusted her dress and ran her hand quickly through her hair and then went downstairs to meet her visitors.

'Good day,' she greeted them politely as she entered the living room.

She wasn't sure she recognised the two gentlemen who rose to give her a handshake. They were accompanied by a young woman, who smiled broadly at her.

'Tare, you don't seem to recognise me, do you?' one of them asked, smiling warmly at her.

'I am Emmanuel. Do you remember rushing a wounded boy to the hospital some years back? You were a secondary school pupil then,' Emmanuel explained.

Tare was silent for a while. She tried to remember the incident, but couldn't. Then all of a sudden, the picture flashed through her mind. She screamed in surprise.

'Ah! Yes, I remember. That was a long time ago. You have changed! Where have you been all these years?'

Without waiting for a reply, she called out to Vero to get some drinks for them. Then she gestured to them to sit down. She slumped on a single sofa next to the young woman.

'I have been in Sweden,' Emmanuel replied animatedly. 'Meet my sister, Stella, and her fiancé, Victor,' he continued as he pointed at the young lady and then to the other young man.

'Welcome, Stella and Victor,' Tare greeted with a smile.

Vero came in with the drinks and served the guests. Emmanuel requested for a glass of cold water, while Victor and Stella took a bottle of bitter lemon each. They drank silently for a while, and then Tare suddenly broke the silence.

'So what took you to Sweden?' she asked Emmanuel with keen interest.

'Studies. I went to a medical school,' Emmanuel replied as he gulped down what was left of his cold water.

'Quite interesting, Emmanuel. You mean you are now a qualified medical doctor?' Tare asked, enthralled.

Emmanuel smiled broadly. He heaved a sigh and then began to narrate the story of his life in Sweden and what he had achieved after the medical college.

'All is now set to formally open my hospital,' he continued confidently. 'Actually, it isn't a business venture. It will offer free services to the poor and needy. I will continue to get support from big charity organisations in Europe and America for as long as the hospital functions,' he concluded.

'Are you kidding me?' Tare asked in admiration. She shifted on her sofa. Her face lit up with excitement.

Who would have thought that this chap would make it in life? What a world we are living in! she thought to herself.

The humanitarian aspect of the hospital project gave her joy because she had always had the passion to help the poor and the needy.

'Health inspectors will be coming tomorrow to assess the standard of the hospital. I would love you to be there,' Emmanuel requested as he rose up to leave. 'My would-be in-law will pick you up if you accept my invitation.'

'Sure! I would love to be there. Just let me know when he will arrive,' Tare replied.

'Twelve noon will be fine,' he said as they walked towards his car.

Tare watched them drive off before retiring to the house.

Her mind was occupied with what she had just seen and heard. She just couldn't believe it. Emmanuel was the last person she expected to see again, let alone receiving him as a medical doctor. It was a pleasant surprise. Concentrating on anything became a task for her. She forgot about dinner. Her thoughts ran riot.

Is this some kind of a dream? A joke or just my imagination? Did Emmanuel just visit me? The injured, bleeding poor boy? she thought aloud.

Her mind flashed back to the day she met Emmanuel.

Yes! I remember vividly. It was on a hot afternoon. Yes! It was on my way back from school. I was in the company of my two intimate friends. I remember that day. Yes, I remember. Oh! That face! I remember the face. I remember the agony in his eyes, the fear in his voice as he pleaded for help. Yes! I remember that day. He was helpless. The picture is clearer now. Oh, Emmanuel! Thank God I helped him. I am happy I took the risk, Tare kept thinking aloud.

She still couldn't believe she had just seen Emmanuel.

The event of that afternoon kept replaying in her mind. Tare and her friends saw a young man by the roadside, groaning and begging for help. He had wounds and bruises all over his body and was bleeding from his left knee. He had a broken limb. People just walked past him. Some stood watching him from a distance. Tare was the first to see him. She went closer to him and tried to touch him.

'Are you out of your mind?' Ifeoma, the oldest of the three of them, queried.

'Don't you see he is injured and in pain?'

'Yes, but you do not know what happened to him?'

'That is the more reason why he should be helped,' Tare replied.

Her friends watched her as she bent over to touch the injured man.

'He is a thief,' came a rather croaky voice from the crowd that had begun to gather. Tare turned to look at the person who spoke. It was a stocky man, wearing a pair of worn-out trousers and an old blue shirt.

Tare stood upright. She fixed her gaze on him and very calmly told him, 'He is a thief, but I will help him.'

Tare was a firm person. When she set her mind on anything, it was difficult for anyone to discourage her. She was known for challenging anybody, including her teachers, if the occasion arose. Once, she got suspended from school because she did not allow her mathematics teacher to punish her for coming late to school. She insisted she did not come late out of her own fault but that the taxi she booked had a minor accident on the way.

Her friends, Ifeoma and Felicia, had advised her to leave the injured man alone. Tare refused. She began waving down taxicabs, but many drivers ignored her. She looked around her. People were watching her. Her classmates had begun to leave. She was almost ashamed of herself, but she wasn't deterred. She racked her brain, trying to think what she could do to save the situation. Then it occurred to her that she could offer a higher taxi fare. The trick worked. She had wealthy parents and always came to school with enough money. She hardly ever exhausted all her pocket money during break times in the school.

'Holy Cross Hospital. Two hundred naira,' she offered.

It wasn't long before she saw a cab pull up in front of her. She pleaded with the driver to help her carry the injured man into the taxi. He flinched as he was lifted. Tare had managed to tie up his bleeding limb with his own shirt. The taxi drove off, meandering through the traffic jam. Tare sat next to the taxi driver but kept an eye on the injured man. When they got to the hospital, she quickly went to the emergency department to inform the nurses of a patient in a critical condition. A stretcher was brought to take him in immediately.

Tare and the taxi driver followed behind them until the wounded man was taken into the emergency unit.

'He does not look like an accident victim to me,' the doctor said to Tare after a close examination of his wounds.

'Doctor, please treat him. I will pay the bills. He is dying,' Tare pleaded helplessly.

'OK. I will treat him,' the doctor said after pondering for a while.

'I am grateful, Doctor. Thank you,' Tare said as she heaved a sigh of relief.

'He has a broken limb and has lost much blood. He would have died if he wasn't brought here on time,' the doctor explained further. 'I will commence initial treatment now. But you would have to make some payments first. Go to the reception desk and enquire where you can make payment,' he concluded.

Tare was not happy. She wondered why doctors would place money above saving lives. She went to the reception desk from where she was directed to the accounts department; she was oblivious of the fact that the taxi driver was still following her.

'You have to make a deposit of 3,000 naira,' the accounts clerk said emphatically.

'OK, let me go home to get the money.'

'What is the guarantee that you will come back?' the accounts clerk queried.

'Give her your school bag,' a voice from behind Tare echoed.

Tare turned. It was the taxi driver. Then it occurred to her that she had kept the man waiting but was also pleased with his patience. She did as he suggested. She also wrote down her name and school address on a paper the accounts clerk gave her. Then she left. Outside, she paid the driver and pleaded with him to drop her at home for a 100 naira extra. He agreed to do so. Tare went home feeling more confused than ever.

The taxi driver drove off. Tare watched as he sped off, leaving a whirl of dust behind, and houses and trees went past them. As soon as the cab pulled to a stop in front of her home, she alighted and made for the gate. She looked at her watch. It was 3 p.m. Several thoughts ran through her mind. She was still at a loss as to how she would get the deposit for the injured young man she had just left at the hospital. She wondered if her mother would be willing to help. She couldn't answer that question, but she decided to give it a try. She gently opened the gate and walked towards the kitchen where she was sure to meet her mother. She passed by the security guard without saying a word because her mind was occupied with the thoughts of the injured man in the hospital. She didn't even notice the guard standing by as she walked past him absent-mindedly.

She met her mum in the kitchen in the company of her employees. She wondered what they were doing with her mother in the kitchen at that time. It was unusual.

'Mother, can I please speak with you?' she asked almost impatiently.

'My daughter, we can talk here,' her mother replied as she requested the two employees to excuse them.

'Tare, your friends were here. Your father and I know what happened,' her mother said with a frown.

'They were here?' Tare was perplexed.

'Tare, why would you help a thief?'

'Mother, he is a human being!' Tare said defensively.

'You are endangering yourself. He will come out and become a problem to the society. In fact, he deserved to die where you found him.'

'Mother, was that a good-enough reason for a mob to beat him instead of calling the police?' Tare queried.

'Yes, you would always argue instead of listening.'

'Mother, please do not say so. Let's help him, please. I know nothing about him, just like you do not. It's compassion.'

'How could you allow your emotion to becloud your sense of reasoning?'

'OK, Mum. I will not do it again, but please, I need 3,000 naira to pay the deposit. If not, the treatment wouldn't commence.'

'You can never have that,' retorted her mother.

Mrs Riega was furious. Tare was dejected. Her school bag and school name were mortgaged at the hospital. She went up to her room. Her mum was her last hope. She thought of going back to the hospital to tell them she could not get the deposit.

There was sudden lightning, and it began to rain. Tare watched as raindrops rolled down the window of her room. She could see Musa, the night guard, and Ebi, the gardener, playing chess in the security post. She thought about borrowing the money from them. She sprang to her feet and went to them without a second thought. She was desperate; she needed the money anyhow now. She greeted them warmly but unsure of herself. Then she made her request.

'Young girl, why don't you meet your parents?' Musa asked.

'Musa, I will return it. Trust me. It's urgent, and I wouldn't want to go into the details now.'

'Well, Tare, I wouldn't be able to help. I will get into trouble if I did.'

'Ebi, please, could you help?' Tare pleaded.

'How much is it?'

'Three thousand naira.'

'Well, I can afford only two,' he said after a while.

Tare's face shone. That wasn't the amount she needed, but it was better than nothing.

'Thank you, Ebi,' Tare replied with relief.

'It's OK. Wait here while I go get the money.'

Ebi lived in the staff quarters provided by Chief Riega for his domestic workers. The apartments were directly behind Chief Riega's house.

Tare sat down in one of the chairs and waited patiently for him. Her eyes followed him until he disappeared around a corner. He appeared about ten minutes later and handed her the money.

'Thank you, Ebi. I promise to pay it back soon,' Tare said with gratitude and rushed back to her room.

How do I get the remaining 1,000 naira? she thought to herself.

She looked at the time; it was too late to go to Holy Cross Hospital. She decided to return the following day on her way to school.

Tare got to the hospital and went straight to the accounts clerk's desk and gave her the money. But she frowned and questioned her as to why she did not bring the complete amount.

'Please, this is all I have at the moment. I will run around for the rest,' she pleaded.

'Young girl, this is a hospital and not a charity home. What happens if you don't show up again?' she asked suspiciously.

'You can still keep my school ID,' Tare said, trying to assure her.

The accounts clerk looked intently at her before responding.

'Then you may go,' the accounts clerk said as she handed her the school bag.

Tare left the hospital for school. She arrived just as the assembly bell tolled.

She joined the other pupils, walking past Felicia and Ifeoma, who stared at her as if she was a stranger. During break time, both girls came to meet her.

'Why did you girls tell my parents about what happened?' Tare demanded in anger.

'Tare, you did the wrong thing. You were told he was a thief!'

'Who appointed you as the judges? I followed my instincts. And could you both please leave me alone? I really want to be alone,' she snapped.

Felicia and Ifeoma exchanged glances. They had never seen her so angry. They quietly left without uttering another word.

Tare was more preoccupied with how to raise the money for the hospital bill than worry about how her friends felt. She couldn't concentrate the whole day at school because her mind was troubled. She walked home alone along the lonely road that passed through the farm behind her school. She wanted to avoid talking to her friends who criticised her actions so much.

More troubles waited for Tare at home. She met her angry father, who lashed out at her, like never before, in the living room.

'You will not go to England for holidays any more as planned. You seem to have grown wings,' he chided.

'But I was only helping someone in need. Dad, please don't take such a decision,' she pleaded.

Mr Riega ignored his daughter's plea. He stormed out of the living room, leaving Tare speechless. He left the house almost immediately in his car. Tare watched him zoom off but was resilient. She wondered if their housemaid could lend her the remaining balance. She ate her lunch quickly and hurried to Nancy, the housemaid. Nancy's room was next to Ebi's room. She knocked softly on the door and waited to be allowed in. Nancy lifted the curtain from her window to see who it was.

'Oh! It's you, Tare,' Nancy said, opening the door at the same time.

Tare entered the room, looking gloomy. Nancy could tell all was not well, so she enquired what the matter was. Tare told Nancy all about the young man she helped to get to the hospital. Nancy shook her head and stood up.

'I will lend you the money. My boss shouldn't have refused to give you the money. But, Tare, with something like this happening, why could you not tell me?'

Tare looked down. She tried to dig with her big left toe into the floor.

'I was all confused, and it did not occur to me, Nancy.'

She was very friendly with Nancy, and both ladies often exchanged pleasantries. Nancy reached for her small suitcase behind the door and brought out a small plastic bag in which she had wrapped in some money. She counted 1,000 naira and handed them to Tare. Tare took the money excitedly and hugged Nancy.

'I'm so very grateful, Nancy.'

'It is God we should thank for the young man's life,' Nancy insisted.

Tare dashed out of Nancy's room and ran as fast as her limbs could carry her. She boarded a taxicab which took her to the hospital. Tare made straight to the accounts clerk to pay the balance.

She looked at Tare and then at the money. Tare ignored her.

After paying the balance, she went to see Emmanuel. He was sleeping when she arrived. His broken limb was wrapped in bandage. The sound of the creaking door woke him up.

'Sorry, I woke you up. How're you feeling?'

'Much better, but the doctor said I have to stay for some time.'

He introduced himself to Tare and narrated what led to the ugly incident.

'I had gone with my friends to steal bread from a shop because I wanted to get something for myself and my siblings to eat. We had nothing at home. Not even a grain of rice,' he explained shyly, feeling embarrassed.

He requested that Tare locate his family and tell them what happened. She accepted.

'Emmanuel, I am sorry about what happened. I understand the situation. I will leave now. I need enough time to locate your family so I can go back home early too. I am going to be a bit late, but I know what to say when I get home.' She left.

Emmanuel was full of gratitude.

Tare was able to locate Emmanuel's house. It was in a very poor neighbourhood, full of one-room apartments and houses made of wood. Dirt was littered here and there. The stench that emanated from the surrounding gutters was unbearable.

The only good buildings seen around there were those of the colonial times. Half-naked children played freely outside. Some women had their small stalls across the gutters. It was a disgusting sight for Tare. Emmanuel's house was a bit hidden, but following his description, Tare was able to locate it. The house was an old bungalow with each family having a room located opposite one another. On the corridor, which led from the entrance to the back of the house, were kerosene stoves and different items belonging to different families. A woman was cooking when Tare entered. The stove, on which she was cooking, had soot. She coughed and fanned the flames from the stove and, at the same time, tried to shield her eyes from the smoke. Tare walked towards her and greeted courteously. She asked the woman about Emmanuel's family.

'There,' the woman said, pointing.

'Thank you, madam.'

Tare knocked on the door. Without asking who it was, a lady opened.

'Good day, Ma!'

'Good day, my daughter.'

'Emmanuel sent me here.'

'Emmanuel?' she asked in surprise. 'Please come in, come in. We have been looking for him.'

Tare followed the lady. Every object in the room whispered poverty.

There was an old bed by the right corner of the room, a wooden cupboard beside the bed, two old spring chairs, and a table in the centre of the room. Three wooden boxes were stacked behind the door. Clothes, books, shoes, sandals, and other items protruded from under the bed. A torn curtain hung from the window. It was obvious that it had not been washed for a very long time. Flies buzzed in and out through the window. Two small children were sitting on the floor eating garri and some white watery soup. Emmanuel had told Tare that they were six. She wondered how all six children and two adults could live in such a small room. She could now understand Emmanuel's condition even more. He had to steal to keep life going here. *How long had he been stealing?* Tare wondered.

'Welcome, my child, please sit down,' she said, pointing to a chair.

Tare sat down, trying hard to suppress her discomfort as the chair sank in the middle.

The lady explained that she was Emmanuel's mother and that her husband and two of Emmanuel's siblings had gone to some of their relatives' homes to plan how to continue the search for him. Tare narrated Emmanuel's ordeals. The woman was stunned. She thanked Tare for her kindness. Tears rolled down her cheeks. They were tears of bitterness and gratitude at the same time. Tare felt the woman's pain. She wished she could do more. She rushed out a few minutes later and hurried home. She walked as fast as she could so as to beat time. She didn't want her father to lose his temper again on the same account.

That year Mr Riega kept his word. Tare did not travel to England, but her two siblings did. In spite of her mother's effort to change her father's mind, he still stood his ground. Tare was greatly disappointed, but then, she was able to engage in some other activities throughout the holiday.

Staying back wasn't a bad idea after all, she concluded.

Victor came at exactly twelve noon as agreed.

'You are right on time, Victor.'

'Yes. I am glad you are ready,' Victor said.

'How is Stella?' Tare asked, somewhat excited.

'She is with her brother. Can we go now?'

'Yes! Of course, we could. I'm set.'

They climbed into the car, and Victor sped off. They headed towards the hospital.

'So what have you been doing with yourself today?' Victor asked.

'I have been indoors. I have been reading a novel.'

'Hmmm, that's good.'

There was silence until Victor spoke again. 'We would soon be there,' he told her.

'No problem, Victor.'

Victor negotiated a bend and drove into a compound. The compound had two imposing buildings, one much bigger than the other. Both buildings were of contemporary designs. Without being told, Tare knew they were in the hospital.

'So here we are,' Victor announced.

Victor led the way as they got out of the car. Stella was already at the door, waiting anxiously to welcome Tare.

'Good to see you again,' she said giving Tare a big wide smile.

Victor and Stella took Tare to Emmanuel. He was seated comfortably in a plush room. On the walls hung some pictures he had taken during his time in Sweden and some award plaques.

Emmanuel rose to greet Tare as soon as she stepped into the room, while Victor and Stella left them for the reception to wait for the inspectors.

'I am glad you made it. You are part of this dream.'

'Thank you, Emmanuel, but what do you mean?'

'You may not understand. Please sit down.'

Tare sat down on the sofa. Emmanuel sat beside her.

'So what can I offer you? The inspectors will be here in half an hour.'

Emmanuel wanted to say everything at once. He beamed with a lot of excitement.

'I don't really need anything now. Perhaps later.'

'That's OK.'

'This project must have cost you a fortune,' Tare remarked, looking round the office impressively.

'All the money didn't come from my own pocket. I got some grants from some international organisations. Victor is an architect from Ambrose Ali University, Ekpoma. He designed the whole building without taking a penny. I persuaded him to take at least half, but he refused. He asked me if Stella and their children could avail medical care in my hospital when they start having children.'

'He is right!'

Just at that moment, Victor called out to Emmanuel that the inspectors had arrived.

He left immediately for the hall to meet them, asking Tare to follow him.

Emmanuel showed the two gentlemen around the hospital. They did a thorough inspection which lasted for about an hour. They were satisfied with what they saw. It could be seen on their facial expressions.

When the inspectors left, Emmanuel decided they'd all go for lunch at one of the new restaurants in town. The idea was welcomed.

Stella suggested they all go to Sizzlers. She explained that they offered excellent range of menus. She spoke so convincingly about the restaurant that one would think she was its public relations officer.

At Sizzlers, they all made their choices from the menu and settled down to eat. Everyone appeared to be hungry, so they ate silently for the better part.

Victor and Stella left after the meal because they had to catch up with an appointment.

Their departure gave Emmanuel and Tare ample time to discuss. He wanted to tell Tare how life had been since they last met. He started from when he was discharged from the hospital. They had to borrow to make up the deposit Tare had paid.

'My mother had borrowed 500 naira from different neighbours, while my father offered to work for the hospital without pay for two months. Shortly after I was discharged, my father sent me to Lagos to work as an apprentice for an uncle of my father's friend who lived there,' Emmanuel said with a pain-laden voice as the bitter memories flashed back to his mind.

There was a heavy silence.

'My sister Stella went to work as a househelp in a Catholic convent. That event really changed our family for good though the beginning was difficult,' Emmanuel continued.

'My other siblings stayed with my parents but could not go to school because there was no money. There were three other young men of my age already living with Mr Nwachukwu when I arrived in Lagos. He had three big shops with warehouses in Lagos where he sold electrical appliances. He travelled to China and Taiwan to get his goods. Mr Nwachukwu was wealthy. His house was a mansion. He had a big garage where he had his fleet of cars parked. Behind his mansion was a bungalow, housing his workers. They all had their own rooms except the apprentices who shared a single room,' Emmanuel explained.

There was another silence.

Emmanuel came from the same tribe as Mr Nwachukwu, where there is an unwritten tradition of allowing young men to serve a master. The master must be in a particular trade to enable the young man to learn the art of the trade from him for a number of years. After the period of service, the master usually gives certain amount of money to the servant as a reward. This will enable the servant start a trade of his own in the line of his master.

'So what happened next?' Tare asked.

'About two years into the apprenticeship, I made friends with some young Christian boys who came to preach in our shop. They introduced me into the art of reading and browsing the Internet. I found it interesting and devoted some evenings and leisure time to browsing the Internet. I learnt fast and did not need to wait for my friends before going to the cyber cafe. Browsing the Internet was like being ushered into a new world. My Christian friends told me that I could learn from home and take exams. They got me some of the books they had used and encouraged me to register for the Ordinary Level General Certificate of Education exams a year and a half later. I did, and to God be the glory, I passed. I started yearning for a university education. One day, I stumbled on to information about studying in Sweden while browsing. I applied, and surprisingly, I was admitted. So were two of my friends. A Christian organisation offered the three of us scholarships. That was it! Mr Nwachukwu was a kind and understanding man. He rejoiced with me and gave me some financial support as compensation for the number of years I had served him. So this is my story, Tare,' he concluded.

'Wow! I am impressed. This is great, Emmanuel. See how fortune suddenly smiled on you! I am happy for you.'

'Thank you, Tare. But am a bit curious, why are you not married yet?' Emmanuel asked, changing the topic.

'Well, Emmanuel, this is something I don't like talking about, but I have gone through three heartbreaks. First, I dated a boy from my third year in the secondary school till my first year in the university. We were together for seven years. He died in a car accident. It took me some years to get over the shock of losing him. Then during my National Youth Service year, I met a young man who grew up in London but only came home for the law school. He wanted to experience the system. We dated for two years. We planned to get married, but I opted out of the relationship because he did not want to leave his Eckankar religion. A year later, I met a man who was from my ethnic group. We hit it off immediately. He was the principal of one of the government secondary schools. We courted for six months, planned our wedding, and did introduction, only to find out that he was already married. Thereafter, I became weary of relationships.'

'You really have passed through a lot. You will find your man one day.'

'Thank you, Emmanuel, so are you married?'

'Actually, I'm considering a lady, and my mother has been reminding me of the need to settle down.'

'Well, Emmanuel, I'd like to go home now. It's almost 7 p.m. I really enjoyed spending some time with you,' Tare said as she stood up.

She adjusted her dress and heaved a sigh.

'So soon? Anyway, before I forget, I'd be having the formal opening of the hospital in about three weeks from now. It is also going to be an award night. I'd like you to be there,' Emmanuel requested.

'Oh, Emmanuel, I'm so sorry, but I already planned to travel to Abuja to spend time with a friend of mine who just had a baby.'

'That's OK. You could travel to see your friend and then come back on the eve of the occasion. How about that? My Swedish friends would be in the country, and there would be seminars on some topics that you would like.'

'Let me see how it goes, but I can't promise you anything right now,' Tare said, yawning.

'It would be an honour for me to see you there. Please don't fail me,' Emmanuel told her.

Emmanuel drove Tare home. On their way, she told Emmanuel how she had missed her holiday because she helped him and how long it had taken to pay the money she took from her father's workers.

'Oh, Tare, if not for that singular act of kindness, I do not know what would have become of me. After that incident, a lot of good things happened to us. You know, one of the reverend sisters that

Stella served eventually sent her to a nursing school,' Emmanuel told Tare.

They arrived at Tare's house after a short drive. He dropped her off and bid her goodbye.

The next day, Stella paid Tare an unscheduled visit. She urged her to attend the opening ceremony and that it would be fun for them to be together again. Tare made a promise that she would be there. Stella left after a while.

'Regards to Victor and your brother,' she told her as she drove off.

Tare thought it would be a wise thing to support Emmanuel and his family once more. She wanted to witness the honourable celebration of the achievement of a man who once was seen as a dying thief. So she decided to travel to Abuja earlier than scheduled. She informed her friend about the change. Ifeoma couldn't see anything wrong. For her, it made no difference if she came earlier or later.

Tare called Stella to confirm that she was coming, and Stella was relieved that she could make it. Stella encouraged Tare to invite her parents which she promised to do as well.

The opening ceremony took place as planned. Tare and her parents were there. Tare had told them all about Emmanuel. They were surprised to know that he had become a medical doctor. The hospital hall had about fifty guests. Victor was the master of ceremony. Stella and her siblings and some other relatives were the ushers. The representative of the ministry of health gave a short speech followed by a cultural display and light refreshment. Emmanuel mounted the podium again. He announced to the guests he wanted to give awards to a few people. He called two of his friends who had taught him and encouraged him to further his education. He thanked them and gave each of them a plaque.

'The last award goes to Tare Riega, the woman who saved my life and made me what I am today.'

Tare looked around. Stella walked up to her and led her to the podium where she was to receive her award from Emmanuel. But before handing her the award, he begged to tell the guests a few more things.

'Ladies and gentlemen, this lady saved my life. When I was dying, she stood against all odds to save me, and today, I am giving her the greatest award that can be bestowed on a woman.'

He turned to Tare.

'Tare, will you marry me?' he asked.

Tare was stunned; she did not expect a marriage proposal. She looked at the guests and then at Stella who was now smiling. She covered her face with her hands. She was too shocked and shy to look at anyone. Emmanuel moved closer to her and embraced her. The guests gave them a standing ovation.

It then dawned on Tare that Stella's insistence that she attends the opening ceremony was a ploy to carry out the marriage proposal.

Tare and Emmanuel married a month later. Mrs Riega told her daughter the help she gave Emmanuel was like an investment for her future. Her father was short of words. Emmanuel told Tare that he had been monitoring her even while he was in Sweden. He got feedback from Stella and that he had secretly prayed that she should remain single until he was ready for marriage.

'Today, that prayer has been answered,' he said as he planted a kiss on her lips.

UNBELIEVABLE MARRIAGE

Lukas Koenig felt at home in Nigeria. He had worked there for twenty years. Throughout those years, he made a lot of friends and had a lot of Nigerian contacts. He planned his retirement and return to Germany that year. At fifty-two, Lukas was still a bachelor. His colleagues at his office organised a farewell party in his honour. On that day, he announced to his colleagues that he wished to get married to Edore. She was one of the Nigerian girls who worked in his office.

Edore herself and her other colleagues were surprised. Edore and Lukas were close friends, and she had no idea that Lukas loved her. In fact, he had never revealed his feelings for her. Edore had visited Lukas after the gathering, still in her usual manner. Lukas confessed to her that he had secretly loved her but had been waiting for the right time to reveal it to her. Edore, though still surprised, hugged him. Lukas told her he wanted them to get married as soon as possible. Edore told him it was common in Nigeria to have the customary marriage alongside church, Islamic, or court marriages. Lukas was interested.

'You have to find time to teach me all about the traditional marriage thing,' he pleaded with Edore.

Edore took a break from her job shortly. She explained all she knew about the traditional marriage to Lukas. He had no problem with the Nigerian culture. He wanted Edore to teach him every evening about each stage of the traditional marriage. Edore laughed. She told Lukas there was no written stage of the traditional marriage that must be adhered to, but it would be best to explain to him as much as possible all that would be involved.

Edore took Lukas to her family not before long. They were glad Edore would be marrying a German. Edore's uncle called her aside and asked her if she could really cope with the differences in their cultures. It was then that Edore told him Lukas could eat garri and cope well with her culture. Her uncle was amazed. The traditional marriage was fixed for the following year.

Lukas and Edore donned the traditional Urhobo attire. Edore looked gorgeous in her head gear and two-piece cloth. Lukas didn't look so good in his hat and cloth. He held a walking staff to complement his dressing. The ceremony was well attended by some Germans who lived in Nigeria and many of their colleagues from their office. Lukas met all the requirements of the traditional marriage. He was accompanied by his three intimate Nigerian friends. None of his family members was present at the ceremony. He was an only child, and his parents were long dead.

Lukas presented kola nuts, bottles of hard drink, three bags of salt, a bag of rice, a bag of black-eyed beans, two gallons of red palm oil, and twenty-four yards of Nigerian wax. The bride price was a token of 20 naira. Lukas smiled during each step of the ceremony. The first step involved the presentation of a fake bride to the bridegroom. Edore's elder sister, Najite, was presented to Lukas. He told them she wasn't his bride as he had been tutored earlier by Edore. He gave her some amount of money, and she left with her entourage. Again Edore's younger sister, Eruona, was presented to Lukas. Lukas said the same thing and gave her money, and she left with her entourage. Finally, Edore was escorted to the stage by her entourage amidst encomiums.

As soon as he saw her, Lukas announced with pride, 'That's the bride for the bridegroom.'

The announcement was followed by jubilation and ovation. Drums echoed. Relatives and friends stormed the stage, dancing; women threw their cloths on the ground. Lukas enjoyed every moment of the ceremony; he smiled throughout. The guests ate and drank to the occasion. There was great festivity throughout the ceremony. The church wedding was held the next Saturday. Lukas had very little time. He wouldn't want to leave the village without Edore.

Lukas was to board a ship back to Germany. His friends and Edore's family found it a bit unusual. He explained that he had lots of goods to carry. They were things for the private museum he planned to open in Germany. He bought five wooden canoes, locally made cooking tripod stands, a model of bamboo hut, seedlings, budding palm nuts, cocoa, and many other things. Lukas loved nature. He enjoyed every bit of his time in Nigeria, Africa, but he thought he could go back to his homeland and set up a business or something that would keep him busy in Germany. Edore was worried he had too many things to carry.

'Don't worry, darling. We'd be fine,' he consoled her.

The next day, he was driven in the company of Edore, her parents, and a few relatives to the Apapa Port in Lagos. He had arranged with his friend Johannes Mueller, who was a sea captain, to ship his belongings back to Germany. Johannes Mueller accompanied Lukas and Edore to Europe. Lukas wanted to experience how it felt to travel to Europe by sea. He had never done it before, but he liked the adventure, a voyage to Europe. Johannes told him that it would take about three weeks to arrive in Germany. Lukas and Edore boarded the ship and bid everyone goodbye. Edore, like Lukas, had never travelled by ship.

When they got inside the ship, Edore was surprised to see that the interior was built like a house.

Everything you find inside a house is here, she thought, surprised.

They were ushered in through a white padded door into a long corridor. They passed through several doors, turned right, and took a staircase up to the first floor of the ship. The corridor was covered with a red carpet. The corridor opened to a shining large parlour with a bright red carpet. Five sofas were arranged at the centre of the parlour, several stools lined the wall, and a bar that completely occupied the left corner of the parlour. Reggae blasted from the sound system, and the room vibrated with every beat of the bass. Edore felt her heart shaking too. Accessory bulbs on the white ceiling were shining. It reminded Edore of the picture she saw of Queen Elizabeth's ballroom. Edore wondered if she was still inside the ship and if she was still floating on top of the water. She moved towards a small glass window and took a look of the sea.

'Lukas, it's beautiful, isn't it?'

Lukas was glad she liked it. 'It sure is,' he said, smiling.

Just then Johannes offered to show them their cabin. Johannes took them down the corridor and opened the cabin numbered '6'.

'Have a good rest,' he said.

Without answering, Lukas went inside and Edore followed.

'Dinner is 8 p.m., and I will come for you,' Johannes explained as if it was a duty.

'See you then, buddy,' Lukas replied.

The room was quite small but could carry two. It was dark, and Edore wondered if none of those beautiful bulbs was fitted here. Lukas stared at something on the wall, pressed it, and the room was alight with tiny yellowish bulbs. There was a bed on the right corner of the room, and on the left was a door with inscription 'Shower/Toilet'. Edore undressed and had a shower and went to rest on the bed while Lukas took his. When she woke up, it was 7.30 p.m.; she had slept for two hours. Lukas was awake and reading a German newspaper. There was a knock on their door. Lukas opened, and it was Johannes.

THE DYING THIEF

'I thought we could walk around before dinner,' he said.

Lukas and Edore loved the idea. Johannes took them around the ship and introduced them to other crew members. The senior captain was from Ukraine. There were six sailors with him. They were all friendly. Johannes later went with them to the deck where they had a better view of the sea. Edore looked at the fast moving water current. It reminded her of her history classes. She had read about Mungo Park and the slave trade. She wondered if the sea she was seeing is the same sea on which Mungo Park had sailed, and if there could be bones of dead slaves deep in the seabed beneath them now. Edore shuddered and shivered at the thought. She quickly looked away, her throat thickened. Lukas walked up to her. He had noticed her discomfort.

'Are you all right, darling?' he enquired.

'I'm just thinking, Lukas. The sea reminded me of the slave trade era. Thank God, it's now history.'

Lukas put a hand on her shoulder and pulled her closer, and they both went to meet Johannes where he sat on the deck.

'We're not yet on the high sea,' Johannes explained to them.

Johannes was an experienced seaman. He had gone on voyages to almost every continent. He had so much to tell virtually about every country. He told Lukas and Edore how he saw blacks for the first time in the Indonesian Island of Irian Jaya. Edore had thought all blacks were found in Africa alone. Her mind went back again to history. She thought to herself that it was the slave trade that could have sent blacks there and other places. But then she loathed when Africans were addressed as blacks and scorned the Europeans who came to buy slaves from Africa. She wondered how people could be so callous. She remembered the story of Olaudah Equiano, who was sold into slavery by his own kinsmen. Her history teacher, Mr Nduka, had told them that Africans themselves could be blamed for the slave trade menace because they sold their own brothers to the Europeans in exchange for petty articles like mirrors.

They are foolish, Edore thought, closing her eyes.

'Are you all right?' Johannes asked her once again.

'Yes.'

She became very emotional whenever she thought about the slave trade issues. Lukas rubbed her shoulders. Johannes further told them about how the blacks of Irian Jaya fought for independence. Lukas added that Irian Jaya shared border with Papua New Guinea and that both of them formed the New Guinean Island.

'You know about it too?' Edore asked Lukas.

'Just that bit.'

The cook came before Lukas could explain further and told them dinner was ready. Johannes led the way, and Lukas took Edore's hand. He walked her to the small kitchen located at the base of the ship. There was enough space in the basement for the dining tables and chairs. Lukas pulled out a chair for Edore, and she sat. The other sailors were already seated. They were waiting for Johannes and his friends to join them. The food was steaming hot. Rodriguez had made pork cutlet served with potato dumplings and brown sauce. There was also salad with sliced tomatoes and yoghurt dressing. Johannes relished the food.

'Ich habe schon hunger,' he said in German.

They all laughed except Edore. Lukas whispered to her that Johannes only said he was already hungry.

Johannes quickly realised he had made a mistake when he saw Lukas whisper to Edore.

'Sorry, Edore, I forgot you don't speak German.'

Lukas served Edore himself. Edore prayed over her meal and began eating. Lukas quickly made the sign of the cross. He knew his wife could be very religious, so he wanted to show her some solidarity and erase his own guilt.

'I think people in Africa and Latin America are much more religious than people in Europe these days,' Lukas joked.

'Yes,' Johannes consented.

'My grandmother always reminded us to pray before meals when we were in Brazil,' Rodriguez added.

'You lived in Brazil?' Lukas asked.

'Yes.'

'How did you get there?' Lukas asked, stuffing his mouth with the salad.

'My grandparents migrated to Brazil from Germany in the early 1940s with my father and his siblings. My father got married to a German migrant whose mother is half-Spanish and half-Peruvian Indian, but her father is pure German. So I was born there.'

'Hmmm, your family is so mixed. How did you learn German?' Lukas asked Rodriguez again.

'In Germany. My father came back to Germany when I was nineteen and when my grandfather died. He said he no longer liked the life in Brazil. As soon as we returned to Germany, we were enrolled in a German school, and arrangements for extra German classes were made. Although, we spoke little German while we were in Brazil . . .'

Edore got up and ran towards the kitchen window. She threw up as soon as she got there. Lukas ran to her side. The others watched them.

'What kind of food is that, Lukas? No pepper and that round stuff like pounded yam.'

'Sorry, darling. That's very German. I forgot to serve you pepper.'

Johannes came up to them.

'Is she all right?' he asked.

Lukas explained to him that Edore had never eaten German food and that she needed some time to get accustomed to it. She needed chilli too. Johannes offered to prepare Edore some rice. He informed them he had some pepperoni, which would do.

'Thank you,' Edore blushed.

Lukas cleaned Edore's vomit. He gave her a cup of sour wine to warm her cold stomach. Edore walked up to Johannes. She insisted on making the food herself so that Johannes could continue eating with his colleagues. Edore cooked the rice and made a tomato sauce full of sliced onions and chopped pepperoni. Edore felt better eating something she was used to.

'Do you feel better now?' Lukas asked her.

'Yes,' she replied.

He was glad that Johannes had some pepperoni. Rodriguez told them they also ate sharp and spicy foods in Brazil. He told Edore he could do without pepper if ever there was none.

'You would get use to it,' he assured her.

'I hope so,' she said, leaning on Lukas.

Johannes asked Rodriguez to serve them some oranges. Johannes usually took fruits after every meal. A day without fruits to him is like a day without water to drink. Rodriguez served the oranges. He cut them into wedges and passed them round. Edore declined to eat the oranges. She thought she may upset her stomach eating them. Captain Anton came to join them. The co-captain just took charge and relieved him. He took some oranges and then sat down to play his guitar.

'Is Anton the same as Anthony?' Edore asked Lukas.

'Yes, darling. Anton is the Russian and Ukrainian version name of Anthony.'

Johannes shook his head to the rhythm of Anton's song.

'You guys did well by breaking up from the old Soviet bloc,' Johannes began.

'Yes, it is good for us.'

'We used to be one of the world's superpowers, a major rival of the USA,' Anton said with pride.

Anton continued to play his guitar. He was playing a Russian traditional folk by Nadezhda Kadisheva. Edore thought Johannes liked politics too.

'Do you think the people of Irian Jaya will ever get independence?' she asked Johannes.

'That depends on how hard they fight. East Timor was able to gain independence. I think the Portuguese backed them,' Johannes explained.

'East Timor is now Timor Leste,' Lukas told Johannes.

'I think it is interchangeable. It is all politics, Edore. I think they will be free one day.'

Edore sighed and looked again towards the sea. *The world is unfair to the weak*, she thought.

Anton suddenly stopped playing his guitar. 'I'm running out of songs. I need some wine to restock myself.'

They all laughed and headed to the parlour that also served as the dance hall. Anton headed straight to the bar and gulped down a glass of whisky and then settled on a high stool and began to play his guitar again. The sound was loud; they had glasses in their hands now. They danced salsa. Lukas was a good dancer, but Edore never liked dancing, so she could not match Lukas's steps. Johannes was a lively man and full of ideas. He could sometimes talk too much. He invited everyone to the deck and handed each person a small stone. Edore declined his offer politely. She knew he was up to something. She preferred to watch him and the other men, so she sat back on the camping bed from where she could see them. She longed to see land. The long stretch of sea was becoming boring to her.

'I won,' Rodriguez screamed like one who would be given a trophy.

'Yes, capoeira knowledge aided you, Roddie.' Johannes fondly called Rodriguez Roddie.

'Not at all,' Rodriguez said defensively.

'You people in Brazil know how to throw your hands and legs during your capoeira training.'

'It has no connection,' Rodriguez laughed.

'What is capoeira?' Edore asked her husband softly.

'It's Brazilian fighting sport for self-defence. It consists of African songs too.'

'All with slave trade root, I suppose,' Edore quickly added.

They all soon returned inside to continue dancing. Lukas held Edore and occasionally waited to match his steps with hers. The dance was over, and they returned to their cabins.

The weeks passed by quickly. Then one day, the captain told them they would arrive in Hamburg the next day. Edore, even though enjoying the journey, thought sometimes that it was taking too long to reach Germany.

There was excitement everywhere on the day the ship was to arrive Hamburg. Edore had sought leave from the usual evening party which routinely preceded their supper. She had tasted alcohol, she was tipsy, and she needed a sleep. As soon as her back touched the bed, she was gone.

Lukas, Johannes, and the rest stayed up until late in the night. Suddenly, lightning struck followed by a low rumbling of thunder. Wind began to blow slowly but gained strength gradually. The party dispersed; Lukas went briefly to cabin 6 with the intention of returning to the parlour, while the sailors went to work. It was raining heavily now, and the sea current was building into a storm.

'What's the depth, Boris?' came Anton's voice.

He was behind Boris, the sailing captain.

'Under control,' he retorted nervously.

Boris was a young sailor who joined the crew seven months ago after his graduation from the Royal Dutch Marine College. The water was rising higher than ever, and the communication signal was breaking. The waves became stronger, and one could feel the ship swaying to its currents. Anton glanced at the compass but quickly looked away because there was a huge blast from the sky.

'I think the mast is broken. We are unable to signal,' Boris said.

'All right, let me in,' Anton said, sliding behind Boris.

He took charge of the ship and navigated it towards shallow waters when suddenly a loud cranking sound emanated from the engine below them. Johannes climbed the crest to see if there was any sign of help out there, but they were alone. There was no sign of life near them. He narrowed his eyes to see further, but he was blinded by a lightning that tore the sky apart just that moment. As soon as he could see again, he ran down to meet the other sailors.

'We need to ring Hamburg as quickly as possible for help,' he advised.

'We are unable to signal, and the mast is broken,' replied Boris.

The cranking noise grew louder and louder; Anton slowed the engine down to reduce the noise.

'All right, I will try the satellite phone from the basement,' Johannes said.

He took two steps at a time as he ran down the stairs. He grabbed the radio and punched in the coast guard's codes. The ship vibrated vigorously and came to a standstill. The radio signal went dead. The ship had hit a rock.

It was just 5 a.m. in the morning, two hours before the ship would arrive at Hamburg port. The base of the ship cracked, and water began to leak in. There was panic. Lukas ran down to cabin 6. He had returned to join the men after leaving for the cabin with Edore. Edore was awake but could not comprehend what was happening. Panic was written all over her face.

'Wake up, Edore, the ship is sinking,' he broke in with the words.

Just then, Boris pushed in with a lifebuoy and threw it at Edore.

'Wear it and follow him,' Lukas instructed Edore.

She was terrified.

Lukas hurriedly pulled down the lifebuoy on her. He waited until another lifebuoy was brought for him. Where they had been standing was now a pool of water, and it was rising. They started climbing up. But the higher they climbed, the lower they got until the ship completely sank. It took the rescue helicopter about thirty minutes to arrive at the scene. Divers were at hand to search for all the missing persons. Edore was seen floating on the sea near the ship's mast. She was quickly carried to safety by one of the rescuers. Two more men were rescued before the helicopter flew to the hospital.

They had to leave with just three people because Jahlid, the Moroccan sailor, was critically injured. He had a broken limb and a lacerated head. Edore had bruises all over her face and was frail. The head of the rescue team had sent for reinforcement to enable the search for other survivors. Edore was taken to St. Maria Hospital. She was moved to the female ward where she was given intravenous transfusion. She woke up five hours later, surrounded by a team of doctors and nurses. It was the routine ward visit. The chief medical officer, Dr Weiss, smiled broadly at Edore. She returned a weak smile. He tried talking to her, but she only stared at him. It was only then that Dr Weiss realised there was a language barrier.

'English?' he asked.

'Yes,' Edore replied.

Seeing the puzzled look on her face, Dr Weiss tried calming her down by explaining to her about the ship mishap and how she was brought to the hospital but assured her that she would be well in a short time. A nurse came in and took her details.

'Edore Koenig,' she told the nurse. Then turning to the doctor, she asked, 'Where's Lukas?'

'We have no record of any Mr Lukas. Hope they find him in the next round of search,' Dr Weiss said.

Edore tried to turn to the other side of the bed, but she felt a sharp pain in her abdomen. She let out a low moan. Dr Weiss enquired to know if she was all right, but before Edore could answer, the doctor noticed blood soaking up the white bed sheet where she lay.

'Are you pregnant?' he asked Edore.

The pain had become intense, so she could not respond.

The nurses hurriedly pulled over a wheeled stretcher and put her on it and wheeled her to the theatre. The medical examination suggested that she was three months pregnant, and she had suffered a miscarriage. She had lost a good amount of blood and needed transfusion.

In the weeks that followed, Edore suffered more pains, and it was discovered she had further complications to her health. Even in her condition she never stopped asking about her husband. She was told that only three people survived – she and two other men. The others had been transferred to a specialist hospital because of the seriousness of their case. Edore was devastated. She had lost her husband and everything she hoped on. Her marriage certificate, international passport, school certificates, and other vital documents were all locked up in that luggage that must be sitting on the belly of the sea by now. The only option was to go back to Nigeria, but she wondered how to go with almost everything gone. It was all a nightmare. She could not believe her husband was gone too soon. Unconsciously, Edore got up and began to run down the corridor of the hospital, screaming. The nurses ran after her. They caught her and held her down. She was bound and injected with tranquillisers. She drifted into trauma as soon as the tranquillisers wore off. Edore cursed the day she boarded that ship. That ship that took all that mattered to her life!

Some Ghanaians were in St Maria Hospital, visiting one of their countrywomen who had delivered a baby. It was then, one of the cleaners, a Turk, informed them that an African had been in the hospital for over a month. Alena, the cleaner, knew what it meant to be in a hospital without relatives coming to visit. This conviction prompted her to speak with Kofi, one of the Ghanaians, who decided to check the ward pointed to him by Alena. She had also told him the African occupied the second room after the

CHOVWE INISIAGHO

entrance to the ward. Kofi had no problem locating the room. He knocked and, with uncertainty, entered the room where Edore had been receiving treatment for some time now. Kofi did not see any African woman there, so he asked a lady, whom he supposed was an occupant of the room, about the African lady.

'Ah, I think she had gone for her routine ultrasound,' she told him.

'Thanks,' Kofi said. 'I will come back,' he added.

Edore came back from her check-up late in the afternoon.

'One of your countrymen asked about you,' the room occupant whom Kofi had met told her.

Edore couldn't understand her.

She had attempted to translate German into English for Edore. It was when one of the nurses came around with Edore's lunch that the lady explained to her that she was trying to tell Edore that an African man had come to ask after her.

The nurse relayed the message to her as much as she could in English. Communication had been a big problem between Edore and the staff. Few of the medical staff spoke English except for the chief medical officer and two of his assistants, who spoke English fluently. It was always a relief for her to see someone speak English. She wondered who that person could have been. A few days later, Kofi showed up with another lady. They greeted Edore with some familiarity. They already knew she spoke English. Kofi introduced himself and the lady that accompanied him. He told Edore how they got the information about the shipwreck and her presence in the hospital. Kofi explained further to her that as Africans, it was duty bound for them to pay her a visit.

Edore was elated. It was the first time she saw Africans in about six weeks. She told them all that had happened and how she planned to go back home. Kofi told her that she could stay back in Germany and make a living with her story. He promised to come back with a Nigerian he knew. Both Kofi and Annabel, the lady with whom he came, stayed a while longer and left. They came the next day with Steve Osas, a Nigerian. Annabel brought her some Ghanaian food, fruits, and new clothes to change from those given to her by the hospital on her arrival.

'You have been wearing only these hospital clothes, so have a change of clothes,' she said.

Edore had braided her hair before the journey, so it wasn't much of a problem keeping that still. Edore spoke at length with Steve. They all left after spending an hour with her. Steve continued the visit once in a week. He had told Edore that he could inform the Nigerian embassy in Germany about her situation. He took an undertaking with the hospital that he would hand Edore over to the Nigerian embassy. Edore was discharged after nine weeks in the hospital. The hospital authorities gave her documents to present to the foreign office which would enable her get permission to stay in Germany pending the time she completed arrangements with the Nigerian embassy to travel back to Nigeria. She was allowed to leave with Steve. He helped her to carry her few belongings, which consisted of a small suitcase, five pairs of trousers and five blouses, two pullovers, and a jacket packed in a polythene bag. It was June when she got discharged, so the weather was warm.

'You are fortunate that you did not come in the heart of winter. Winter is not a good season to visit Germany,' Steve told her.

'Really?' she asked him.

Steve nodded in affirmation.

They got to the taxi park nearby from where they boarded a taxi to Steve's home. His fiancée had been away in America and was due to return the following day. He had invited her cousin, Kate, to spend the night with them. He thought it wasn't proper for him to be alone in his flat with Edore. Kate came well ahead of his arrival with Edore from the hospital.

Kate knew it was Steve and Edore as soon as the doorbell rang. She opened the door and greeted both of them. She motioned for her to sit down. Steve took her luggage to his room. Edore looked around the small apartment. She loved its modesty. Kate walked up to her.

'Would you like to take your bath first or eat?' she asked her.

'Please give me a glass of water first. I prefer to rest and eat anytime from midday.'

'Just let me know when you are ready,' Kate told her.

Steve entered the living room again.

'Feel at home. My fiancée should be here later today or tomorrow', he told Edore.

Kate persuaded Edore to take her bath. She showed her the bathroom and where her suitcase was. Kate switched on the computer.

'I'm sure you would like to check your email or send one,' she offered Osas.

'Yes, my dear cousin,' Steve told Kate, trying to suppress his laughter.

'I hope she likes this pounded yam,' Kate said, placing a plate on the dining table.

'Yes, she will,' Steve told Kate without looking at her.

'You computer freak! You can't even remove your gaze from it for a second to look at me.'

Steve grinned and continued browsing the Internet. Edore came again into the living room. Kate invited her and Steve to the dining table.

'Please help yourself,' Steve told Edore.

She was surprised to see pounded yam and okra soup. She enquired where they were from. Kate told her they had bought them from an African shop.

'Thank God for this meal. It has been German food all this while save for some Ghanaian food I ate just once. I managed to eat without pepper. I'm just eating the real food now.'

Edore got her hosts laughing with her remark.

She ate every morsel of the pounded yam she served herself. Kate cleared the table after the meal. Steve showed Edore how the remote control functions. Edore turned on the television. She preferred to watch *BBC News*, hoping to hear something about the ship mishap. She paid close attention to every detail as the news went on, but there was no mention of any accident at all. She felt weak after a while and knew then that she needed a rest.

'I think you need some rest,' Kate, who was still cleaning the table, told Edore.

'As if you know my mind,' Edore told Kate half-asleep.

Steve thought it was wise for some experienced Nigerians to know about Edore's story. He invited three of his close friends to his house that afternoon. One of them, Uchedike, suggested she should not go back to Nigeria but seek asylum in Germany. He explained that since she had the opportunity to be in Europe, she did not need to go back because her story was credible enough to get her a residence permit in Germany.

Edore did not really understand Uchedike. He explained to her all about seeking asylum.

Osas thought it was a good idea. Uchedike did all the planning. Akpos, the third friend, thought it was better if she told the whole truth. After a long deliberation, the three men decided it was better if Edore said she was involved in a ship mishap where she lost her husband and that when she returns to Nigeria, people would be after her life. To give more impetus to her claim, the men added that she should say that her husband was a very wealthy man and that it was the belief of the Niger-Delta militants that all foreigners who worked in the area prevented the indigenes and Nigerian citizens from getting good jobs, a development that could endanger her life. They warned that she should not present any document from the hospital to the asylum office authorities because it could vitiate her story and cause her deportation to Nigeria without delay. Edore had been listening with rapt attention and did not have much to say. She was confused. She liked the quality of the medical care available in Germany.

Edore thought she would have a better chance if she lived in Germany. Kate had convinced her to stay back.

Angelique, Osas's fiancée, returned from her work at the airport just before they finished the discussion. She was just in time to prepare lunch. Whenever Nigerian men got together, they seized the opportunity to discuss politics. Osas and his friends soon delved into Nigerian politics. They were not satisfied with the current political situation. Uchedike lashed out at the employment policy in Nigeria, comparing it with that of Germany's.

'You men better go and contest for some position,' Angelique teased them.

She went to the kitchen with Edore. Both ladies had hit it off quickly as friends. Angelique had told Edore that she changed her name from Angela to the French version, Angelique, because she thought it sounded more modern. Besides, she loved the music of Angélique Kidjo, the songstress from the Republic of Benin.

'It was from her I first heard the name, so I immediately fell in love with it. I had to change my name fast,' she had told Edore.

Osas came into the kitchen to say his friends were leaving. Edore and Angelique went back to the living room to bid them goodbye. Edore expressed her gratitude for their advice and concern.

'We are our brother's keepers,' Akpos told her.

Osas took Edore to the Asylum Seekers Authority. He pointed the office to her from the other side of the road. He embraced her and bid her goodbye. She crossed the road and then went into the office. Before he left, Osas watched her as she entered the building. She had with her a few clothes and all the documents she had acquired in Germany. Osas had wanted her to leave them behind, but she preferred to have them with her.

'Do not let the authorities see them,' he cautioned her.

Edore met a uniformed man at the entrance. She told him just a word in German. A word which Osas and his friends had taught her. She had to rehearse it several times.

'Asyl,' she told the man in German, meaning asylum.

With that, he knew what she wanted. Then the man asked her, 'Deutsch, Englisch, Französisch?'

Edore knew from what she had been told that she would be asked what language she spoke.

'English,' she told him.

He gestured to her to sit on a chair in front of his desk.

He went into the room adjacent to his office and came out with a lady. She spoke warmly to Edore in English. She greeted her and gave her some forms to fill out in English. She asked her to wait a while so that her initial application could be processed. The man whom she had met on her arrival came back with a basketful of takeaway food consisting of sandwich and juice. There were about nine other people there that morning. They took one plastic bag each from him. The lady with whom Edore spoke came out again and handed her some papers. In it was her new posting as an asylum seeker. One paper was in German and the other in English. She understood from the paper that she had been posted to Schweinfurt in southern Germany. Another man came out and handed them each an envelope. She was made to understand it contained the train ticket to her new destination.

Edore asked how she could get to the train station. She was told a bus would drop them off there. About ten minutes later, a HILUX van pulled in. It took them to the train station. They were directed to the various platforms which would take them to their destinations. Osas had told Edore not to be afraid. He had explained the whole process to her. He told her the duration of travel was always written on the train ticket and that each intermediate stop in the course of the journey would be announced. Edore had never travelled by train before. She simply followed other passengers entering and sat down on the nearest seat. She clutched her plastic bag tight as if her life was hidden in it. A young African came from behind the back row of seats and sat next to her. She looked wearyingly at him and looked away again. The young man smiled and muttered some greetings. The train conductor blew his whistle. All doors closed and the train began to move at a slow pace. Edore leant back on her seat and began to sleep with her plastic bag held tightly to her chest. She had slept for less than thirty minutes when she felt someone tapping on her shoulder.

It was the young man sitting next to her.

'Sister, do not sleep off when you are on a journey. You may miss where you are going.'

Edore yawned and thanked him.

They soon got into conversation. He introduced himself to Edore as Camara from Sierra Leone, working as a Christian missionary. He informed her that he had a meeting in Aschaffenburg, a small city about two hours from Schweinfurt. Edore told him she was going to her asylum posting.

'Why did you not go back home?' he asked Edore.

'I think I will have a better chance here,' she told him.

Camara had told her that asylum life wasn't all that a pleasant one and that recognition depended on the individual's circumstance. He said he left Sierra Leone during the civil war and was given a German passport because it was clear that his country was at war. Camara was the only surviving child of his parents. The rebels had killed his only sister and three brothers. His aged parents were not killed. He ran away when they tried to shoot him. He was fortunate that the bullet hit his leg but could still run with the leg. He was by the roadside, bleeding and weeping when a UN truck drove past him. The army officer had to reverse to find out what he was doing all alone there. He told him he managed to escape from some rebels who shot him in the leg. While they were still talking, they heard gunshots. He was quickly hurled into the van. The army officer made arrangement for the treatment of his wounded leg in Germany. The condition of his leg was deteriorating fast. The army officer had to return to war, so he recommended him for asylum.

'Till date, I still limp, but thank God, my life was saved. Since that time, I became more serious with my Christian faith.'

The train stopped in Koblenz for some passengers to disembark and then resumed its journey. Camara knew the routes very well. He had been in Germany almost ten years and did an apprenticeship with a furniture company. He told Edore some history or geography of any town they passed. Edore told him she loved the landscapes, especially the rolling hills.

'Nature is simply wonderful,' she told Camara.

In Frankfurt, Edore ate her sandwich. Camara offered to buy her more food on the train if she was ever hungry. Edore thanked him. She told him she would let him know if she was hungry. There was a brief silence between them. Edore looked out of the window while Camara read his Bible. He broke the silence again when he told Edore the train would soon be in Aschaffenburg. He gave Edore his contact number.

'Let me know if you need help.'

At exactly 2 p.m., the train stopped in Aschaffenburg. Camara alighted and reminded Edore that she would arrive in Schweinfurt in less than two hours.

'Don't forget to contact me,' he told her, waving goodbye.

Edore sat upright and paid more attention to her arrival time in Schweinfurt. She never knew travelling alone on a train could be boring. Camara's departure left her longing for company. She recalled all that Camara had told her about the war in Sierra Leone. Her ticket was inspected for a second time by the train conductor. The train arrived in Schweinfurt at about 3.43 p.m. She was directed to the exit by a German who spoke little English. Edore had spotted the difference between trains in big and small cities. Schweinfurt's train station was small and had lesser facilities and manpower when compared to the ones she had seen before. She went through the bar and into the hall. There were shops and bookshops just like she saw in Hamburg and Frankfurt stations. She looked around for a telephone booth from where she called Osas. Osas was thrilled to hear her voice. He had been expecting her call. Then he began to tell her what to do next. Osas had always spoken to her like a big brother.

'You either take a taxi by showing the driver the address or go to the information desk to ask how you can get to the address. The authority should have made arrangements for someone to pick you up,' Osas complained bitterly.

'I will be safe. Just send my love to Kate and Angelique.'

Edore looked around for a while until she sighted an African whom she hurriedly walked up to. She waved at him excitedly. Edore greeted him and asked to know if he spoke English.

'No English,' he told her.

Then he motioned to her to wait. Edore was curious. She wondered why he asked her to wait. The young man dashed to a nearby shop and emerged with another African.

'Hello, do you need help?' he asked Edore in flawless English.

'Yes, how do I get to this address?' Edore asked, showing him the letter from the Central Asylum Office in Hamburg.

He told her it was just two bus stops away from the train station.

'When you get on the bus, disembark after two stops from here. Make sure you purchase a ticket from the driver,' he explained further.

Both men took her to the platform from where she could board the bus to her destination. Edore thanked them before boarding the bus. She bought a ticket from the driver. It took another fifteen minutes before the bus left the park. Edore was fully awake and made sure she did not miss the bus stop. It did not take five minutes before the bus came to a halt. Edore alighted. The roads passing through the bus route were narrow, and the houses on both sides of the road were built on top of hills. Edore knew she was in a valley. Edgar, the man with whom she spoke at the train station, had told her the asylum camp was located along the road but she must keep walking through the taxi park. She spent a few seconds looking around before she saw the taxi park. She walked towards the park, and just beside the park was the fence of the asylum camp. She walked along it until she came to the main entrance. She saw three African ladies. They looked at her and then began to talk in hushed tones. Edore showed the security guard at the gate the letter she brought with her. She was now aware that most people do not speak English, so she was not expecting the security guard to speak English with her. The security guard signalled her to follow him. That confirmed her suspicion. He entered her name in a register and went with her to another building beside the gate. It was the first administrative block of the asylum camp. Her details were taken by an administrative officer after which she was handed a kit that contained food, blankets, and beddings. She was taken to a temporary room to sleep. Before the administrative officer left, the ladies whom she had met at the entrance gate approached her. They enquired about her nationality and offered to take her to their room because the temporary room would be boring for her. One of them, Rafa, a Muslim from Nigeria, went to the administrative officer to tell him they were taking her to their room.

Rafa introduced her to the other ladies, Ekua and Adjoa.

'Welcome,' they chorused as if it was rehearsed.

Rafa explained to Edore that the camp used to be an American military base and that they had been there for two weeks awaiting further posting to a permanent place.

Rafa told her she is equally Ghanaian and Nigerian. 'I'm just in the middle of you all,' she exclaimed.

Adjoa and Ekua laughed. Edore smiled but was tired and needed rest. They climbed the staircase to the third floor unto a long corridor. They passed through several doors to their room at the end of the block.

'Thank you,' Edore appreciated them.

She was offered a glass of orange juice, but she preferred to drink water, so she was offered a glass of water instead. She always felt nauseated after a long journey.

'Would you like to eat something?' Rafa offered.

Edore declined the offer politely.

'OK, let us know when you are ready to eat.'

'Thank you, Rafa. I definitely will,' Edore assured her.

Ekua turned the TV on.

'We were about to go out for shopping before you came, so feel free and be at home while we are away.'

'OK,' Edore replied half-closing her eyes.

The three ladies banged the door behind them. Edore drifted away.

After breakfast inside the refectory the following day, Mr Paul, the officer in charge of accommodation, told Edore she could remain with the ladies since they shared a common background. They were Africans. Mr Paul spoke in German, while Rafa translated for Edore. Edore wondered how long she had been in Germany. *Asylum is supposed to be for new arrivals, but there is someone who could speak German fluently*, she thought. It was fluent German, at least to a novice, but grammatically incorrect to a native speaker. Ekua told Edore that most times asylum seekers are put together based on their nationality and ethnic background. There were only two wardrobes in the room, so Ekua and Edore shared one, while Rafa and Adjoa shared another. Edore tucked her belongings inside the wardrobe.

Adjoa made fufu and some Ghanaian sauce which they ate for dinner. Edore did not quite like the sauce. She preferred to cook her meal next time as soon as she knows where the shops were. Ekua took the plates to the kitchen after the meal and washed them.

THE DYING THIEF

Adjoa lit a cigarette. Rafa lay on the bed and was contemplating calling her boyfriend; she missed him very often. The smoke filled the room, and Edore was almost choked by it. Rafa asked her to open the window to let air in and the smoke out. Edore rushed to the window even before Rafa finished the detail. Ekua dragged on her cigarette and puffed out a large cloud of smoke. The highway and the topography were very visible from where she sat. There was a knock at the door. Rafa quickly adjusted herself.

'Ja,' she said.

A young man walked casually in. He had delicately shaped eyebrows. Edore wasn't sure if he was a European. Ekua jumped at him and screamed his name; he held her waist and then fondled her breast. Edore looked away. Ekua put out the cigarette. She enquired after his well-being.

'Gut.' He told her he was fine in a heavy German accent.

Adjoa asked him what he had bought for them from the city. Ahmed, as he was called, promised to take them all to the restaurant over the weekend.

It was about 9 p.m., and Edore felt drowsy. Ekua dressed up quickly and left with Ahmed. Rafa decided to take a walk around the camp. Edore and Adjoa stayed back in the room.

'If you are tired, you can go to sleep,' Adjoa advised.

'I'd like to go to bed, but I still want to stay up a bit more,' Edore said.

Adjoa looked more civil than Rafa and Ekua, Edore thought. She had fixed a golden tooth. Adjoa later explained to her that she got it on a visit to Mecca. She confided to Edore that she had not practised Islam since her arrival in Germany.

'You can become active gradually again,' Edore said.

They laughed. Adjoa looked at her thoughtfully.

'You can make one repent,' Adjoa told her.

Before they slept, Adjoa told Edore Ahmed was Ekua's camp boyfriend but that she had a fiancé for whom she has kids in

53

Oberhausen, a city about seven hours away from Schweinfurt. She told her she was against the relationship, but Ekua would not listen. She told Edore that Rafa had been in Germany for about six years but because she had no permit to stay, she was advised by some Africans to seek asylum. She narrowly escaped being deported a few months before coming to the camp. Rafa came in just as Adjoa finished mentioning her name. Both Edore and Adjoa looked at each other in surprise.

'Hey, you ladies have not slept?' she asked.

'Just about to,' Adjoa told her.

Rafa changed into her pyjamas and hit the bed. Edore and Adjoa followed suit. Ekua usually stayed over with her boyfriend, so she was not expected.

Edore had to change her room. She could not tolerate the smoking habit of Ekua. She was a chain smoker. Besides, she did not like the character of all three of them. She decided to share a room with a lady from Russia. Edore prepared for her interview which would come up in two days. Rafa had advised her not to tender any document nor tell the authority about her husband.

'They would deport you,' she emphasised.

Edore was confused. That evening, she called Osas from a telephone booth in order to seek his opinion. Osas also confirmed Rafa's surmise. Rafa had told her to say she ran away because she was an active trade unionist who rose up against the Nigerian government. Still not satisfied, she called Camara who advised that she tell the truth. Edore had to make up her mind. She hung up and made to go back to her room when she heard people screaming and hurling abuses at each other. It was Ekua and Adjoa. Ekua was calling Adjoa a Muslim hypocrite who slept around with German men. Adjoa told her she was far better.

'You have a husband and two kids at home, yet you sleep about here. I'm not married, so I'm free,' Adjoa hit back.

Before anyone could say a word, both women tore at each other. Ekua stripped Adjoa naked. When she wanted to do the same to Ekua, Rafa and some Africans came between them. A South American lady quickly ran to her with a bed sheet. Adjoa sobbed. Ekua kept yelling and calling Adjoa names and would not stop ranting.

Edore was transfixed. She had never seen such rage and anger in her entire life. She was happy she left the room she shared with Ekua and her friends. Ekua caused a scene that evening.

It was exactly three months since Edore arrived at the asylum camp. Mr Paul came once more to her room and handed her a letter. He got an interpreter to tell her she had been posted to a permanent place of residence. Rafa, Adjoa, and Ekua were no longer in the camp. Rafa was posted to Nuremberg while Adjoa got a place in Aschaffenburg. Ekua had gone to visit her fiancé and never returned. Edore was billed to leave the next day. Later that evening, she called Osas and Camara, updating them of the new development. It was then Osas broke the news to her that Angelique had left him for an American man. Edore was surprised. She had always held Angelique in high esteem.

'God knows best, Osas. He will provide you with the woman you deserve,' she managed to tell him.

'Thank you,' Osas replied with a heavy sigh.

Edore arrived in Randersacker the next afternoon. One of the social workers with whom she became friendly drove her there. An official from the local government in charge of asylum seekers and refugees was there to show her her room. Inge Freitag had to take her leave after dropping her off. She told her she had other appointments to catch up with.

The local government official introduced herself and gave her two forms to sign. She spoke English fluently. She also handed her a food packet. Edore was to receive food packet every Monday with a monthly stipend of eighty deutsche mark. Mrs Maier, the lady from the local government, handed her the key to her room. Edore arranged her things and put her bag into the small wardrobe. She discovered that she was the only African in the refugee home and in the village of about 800 inhabitants. There were two families from Afghanistan, two Kosovar ladies, and a man from Cuba. The home was an old restaurant with poor facilities. Lack of proper maintenance was evident in the weeds already growing behind the building. Rumour had it that the central refugee administration embezzled a large part of the money meant for the funding of refugee homes. No one knew the real story.

Edore made her bed and lay down. Her eyes were riveted on the walls of the room. They had old wallpapers with some edges already peeling off the wall. The floor was tiled half-way. She hoped she would not live there for long. There was a knock at the door. It was the Afghan lady who came to offer Edore some cakes. She tried to explain to Edore that it was her daughter's birthday, but they both had no common language to understand each other with. Not knowing how else to convey the message, she called out to her husband to help. The elated husband who was happy to show off his knowledge of English blurted out clumsily the words, 'Party, party'. Edore was torn between taking food from a total stranger and being polite. Edore took it half-heartedly but felt irresolute. She shook hands with the lady in appreciation, taking the plate from her. Edore placed it on the table and went back to her bed to lie down. She felt all lonely. The thoughts of her husband's death overwhelmed her. She began to regret her decision to seek asylum. She needed to plan out her life again. Edore wanted to secure her future and be productive once more. She hated idleness.

The sunrays from the window woke Edore up. She had slept off without taking dinner. The cake was still on the table uncovered. Edore rushed out of her bed in a frenzy and made for the common bathroom. This was another aspect of the refugee home she hated. She vowed to warn young Nigerians not to venture into the business of seeking asylum. She could hear the Afghan lady talking to her kids. Edore finished taking her bath and went back to her room to dress up. She needed to call Camara and Osas. She wanted to let them know she had arrived in her new home. She planned to tell them too that she needed a television. Edore wore her tracksuit and settled down to eat the cake.

Inge Freitag had promised to visit Edore once in a month, so she came the next month to see to her welfare. Inge visited her in company of her boyfriend who was also a social worker with another organisation. They brought her some English novels and magazines. They discussed at length. For the first time, Edore told her about her husband. She also told her about the documents she brought with her.

'You should have tendered them during your interview and told the truth,' Inge exclaimed.

'I thought it would cause my deportation. I was just scared,' she said.

Inge requested to see the documents so that she could make photocopies. She left with her boyfriend after informing Edore she would be on leave for some time. Edore saw them off to where Inge parked her car. She was grateful Inge brought her two jackets. It was the onset of autumn. Edore had already spent close to ten months in Germany.

She went absent-mindedly into the kitchen and accidentally hit her foot against the vacuum cleaner. Abeda, the Afghan woman who had offered her cake, was in the kitchen. She rushed to her. Abeda tried to ask her if she was hurt. She bent down to rub Edore's foot. Edore gestured to her that she was all right. Abeda raised her hands up. She was thanking God that Edore was fine. Edore found her comical at times but kind-hearted. Edore made her lunch. She managed to cook jollof rice with the ingredients that were in her food packet. She missed eating Nigerian food. After lunch, she lay down to read one of the books Inge had brought her.

Randersacker was a small village with just basic infrastructures. One had to board a bus to the next city to do big shopping. Edore had gotten a shopping coupon from the refugee office department of the local government which she needed to redeem. She woke up early enough one Saturday to buy herself a pair of shoes and new clothes. She was up early because she wanted to take her bath before anyone else in the refugee home. Edore finished bathing and then dressed up. She made sure she was warm. Edore preferred the tropics to temperate Europe. The pair of velvet jeans and padded boots she wore gave her the warmness she craved. She did not forget to wear a scarf round her neck. She ate some cornflakes and rushed to the bus stop because buses arrived every thirty minutes on weekends. It was 8 a.m. Edore met a handful of people at the bus stop. Some villagers stared at her as she walked past. She wished they could appreciate the fact that God created everyone. She could feel their eyes piercing through her skin. It was a small village, and almost everyone knew each other.

Randersacker was famous for its vineyards and wine production. Its narrow road linked many other small settlements. The bus arrived five minutes after Edore got there. She bought her ticket from the driver. Edore took her seat at the back of the bus. She preferred to sit there so she could have a better view of the passengers and the village. Edore could connect with the rolling hills. When it was harvest time, people came from Poland and other east European countries. The German farmers preferred to hire these immigrants because the labour was cheap. The bus got to the city fifteen minutes later. Edore alighted and took her time to go through the major shopping streets. Most shops opened at 9 a.m., so she decided to take a walk. Inge had taken her around the city once, and she had gone with Abeda some other times too. That day was her first time to shop alone in the city. Edore did some window shopping and then went into some shops as soon as they were opened. It was in Woolworth, a clothing store, that she found her choice of designs. Edore took a handbag and a pair of trousers. She held both items in her hands and went through the entrance of the store towards the clothes' hangers outside. She wanted to choose a matching blouse from the wide variety displayed there, but she was abruptly stopped by one of the store assistants who gripped her by the left hand.

'You are a thief,' the assistant shouted in German.

Edore could only stare at her. She did not understand a word of what the assistant said.

'You are a thief, young lady,' she told her again.

'Ja.' Edore had said *yes* in German language, thinking the assistant had asked if she wanted to buy the clothes.

The store assistant called her supervisor. She told him Edore had agreed she was stealing the clothes in her hand. The supervisor looked disdainfully at Edore then requested her to follow him. She stood still, looking terrified and confused. When the supervisor saw she wasn't following him, he shoved her into the shop. It was then that she realised something was wrong. Some passers-by watched the mild drama that was unfolding. Inside the shop, customers peeped in and stole looks at her. She was led through the shopping hall to an office.

The supervisor made a call. All she could do was watch. She could not still piece together what was going on. In less than ten minutes, two police officers, a man and a woman, came into the office.

They discussed briefly with the supervisor. The policewoman told Edore she was to go to the station with them for stealing.

'English, please.' Edore managed to speak up.

The policeman turned to the supervisor. 'Sie scheint kein Deutsch zu verstehen.' She seem not to understand German, he told him.

'You a thief,' the policewoman said in passable English.

'No,' Edore screamed vehemently.

'You come,' continued the officer.

Edore followed them till they came to the police car.

She was driven to the station. Edore was taken into an office for further interrogation. She was interviewed by another officer who spoke better English. He explained to Edore she had agreed to the store assistant that she stole the blouse by saying yes in German. Edore began to weep. She knew it was a misunderstanding as a result of communication barrier. The officer gave her a tissue to wipe her tears but told her the matter would be charged to court. Edore was detained at the station. She pleaded with the police officer to speak to her friend, Inge. She knew her telephone number by heart. Amidst tears, she told Inge all that had transpired. Inge promised to see her. Inge was dissatisfied with the conduct of the supervisor and the police. She knew there was a mistake somewhere.

Inge arrived at the police station at exactly 4 p.m. She introduced herself to the police on duty. She then asked to see Edore. Edore was relieved to see her. Inge hugged her, assuring her that everything would be fine. They were allowed to sit in the visitors' room. Inge opened her bag and gave Edore a pair of trousers, T-shirt, underwear, and something to drink. Inge moved closer to Edore. She held her by the hand and spoke to her soothingly.

'You have a very bright future. You are a very lucky lady.'

Edore shed more tears.

'Get me out of here please, Inge,' she pleaded.

'Yes, you will be out in no time,' she assured her.

Edore took a deep breath 'And promise me you will not be loud because I'm about to tell you something,' she continued.

'I promise,' Edore said, gazing at Inge.

'Your husband is alive!'

Edore rose from her chair and knelt down in praises to God before bursting out into tears again. Inge helped her up.

'It is OK,' Inge said, placating her.

When Edore settled down, she told her how she contacted the hospital in Hamburg to verify her story and see if Edore could be transferred back to Hamburg. It was then that the authorities told her about Lukas. Lukas was found unconscious after three days by some hobby anglers. He was washed ashore by the water currents to another part of River Elbe. He was adrift on the ill-fated ship's wooden cabin door which had ripped off. The anglers ran up to him when they saw him on the beach. They were not sure if he was alive. One of them moved closer to him and could still feel his heart beat slowly. He decided to call an ambulance. Before the ambulance arrived, they tried to clean his face with a wet towel and at least revive him. He was taken immediately to the hospital. He responded slowly to the treatment but remained unconscious.

The first word that Lukas muttered when he regained consciousness was 'Edore'. The nurses asked him to calm down. But throughout that day, he kept on calling Edore's name. In the days that followed, his speech was much more coordinated, so he demanded to speak with the doctors. He was able to recollect how the ship sank, and how he got separated from his wife. He pleaded with them to help find his wife. The police were contacted. They were able to trace Edore's name to the hospital where she was admitted. The authorities there told Lukas that an African man took up Edore's case, promising to take her to the Nigerian embassy. Lukas asked if he left any number behind for contact. He was put on hold while they made a check. 'Ja,' the man with whom he spoke answered. Lukas called the number, but it did not go through. He discovered to his consternation that the telephone number was no longer connected. So he concluded that Edore must have gone back to Nigeria, thinking he was dead. It was a thing of joy when the hospital authorities contacted him months later to inform him that Edore was in south Germany.

Inge left Edore in the police custody. She was refused bail on the grounds that she had admitted to the theft. Inge tried to explain to them that it was a simple misunderstanding created by language barrier. Inge established contact with Lukas. He was upset to know his wife was being detained and was refused bail. Lukas got a lawyer with whom he flew to Munich. From there, they took a train to Schweinfurt. Inge met them at the train station. Together they made for the police station.

After a long and rigorous discussion, Edore was released to her husband. She stepped out of the detention room, running into the waiting arms of Lukas.

THE WITNESS

Kayo was reluctant to wake up when the alarm set off. She went back to bed again. She hated the cleaning job that she got some months ago. She lay on the bed, remembering how she came to Germany and consequently her present state. She had applied to study in Germany. The idea of coming to Germany was that of her uncle who studied in Germany in the early 1980s. Her parents had no objection. Mark, her uncle, studied mechanical engineering in the then West Berlin. He told his brother Denis, Kayo's father, that there was no tuition fee charged in West Germany and that the education was qualitative. Denis was, at first, hesitant. 'What about these neo-Nazis and skinheads?' he questioned.

Mark laughed at his brother's self-knowledge of Germany.

'What is funny?' Denis asked.

'Brother, I can read the fear in your face.' Mark was apt with his answer.

Denis ruffled his hair, trying to avoid his brother's gaze. He knew Mark could be blunt sometimes.

Denis and his brother Mark were the only surviving children of their aged parents. Other siblings died mysteriously. Some elders elected to advise their parents that their sons should stop visiting them to avert any untimely death to them. Such was widely believed in their time.

Mark and his brother were different in all things but united against a common enemy they found in their parents. This singular perception bound them together closely. If they were to send gifts or money to their parents, they sent them in the name of relatives and friends.

Mark was in Germany as a student when he heard about his siblings' deaths. He only saw them once when he visited home all through his years of sojourn in Germany.

'Mark, I do not want Kayo to be attacked by skinheads and some racists,' Denis said, matter-of-factly.

'Brother, I studied there and nothing happened to me. Rest assured that Kayo will be safe,' he affirmed.

Mark did not believe in hearsay. He preferred to find things out for himself. Once he brought up the issue of their dead siblings before Denis, and he told him they could not have died mysteriously but that the family might be jinxed or under a curse. Denis had shuddered. He developed goose pimples. The death of his siblings is an issue he never wanted to recall. Those mysteries that surround their deaths!

'Mark, that topic is best not talked about.'

Mark was an extrovert and very adventurous. He was a sharp contrast to Denis, who was more withdrawn and reserved. He applied for scholarship to study in West Germany from the ministry of education in the then Bendel State, and he was given an admission. At that time, he was in his second year, studying pharmacy, but he opted to study engineering outside Nigeria. His father, who was a school principal, persuaded him to complete his course instead of studying something else and leaving it half done. Mark had his mind made up. He was good at taking decisions that others consider unusual. His friends thought he was an enigma.

Mr Onofere had appealed to Denis to convince his brother Mark to complete his study before leaving for Germany, but Denis reminded his father of Mark's attitude. No one in the family could

THE DYING THIEF

get Mark to change his mind about going to Germany. Mark took another course of action that left his father dumbfounded. He requested his father to go with him to Sagbama in Rivers State to pay the bride price of his girlfriend, a final-year student of political science.

'Mark, but you are too young to marry at twenty-one with no source of income yet.'

'Papa, that is what I want. I am leaving the country, and this girl could marry another man before I return.'

Mark stood his ground. Onofere and some of his kinsmen went with Mark to pay the bride price of his girlfriend, Ebiere. Three months later, Mark left for West Germany.

Denis told Kayo many more stories about his family. Kayo had wondered why Ebiere was no longer with Mark.

'My daughter,' he had told Kayo, our people have an adage which says, "A child is not prevented from growing big teeth, but he must have the lips with which to close them."'

'What does this mean?' Kayo asked curiously.

'Your uncle did not listen to the voice of reasoning. When his wife Ebiere graduated, she got a job in the army. She waited for Mark but to no avail. She met a medical doctor in Yenagoa during a party. The young man proposed to her, she accepted, and her family returned the bride price so that she could marry the medical doctor. Mark was devastated.'

Kayo remembered how her father told her that he was from a closely knit family where brothers cared for each other. Onofere retired and left Ughelli for his home town in Agbarho.

'My father was wise enough to build a small bungalow of five rooms where we, his children and my mother, moved into. He opened the village's only bookshop, and my mother ran a small provision store.'

Kayo's father told her history and events whether they were relevant or not. Denis and two of his brothers were already in the university when their father moved back to the village. They augmented whatever their parents gave them by working as teaching assistants in primary or secondary schools, especially on holidays. Kayo thought of her father with much nostalgia. Mark was the luckiest of them all. He got information about scholarships, and it enabled him to secure a place to study abroad. Denis got admission in the University of Lagos where he studied mass communication.

He met and fell in love with Moyoma, Kayo's mother, at the university. Moyoma studied home economics. She got a job quite easily and later ran a small-eatery business. Kayo was greatly inspired by her mother's cooking skills. Whenever there was party or festival in her school, her classmates approached her to cook or bake for them. At first, Kayo took pleasure in doing it, but later, one of her aunts told her she could make some money out of it. The thought of making money never crossed her mind; it was a hobby. She subsequently requested for little monetary compensation for the time she spent in making pastries and cooking rice on such occasions. Her aunt, Maggie, advised her to save her earnings, which she found very helpful as time progressed. She never asked her parents for money often. She grew to become a fashion icon among her schoolmates and peers. Kayo was grateful to her aunt who constantly encouraged her to save. She would have squandered her money if not for her mentorship. Kayo once consulted her mother on the best gift for Maggie. She gave her a long grateful look.

'That won't be necessary. She would just be glad to know that you appreciate her advice.'

Moyoma thought a gift was unnecessary, but Kayo had a different plan. She bought some towels and neatly wrapped them. The following day, she went to Maggie and presented them to her.

'That is nice of you, my little girl. You have acted older than your age.'

That was the last day she saw Maggie. She died a week later in a car crash. Kayo could not come to terms with her death.

She was too good to die that way, Kayo thought.

Maggie was the first of her father's siblings to die. Kayo remembered her hug, her warmth, and her heartbeat. Maggie's family wished she had a child of her own, but destiny knows best. Her husband, Kayode, requested that she be buried in Ilesha, his home town. It caused a stir in his family. Kayode explained to them it was their tradition and Maggie's wish.

People thought Kayo was an abbreviation of Kayode, but she would explain to them that her full name was Kayoghene. Kayo wept like she never did before during her aunt's burial. Her father chartered a luxury bus which transported all of them to Ilesha for the burial ceremony.

'You people risked your lives,' an elder told Denis. 'Supposing something tragic happened?' he continued.

Denis looked at him, befuddled.

Kayo went to her mother a week after the burial. She leant on her. On the floor of her room were boxes of Maggie's clothes which were to be given to relatives. Some said they should be burnt.

'Mother,' Kayo began.

'Yes,' Moyoma said, stroking Kayo's hair.

'I bought Maggie that yellow towel over there,' Kayo said, pointing at the towel.

Moyoma held Kayo's head up.

'You did well, my daughter.'

Kayo began to cry.

She felt she had something in common with Maggie. She was an only child while Maggie had no children – situational mother and child! Her mother told her that she became pregnant in her second year in the university and had to stay at home until her delivery. After she delivered Kayo, she counted herself fortunate because she did not go for an abortion at the time when abortion was cheap and easy to access. Her mother was supportive.

Mark was the only one who did not attend Maggie's burial. He sent his family a letter of condolence and money.

Denis wasn't the eldest child of his parents but the second of five children. His elder brother, John, joined the army and rarely came home. He was married to a Kanuri woman and, for years, had stayed away from home, so Denis assumed the role of an elder brother. The family was surprised to see John at Maggie's burial. He left almost immediately she was laid down six feet below. John was a man of few words. He was lanky and dark-skinned. He could be mistaken for a Hausa man. He had stayed so long in the northern part of Nigeria that he spoke Hausa fluently. After being posted around many barracks, he settled in Jos where he married his best friend's cousin.

Yusuf, his best friend, had convinced his uncle, Mallam Musa, to allow John to marry his daughter Hawa. They were Muslims and John was a Christian. Mallam Musa would not accept such request easily due to religious barriers. After much persuasion, he consented to marrying off his daughter to John, a Christian. They did the traditional and court marriages not long after. Two years into their marriage, Hawa delivered a set of male twins. John had a big celebration. Hawa gave birth to another baby girl the following year.

She was a prolific young lady and resorted to pill after consultation with a doctor to enable her go back to school and complete her degree. She only had a teacher training qualification in Hausa and Kanuri studies. She thought she could go a bit higher to enable her get promotions in the ministry of education where she worked. John was very supportive, and Yusuf was there for her too.

Hawa got admission to University of Jos to study Hausa education. She went to school from home every day. It was in her third year that John died on a mission. He was drafted from his Twelfth Battalion into anti-terrorism squad to quell a Muslim insurgency in Kano where he was blown in a suicide bomb attack. They were burnt beyond recognition, save the metal name tag that dangled from their necks on a ball chain when rescue workers came to pack their remains. The news soon spread around Agbarho that Onofere had lost his eldest son to terrorist bomb. Kayo wondered why such tragic death befell his uncle, so she asked her mother rhetorically. Kayo could still recall everything that happened that tragic day the news was broken to the family. She visualised her father's countenance on the fateful day. His face lost colour and a strange figure slipped down his feature. Fatefully, John was Onofere's second child to die.

Jite was the immediate younger sister of Mark. She was in school when Mark left for Germany. Mark doted on her for her intelligence. Kayo was told by her father that as a baby, she sucked her thumb always and at eleven months could say a few words. Her father told her it was a generally held belief that children who sucked their thumbs would be intelligent.

'Maybe that could explain her intelligence,' Denis told Kayo.

His eyes shone with pride. Somehow, Kayo was much closer to Maggie than Jite.

Jite lived with Kayo's parents briefly until she gained admission to the Federal University of Technology, Akure, where she studied agricultural sciences. In her second year, she asked her father for a small portion of land to start a poultry farm. She bought five hens and five roosters to start with and sought the help of her cousins to take care of them while she was away at school.

Poultry business booms during Christmas seasons, and she made most of her income during that period. She made it a matter of habit to give Kayo's parents one of her chickens any time she was home. She was a wise and an industrious young girl. One morning, Jite went to her poultry farm very early to feed her birds. Unknown to her was a black cobra curled up in one corner close to the entrance. The chickens squeaked loudly and were jumping helplessly. Before she knew what was happening, the snake stretched forward and bit her on the heel of the left foot. She screamed, but help was not near. It was after several hours when she did not come back to the house that her cousin went to call her for breakfast and saw her lying on the ground lifeless, foaming at the mouth. Three chickens were also dead beside her. Oniovosa, her cousin was alarmed. She saw the dust mark of the snake, and without being told, she knew Jite died of snakebite. Oniovosa ran back to the house, wailing and calling for help. Onofere ran to the poultry and found the lifeless body of his daughter sprawled on the ground. It was exactly four years after John's death.

'What have we done to deserve this?' Onofere lamented.

Relatives and neighbours soon gathered in their house. Onofere's wife fainted when she heard the news of her daughter's death. Neighbouring women tried to revive her. It was a deep sorrow for all who knew her.

Jite was buried three days later.

Mark married a Togolese woman whom he met in Germany and had returned to Nigeria to settle. She was a social worker. She had dreamt of becoming a social worker with one of the ministries, but her dreams were shattered with the difficulties she experienced in getting a job in the field. Instead, she applied for a teaching post. Afi had learnt English during her stay in Germany. It wasn't a problem for her to communicate with people in Nigeria, but with her husband, she spoke German. She could not get a job with any government school. She was discriminated against.

She was always reminded that she was an alien. Mark had to go with her to the ministry of education, but it did not help much. Mark got a job with the Delta Steel Company in Aladja. He tried to get Afi a job as a French teacher in their staff school. The director reluctantly hired her only to relieve her of the job six months later. Afi was impatient. She took their two children and returned to Togo. Mark had pleaded with her to stay. She wrote back to Mark a few months later that she was a commissioner in one of the ministries. Mark visited her and the kids every three months.

Mark was able to convince his brother Denis to send Kayo to Germany to study. It was in 1991, and Germany had reunited as one country two years earlier.

'There won't be much fear of neo-Nazis or skinheads,' Mark told his brother.

Mark asked his friend Hans to help process Kayo's admission. Hans and Mark were coursemates and had kept in touch after graduation. Kayo's father had a small party held in her honour. Her father accompanied her to Lagos, from where she flew to Germany. Denis had categorically told his wife not to travel with him. He remembered the caution given to him by an elder during his sister's burial. Denis saw his daughter to the depature gate. He waited till the plane took off before leaving the airport. It was precautionary. There had been occasions when passengers could not fly even after their relatives had long left the airport.

Kayo arrived in Germany with Hans waiting for her at the Frankfurt Airport. From there, he took her to his house. Hans was married to a Swiss lady, Ingrid. She had gone out of her way to buy an African cookery book in order to prepare African food. Kayo ate some potato dumplings and what looked like melon soup. Kayo did not want to offend her host, so she ate. Ingrid told Kayo that her Gambian friend had helped her with the cooking. Ingrid substituted garri with potato dumplings. Kayo now understood why the melon soup tasted different. It was probably prepared the Gambian way. They finished eating. Ingrid and Hans cleared the table, and Ingrid came back to the living room to sit with her while Hans washed the dishes. This surprised Kayo. She had never seen men in Nigeria, not even her father, do the dishes while the women sat to talk. It was an entirely different culture with the Europeans, she thought. She went to the guest room to have a change of clothes. She thought it was better to take a warm bath too. Kayo entered the bathroom but could not turn on the handle of the tap. It was different from what she had ever known. She wore her clothes and went to the living room to ask Ingrid to show her how to operate it. Kayo spent another two days with Hans and Ingrid before Hans drove her to Offenbach where she was to attend the language school. Hans recommended the language school in Offenbach because of the concentration of Africans. He took her to the administrative office where she was registered. A place had been reserved for her already. Her lessons would start in two days. Hans drove her to the student hostel, which wasn't far from the language school. He helped her to take her luggage up. Kayo was spellbound by the architecture of the hostel. The whole balcony was made of glass, the staircase was spiral, and there was a lift in the middle of the reception hall which housed the mini supermarket, a pharmacy, post office, and two restaurants. Hans called the lift into which they both entered. Kayo's room was on the fourth floor of the five-storey hostel. Hans had picked her keys from the porter at the reception. The lift stopped on the fourth floor. Hans stepped out first with Kayo following behind. He led the way to her room and opened the door.

'Go in,' he gestured to Kayo.

Kayo went in and looked around the room. There was a small refrigerator and a portable TV. By the window were a reading table, a chair, and a door leading to the balcony.

The bed was already laid. At the foot of the bed was an in-built wardrobe. She opened it and found cutleries in one shelf with its own door.

'You can arrange your clothes here,' Hans told her, pointing at some shelves.

'I like this place. It is very comfortable.'

'Yes, you should thank your father and uncle. They made sure you got the best.'

Hans sat on the reading table. He gave Kayo a brief history of Frankfurt and Offenbach before leaving.

'I must go now. You have my number. Give me a call when you need help.'

Hans closed the door behind him and left.

Kayo got a place to study in Frankfurt after completing her language studies. Hans and Ingrid left for the United Arab Emirates the same year she moved back to Frankfurt.

Hans got a new job with Siemens in Dubai. Kayo was sad but managed to get along. She spoke German very well and had made new friends. Just before her second year, she got a message that her parents had died in a car accident. Kayo was shocked but not surprised. The death that ran through her paternal family had caught up with her father. Kayo cried her heart out. She could not go home for the burial because she did not have enough money. Her uncle Mark advised her to stay back in Germany. He took charge of the burial, after which he left for Togo to join his wife. He was afraid. He did not know what would happen to him next.

The death of Kayo's parents changed her life forever. She could not pay her rent. Her visa expired and needed renewal. For her new visa, she had to tender an evidence of sponsorship and means of income. Her parents had been sponsoring her education. Kayo went to the foreign office all the same. The officer she met reminded her of all the requirements. Kayo was dejected and had just a few weeks before her visa would expire. Kayo was facing the greatest challenge of her life. She didn't know what to do or where to go. She was already walking the streets of Frankfurt with an invalid visa. Then she remembered that she had seen an African lady at the church she attended. She decided to ask her for help. The next Sunday, she left for church early and hoped that she saw the lady, but she was not lucky. She did not want to tell her German friends of her plight. Kayo waited another Sunday. She was fortunate to see her. Kayo waited patiently until service was over before approaching the lady.

She greeted her nicely. The lady flashed a smile at her. Kayo wasn't sure if she should discuss her problems with her. She introduced herself and asked if she had any information about jobs. Kayo showed her her identity card. The lady told her she was from Brazil. She told her she knew a lady from Congo who could give her some information. She told her the Congolese lady was married to a German who was her husband's friend. She took Kayo's number and promised to give her a call. Kayo thanked her, praying silently for a quick response.

She returned home, wishing someone would give her a gift of money or food. All she had was some packets of flour and three tins of canned corn. She opened one tin. It was her lunch and supper because she had to ration whatever she had. A week passed, but the lady did not contact her. She was forced to borrow money from one of her German friends. She took the money, not knowing exactly when she would pay back. Kayo went straight to the supermarket where she did a frugal shopping. She crossed the ever-busy Berger Strasse back to her flat. She cooked herself a meal that she had never dreamt of eating. Rice mixed with margarine. She drank a big glass of water and lay on her bed to rest. She fell asleep only to be woken up by a phone call. She picked up the phone and could hardly understand the caller. The line went dead, leaving Kayo confused. The phone rang again. The caller was more audible. It was the lady she met at the church. She was straight to the point after introducing herself. She gave Kayo the phone number of the Congolese. Kayo was appreciative.

She called the Congolese lady immediately. Kayo introduced herself. Kayo's call wasn't a surprise to her. Kayo could sense she was a pleasant person.

'Call me Anita,' she told Kayo.

After a brief conversation, they arranged to meet the next day in the city's central train station. Kayo hung up, hoping Anita could connect her with a job. Her bills were mounting. She dreaded opening any letter she took from her letterbox. Kayo turned on the television. The national news was the only programme she wanted to listen to before going to bed. She was restless all through the night. She could hardly sleep. Kayo met Anita at the train station as agreed. Anita greeted Kayo warmly and then led her to a fast-food restaurant. Anita lit a cigarette and ordered a cup of coffee for herself. She asked Kayo what she would drink. Kayo did not want to bother her. She declined the offer politely. Anita dragged her cigarette, sipped her coffee, and told Kayo that the only job she could introduce her to was housekeeping. Kayo was prepared to do anything to survive. Anita promised to link her up with a family in the next few days. By the time they finished discussion, Kayo had told Anita all about her problems. Anita shook her head.

'Life could be cruel, my dear, especially for students.' Anita promised to see what else she could do to help her.

The alarm rang again. It was then that Kayo realised she had been engrossed in deep thoughts. She rushed to brush her teeth, took her bath as fast as she could, and quickly dressed up. She hurriedly left the house, grabbing some slices of bread and a bottle of water which she tucked in her rucksack. Inside were her working clothes and shoes. She arrived at her work place half an hour late. She apologised to Mrs Braun, her boss, who was already waiting at the door for her. Mrs Braun worked as a nurse in a hospital and was on night shift that day. She was to resume at 4 p.m. Mrs Braun hastily exchanged greetings with her and began to leave. Kayo entered the house. It was a duplex of four bedrooms. She wondered why Mrs Braun and her husband bought such a big place when they had no children. Kayo would have to clean the whole house thoroughly because the Brauns had just returned from a four-week holiday to Spain. Kayo changed into her working clothes and began working slowly coughing intermittently. She was almost choking because of the dust-filled surfaces she cleaned.

Kayo vacuum-cleaned the small dining room and continued cleaning the surfaces. She ensured that each piece of furniture was properly wiped with a slightly wet napkin. She took extra precaution not to do the same with the sofas, couches, and some wooden furniture. Kayo paused a while to admire the painting of a lady dancing the traditional Spanish flamenco when suddenly she heard a bang. She ran out to see what it was but bumped into the horror of Mrs Braun on the ground in her own pool of blood. Beside her was a man holding a gun. Confused, Kayo screamed. The memories of her late young aunt flashed through her mind. She hated life for witnessing the death of yet another person close to her. Her eyes met that of the strange man who, Kayo was convinced, shot Mrs Braun. The man ran towards Kayo, and she knew immediately she was in danger. Kayo ran back into the house but discovered too late that she had closed the door without taking the key. She ran down the stairs past Mrs Braun's body. Her heart was beating rapidly; she did not want to be the next victim of death in their family. She was determined to break that jinx. She came to the end of the stairs and tried to go under it, but she quickly decided against it. She could hear the footsteps of the murderer pounding down the staircase. She needed to act fast. She turned around and saw the door leading to the parking lot. She opened it and ran inside. Though safe for a while, a now confused Kayo did not know what next to do. She looked behind her and saw the handle of the door turning cautiously. It was the man. He ran towards Kayo and shot at her. Kayo screamed and ducked at the same time. In a split second she spotted another door to her left.

She ran towards it and opened it. There she found the working tools and gardening equipments of Mr Braun. In a frenzy, Kayo opened yet another door inside the workroom. It was a cubicle crammed with shovels and rakes. Kayo squeezed herself into it and held the door firmly from behind. She began to say some silent prayers, more of a wish. She cursed whatever spell in which her family had been subjected. Again, she remembered all the deaths that had occurred in her family. Kayo began to weep silently. She stopped when she heard the footsteps close to the door. It was the killer still looking for her. He called out frantically, asking her to come out. He swore to feed her dead body to the vultures. Kayo's heart pounded harder. She began to question why the Brauns lived in such a secluded area. He cursed and raved. He kicked and slammed any door he saw. Then he came to where she was. Kayo crouched. He tried to open the door, but Kayo kept her grip on it from behind. The man ordered her to open the door. Kayo shivered. There were goose pimples all over her body. Kayo began to say her last prayers, asking God to take her to where her parents and grandparents were. She knew the end had come, but she did not open the door. The murderer pulled harder until he was able to force the door open. Without thinking, Kayo took a rake and hit the man hard on the face. He let out a sharp cry, staggered, and fell over. He groaned, vowing to snuff life out of her. She did not wait for a second. She ran out and up the stairs towards the house. Kayo was feeling cold. She wore just sandals and her work clothes. The frightened young lady ran through the main door and into the streets. The Brauns's house was in a very isolated area where houses were far apart from each other.

She ran as long as she could, stopping after a while to catch her breath before running across the field to reach the tarred road. She was unable to think straight. Kayo managed to get to the bus stop, panting. Some passengers stared at her curiously. She looked away, wishing someone could offer her a jacket. Kayo got into the bus as soon as it arrived. She told the driver that she had no ticket because she was running away from danger in her home. The driver shook his head in disbelief. He told her it was the antics employed by many foreigners, especially Africans, when they know they do not have tickets. The driver demanded that she leave the bus or risk being arrested by the police. Kayo chose the last option. She agreed that the police should be called. The bus driver grinned and sent a radio message for police. There was a delay in the bus schedule. The argument between Kayo and the driver had to be resolved. The driver asked the passengers to disembark and board the next bus. The police arrived shortly and took Kayo with them. Kayo was shown a bench to sit on at the station. She pleaded with them for a jacket because she was cold and already shivering.

'How could you have gone out without a jacket?' one of them asked her.

Kayo explained again that she had to save her life. The police officer went into their lost-but-found room. He found an old jacket which he threw at Kayo.

'Let me check if there are any shoes that will fit you.'

Kayo took the jacket gratefully and put it on. Another officer offered her warm tea which she also gladly took. An old pair of garden boots was placed near her feet. Kayo looked at them; they were boots she would have never thought of wearing. She thanked the police officer that brought them. She placed her mug of tea on the bench. Kayo took one of the boots and tried it on her left foot. The boot was small, so she had to force it on. All she wanted was something to keep her feet warm. She was given time to drink her tea and settle down to give statement. The senior police officer took her details later. He checked the computer and saw her visa had expired over a year.

'Your visa expired long ago, and you are still here in Germany?'

Kayo was silent. She did not know what to say.

'How am I not sure these are all cooked-up stories for you to elicit sympathy?'

Those words hit Kayo hard. She knew she had been living illegally in Germany.

'You would be transferred to the deportation camp tomorrow.'

Kayo insisted her story was true. She was given a mattress and a duvet for the night in another room. The next day, she was

THE DYING THIEF

driven to the immigration office where she was handed over to the officials. She was given a change of clothes. She continued her plea of being a witness to a murder case, but she was ignored.

Mr Braun came back from his official trip three days later to see the decomposing body of his wife. He was shocked. He called in the police who came to the crime scene immediately.

Forensic experts were invited to take samples and pictures. Detectives interrogated him and wanted to know who else was in the house. He said he suspected the cleaner, Kayo, was there. He saw her bag and clothes but could not understand why they were there. She became a prime suspect, and the police planned to circulate Kayo's name around all police stations in Germany. Mrs Braun's corpse was taken to the hospital for autopsy and DNA examination. Investigations into her death continued. Unknown to Mr Braun, Kayo was being prepared for deportation. Amidst tears, Kayo narrated all that happened to the immigration officer. She told him she would like to speak with Mr Braun. This time, she gave his name and address because the immigration officer listened to her. He promised to contact Mr Braun as soon as possible.

The officer ended his shift and went home. He did not show up for another five days. Kayo reminded his colleagues of her story and the officer to whom she had given Mr Braun's details. She was informed that he had gone on leave and would be back towards the end of the month. Kayo was disappointed. It was clear to her that fate was working against her. She was taken to the airport and was put on the plane bound for Nigeria. She never stopped telling the authorities of being a witness to a crime and not being given a fair chance. She explained she was an orphan and a victim of circumstances. She was led to the airport accompanied by two stern-looking policemen. She could not understand why the Nigerian embassy issued a travelling certificate to facilitate her deportation. Kayo wept for many reasons. Her parents were dead. She left Germany unceremoniously. Her documents and certificates were all left behind under no one's care. She kept a straight face, and it did not matter to her that other passengers looked at her. She sat down with a thump on her seat and took a view of the airport through the window. She was leaving a country without getting what she set out to achieve. She squeezed her eyes shut, forcing tears to trickle down her cheeks. She had been thrown into the path of thoughts and pain. Pain that can only be quantified by emotion! She was returning home unprepared, with neither money nor a home to go to. The plane took off, and in no time, she fell asleep. She was woken up by the air hostess who served her food.

'That's your food,' she said.

'Thanks,' she mumbled.

She gulped down the juice and continued with her sleep. It was when the plane touched down at the Murtala Mohammed Airport, Lagos, that she woke up. All the passengers disembarked. They all went through immigration except Kayo who was treated differently. She had not been in Nigeria in some years. She was led away by some security operatives who interrogated her for two hours. They were at a loss as to where she would live. She was taken to their boss whom they referred to as Hajia. She listened keenly to Kayo's story. Hajia told her that many young Nigerian girls had gone abroad as prostitutes. She told her the only thing they could do for her was to send her to the NGOs, who helped in the rehabilitation of young girls deported because of prostitution or who suffered abuse. Kayo was partially relieved. At least, there was a guarantee that she would have a roof over her head.

The police investigation into Mrs Braun's death went on. The immigration officer returned and was angry that Kayo had been deported. His colleagues blamed him for not giving a follow-up note. He decided to contact Mr Braun. Mr Braun was happy to know someone knew something about Kayo. Mr Braun asked to speak with Kayo.

'I'm sorry that she was sent back to Nigeria before I came back from my leave.'

'But why is that?' Mr Braun asked slightly miffed.

The immigration officer tried to placate him. He suggested Kayo be contacted in Nigeria, but Mr Braun was pessimistic. He knew it would be a Herculean task to establish contact with Kayo.

His wife was buried after three months. Mr Braun was devastated.

There was a vacuum in his life, and he thought another holiday would be good for him. He decided against the idea. He thought of seeing a therapist. He kept thinking of what best to do. He did not know exactly what to do. He felt his head splitting. He felt the room spinning, but he managed to call an ambulance. He slumped when he tried to open the door for the paramedics that came after he made the call. The medics were fortunate that he had opened the door before collapsing. He was lifted on a stretcher and driven to the hospital. Mr Braun woke up in the hospital and wondered why he was there.

He told the doctor about his wife's death and his fear of going back into the house. The doctor knew Mr Braun was traumatic. Mr Braun swore to the doctor that his wife's spirit would not rest if the murderer was not found. The doctor was empathic. He enquired from Mr Braun if the police had stopped investigation. Mr Braun hissed. He told the doctor that the police and their immigration counterparts wrongly deported the crown witness to her home country. He held the doctor's hand.

'Please, Doctor, I would die if the witness is not brought back to testify. I do not want the murderer of my wife go unpunished.'

The doctor asked for some tranquilisers to be given to him. Mr Braun slept off again. He needed plenty of rest. Two days later, some police visited him at the hospital. They asked if he knew the full names of Kayo. He wasn't very sure, but he told them she was a student. They made a few notes and left. Visitation took place after all patients had their breakfast. The chief medical officer spoke with Mr Braun. He advised him to go on a holiday. Mr Braun recounted again how he came upon his wife's corpse. Dr Schneider, the chief medical officer patted him on the back.

'You have to rest. The police will investigate the case, and we hope the culprit would be found, Mr Braun.'

He returned home but dreaded to be in his own home. He imagined his wife's ghost in the house. He was determined to find Kayo. He planned to travel to Nigeria in search of her. He got a visa and bought a ticket. He informed the police he was going to search for Kayo alone. They advised him not go because he did not know exactly where Kayo would be. The psychologist attached to the police knew Mr Braun's behaviour was rooted in depression. They reminded him that Nigeria was vast, and he could not possibly board a plane and begin to ask anyone he met who Kayo was. He advised him to get a friend to live with him for some time. The idea sounded good. He arranged for a male care worker to keep him company in the evenings and weekends. He also paid for a housekeeper to cook his meals and clean his house. He gave her a room to live in. That was the only way he could manage his situation.

Kayo was taken to the Mother of the Redeemer Charity Centre in Lagos. It was a centre for the rehabilitation of young girls and young female adults with special needs. It was run by the Catholic Church. Emphasis was to equip the young ladies with vocational skills and integrate them into the society. There were about thirty young girls in all. Most of them had a tale of woe to tell. Kayo was withdrawn. She wanted to be alone each time. She knew she wasn't supposed to be there. She remembered her aunt Maggie each time they baked. During Kayo's third month there, the bishop of the Catholic diocese visited them. The girls were told that they would have to prepare for the visit, which was the presentation of welcome songs and display of some of their products. Mrs Aigbe, the director of the centre, took charge of the preparation. The bishop came a week later. He came with two other visiting priests from Rome. At the end of the performance, one of the priests, Father Angelo Nwokocha, gave each girl the sum of 300 naira. It was a gift no one expected. The money was the first cash she got since her return from Germany. Kayo returned to her room. She had an urgent use for her windfall. She planned to write a letter to Mr Braun. She needed to post the letter. She settled down on her bed that night and began to write a very lengthy letter to Mr Braun. She gave details of how his wife was murdered and what followed thereafter. Kayo did not want the administration to know about the letter. She hatched a plan. She lied to Mrs Aigbe that she wanted to have some meditation inside the church. She sneaked out with the only friend she made there. Priscilla told her she was a victim of sexual abuse. Priscilla's father, who had long separated from her mother, had impregnated her and had wanted her to abort the baby, but she had refused.

'My father wanted to kill me, so I fled to the Catholic Church near our house. That was how I was brought here.'

Priscilla took Kayo to the post office where she posted the letter. Kayo and Priscilla strode back slowly to the women's shelter. The shelter was located behind the Catholic Church in the Aguda area of Surelere. It was some twenty minutes' walk from the post office to the shelter.

'And how is your baby?'

'She is being cared for at the children's village. I am here to learn a handiwork.'

There was a loud screech from a car. A motorist had hit a stray goat.

A group of young boys were running after it from behind. The motorist came out briefly and drove off again in full speed.

'Oloshi,' one of the boys cursed the motorist out in Yoruba language.

'I was scared,' Kayo told Priscilla.

'Me too,' she said.

Mrs Aigbe was waiting for them at the gate. They were shocked.

'Where are you ladies coming from?' She demanded.

The girls stared at each other and then Priscilla spoke first.

'Hmm, we thought we could look at some second-hand clothes at the Aguda market.'

Kayo was silent.

'Good, you ladies are now after fashion. And, Kayo, you lied. Both of you will wash the bathroom and toilets for rest of the week.'

Mr Braun received the letter. He rushed to the police who assured him they would send for Kayo. Mr Braun asked Wiebke, his newly employed housekeeper, to prepare meat steak and salad for five people. He wanted to celebrate a new chapter of the investigation into his wife's death.

Mrs Aigbe was surprised to see two police officers and a European at their shelter. The senior police officer spoke first. He told Mrs Aigbe the European was from the German embassy. They requested to see Kayo who was a crown witness to a murder case. They showed her a copy of the letter she sent to Mr Braun. Mrs Aigbe asked the men to wait while she summoned Kayo. Kayo did not know that her letter would yield a fast response. The men told Kayo who they were and that she had to return to Germany to aid the police in the murder case of Mrs Braun. When the men left, Mrs Aigbe called Kayo to her office.

'So you were in Germany?'

Kayo answered in the affirmative. She told her about the murder and her parents. When she finished, Mrs Aigbe queried her for not speaking up about it earlier. She also lamented not being given the true story of Kayo by the security operatives that brought her to the shelter.

'We thank God,' she said.

The German diplomat came back to take Kayo. She hugged Priscilla.

'I will be back after the investigation,' she told them.

Mrs Aigbe hugged her too. Kayo travelled that night to Germany. Mr Braun picked her up from the airport to his house.

Kayo gave a vivid description of the man and how she managed to escape him. It was only then that Mr Braun knew for the first time that Kayo was a student who had problems with her residence permit. Mr Braun went with her to the police. He insisted she should be given the 10,000 deutschmark reward for the person who could give information on the murder of Mrs Braun. Mr Braun took another step. He took Kayo to the foreign office. He requested that Kayo's student visa be renewed because her presence in Germany was highly needed.

Kayo wrote back to Priscilla and Mrs Aigbe. She told them she lost most of her documents and photographs in her former house. The landlord broke into it and disposed of her belongings. She told Priscilla that the housekeeper had a baby girl for Mr Braun. She promised to send her some money.

A BASKET OF FORTUNE

Izah was revered for his farming skills and hunting prowess. He maintained his two wives even when the missionaries came to their village to preach against polygamous family as a Christian virtue. He told them it was the traditional African way of life, and he must continue with what his forefathers began.

Despite the fact that his huge frame intimidated his acquaintances, he remained kind to a fault and would never hurt a fly. His main worry was his second wife, Eruke, who had not been able to conceive after twelve years of their marriage. Eruke was just eighteen when he married her, and there were rumours round the village that she was a witch and had seduced Izah into the marriage.

When all hope was gone, Eruke conceived and gave birth to a baby girl. The whole village went to the rumour mill again and started another rumour that the child must have come from her witch world. In spite of the rumour, Izah was nonetheless overjoyed and named the newborn baby Adede, after his own mother. Eruke loved her daughter so much and adored her and always wanted the best for her so that when she was six, she pleaded with her husband to allow Adede to attend the only village school. At first, Izah insisted that schools are for boys and not for girls.

'After all, she would be married, and all the money used in training her will come to nothing,' he told Eruke.

Eruke wouldn't give up.

She not only knew how to convince her husband but knew the way to win his heart as well. She was determined to have her daughter go to school. Two days after telling Izah about sending Adede to school, Eruke went to the market to buy some fresh fish and melon seed with which she made some soup. She added periwinkle and crayfish and served it with *usi*, a staple food made from cassava starch. Eruke knew periwinkle was rarely eaten in the house, so she grasped the opportunity to thrill her husband with a new delicacy. Eruke waited until dinner time to serve Izah the food. The earthen bowls in which the food was served were steaming hot. Izah took a whiff of the food for an appetiser.

'I know my wife could make magic with her fingers.'

Eruke sat on a mat spread on the floor next to her husband. He took a morsel of the *usi* and a generous portion of the soup laced with some periwinkle.

'I never knew you were such a wonderful cook,' he remarked, savouring the food.

Izah continued eating showering Eruke with accolades between mouthfuls.

'Come, eat with me, my wife.'

Izah invited his wife to join him. Eruke washed her hands and settled down to the delicious meal of which the inviting aroma had taken over the air at least where it was being eaten.

'What is the secret behind this soup?' he enquired from Eruke.

Eruke laughed and promised to tell him after eating. 'I heard it is not good to talk too much while eating.'

'That is true, my dear wife.'

They ate together silently until Izah broke the silence when he asked about the upcoming village feast. Eruke cleared the plate from the mat after eating, giving room for Izah to sprawl himself on the mat. He told Eruke that relaxing after eating makes the food digest faster. Eruke came back from the kitchen and knelt down meekly near her husband and began to massage his feet.

'My husband, Adede can become a great woman with the way she is going. Have you noticed her intelligence?'

'Yes, I have,' Izah agreed with her.

'I heard such children get money from the government only through schools,' Eruke continued subtly, putting forward the issue of Adede's school until her husband agreed that she be sent to the village school.

Eruke was delighted; she stayed with her husband till about midnight before going to her room. She passed her mate on her way.

'Good night, Mama Riode.'

Eruke knew she had been eavesdropping. Isiorho was mute but looked quizzically at her.

Adede was to be the first child of this polygamous family to attend any school properly. Her elder brothers attended but did not progress beyond primary school. That was enough to go back to their father's farm. Their mother, Isiorho, who wasn't literate, saw nothing wrong with them not going beyond primary school; primary school was already enough sophistication. When the farm was not sufficient, they went to Warri, the biggest city in their locality, to work wherever their primary school certificates were viable. She was satisfied with the money and gifts they sent her. They were carried away with stories they heard of the oil city and the Europeans who lived there.

'So you can waste your time sending Adede to school?'

Isiorho asked Eruke one morning. 'I think I made a good decision,' Isiorho adjusted her cloth.

'Well, you should be thinking of who will take care of you in the future, and remember, she would get married too and leave you alone. All the money for training her will become useless.'

'Mama Riode, don't be naive. Do away with this old belief and embrace the new thinking. If I could not go to school, let my daughter go for me.'

'You have been brainwashed.'

Eruke took a long look at Isiorho, shook her head, took her basket, and left Isiorho standing alone. She was not ready to plant a quarrel with her. Isiorho laughed.

'You can go on with your conviction,' she said sarcastically.

The harmattan was the time for harvesting and planting. Izah needed more hands on the farm. He employed more farmhands to help him harvest and weed the land while Isiorho supervised the farmlands. Eruke took care of the sales of the farm produce. Izah had carefully apportioned one role to each of his wives to avoid quarrel between them and save himself the trouble of being his wives' judge. Isiorho felt there was more money and more responsibility in the sales duty, so once she told Izah she wanted a change of roles. Since Izah would not listen to that, Isiorho left his presence, disgruntled. Isiorho could not understand why Izah gave such a sensitive role to Eruke, the second wife. She visited her sister-in-law to complain of what she saw as favouritism and injustice done to her. Madam Najevwe was a very strict and pragmatic woman. She was well-respected for her uprightness and unusual strength for a woman. She fought men and went to farm alone even in the thick of the forest. People likened her to a deity or an Amazon. She brought back her husband's corpse alone from the farm when he fell to his death from a coconut tree.

'Isiorho, please be contented with your role,' she told her.

Isiorho was not satisfied. She trotted off to Izah's uncle's house; he was a drunkard who said he drank at a doctor's recommendation. After hearing Isiorho out, he gestured into the air, dropped down his head, and shook it vigorously.

'You are the first wife. You must be given what you want. I will talk to your husband about it immediately. How could you be relegated to the background? Why does he behave like this? I have told him that he should take care of his father's land by weeding it alone and not turning it to a farm. He should . . .'

'OK, my in-law, I will be expecting your visit.'

Isiorho interrupted, noticing that her complaint was not particularly addressed any more. He was a loquacious man and could rant over nothing all day. But for Isiorho, it was better to talk to him even as he was than have nobody at all. Izah wasn't expecting to see his eldest son late in the evening. Obruche greeted his father and asked about his mother.

'Why did you come so late from Warri?'

'Papa, I put my neighbour's daughter in the family way, and her family is insisting I must marry her. I have to come this late because it is an urgent matter.' Izah looked hard at his son.

'Why didn't you control yourself?' Izah said, slightly fuming.

'Papa, I love the girl, and I'm the first man she knew. She is twenty-three and a seamstress. She loves me too.' Obruche wanted to continue, but his father sprang up again.

'I have heard you. I will talk to my kinsmen tomorrow and let you know about it.'

Obruche went into the compound to meet his mother. He passed Adede who was doing her homework.

'How is school, Adede?' he asked, not stopping for her response.

'Fine, thank you, Brother. You came so late.'

'Yes, I have things to do. That is why,' he said over his shoulder and went on and met his mother in her room. She was preparing to go to sleep.

She was surprised to see her son.

'You are here. Hope all is well?' Without answering, Obruche sat down on the edge of his mother's bed.

He took his shoes off, clasped his hand between his thighs, and gazed on the floor thoughtfully. His mother, who was keeping away her work clothes, did not notice her son's posture.

'Yes, Mother, all's well, but I have impregnated a girl. Her parents are all over me, and I have come home to talk about it.'

His mother broke into a dance and held him in embrace.

'So I'm soon going to be a grandmother,' she echoed.

Obruche was surprised at his mother's reaction. His suppressed joy was betrayed by his glittering eyes.

'My son, you are a man now, and we will talk more about this tomorrow morning. Now you need to eat something.'

Isiorho went into her kitchen. She knew it was late, but she wanted to show her son her support by preparing him some food. Obruche lay on his mother's bed. Isiorho came later with two earthen bowls which held some yam and the traditional *egbagba* soup for Obruche. He took the bowls thankfully from his mother after which he went into the kitchen to wash his hands and get some water to drink. Isiorho, still excited with the news her son brought, asked more questions. She stood up again and danced round the room. She sat down and suddenly put on a gloomy look.

'Obruche, I told your father that I want charge of the sales of the farm produce now, but he would not hear of it.'

'Mama, I think you should not worry about that.' Isiorho disagreed with her son.

'Your granduncle, Ovedje, plans to talk to your father about it soon.' Obruche stopped eating at the mention of Ovedje.

He stared at his mother and burst out into a long laughter. His mother was confused.

★ ★ ★

Ovedje was the loudest and the only one who finished a whole keg of palm wine when they went for Obruche's traditional wedding. Isiorho wasn't happy with him. He did not keep his promise of talking to Izah on her behalf. She walked up to him and took away his glass of wine.

'You should be ashamed of yourself,' she told him.

'Don't worry, I will marry you when my son dies,' Ovedje said.

Everyone turned to look at him. He got up staggering and struggling to keep his cloth in place. Izah did not want to leave his in-laws' presence to caution him. He knew his uncle could cause him lots of embarrassment. Izah bowed his head in shame, but his friend Oseh whispered to him to ignore him. Oteri was brought in by the women. Obruche stepped forward to spray her some money. His father and uncles accompanied him amidst drum and singing and the loud live band that sang Izah's praises. The guests were not left out in the spraying galore. They seemed to want to outdo each other while at it. Oteri danced lightly to the music, with Obruche holding her hands. Her stomach was now well-grown and bouncing under her cloth.

'It could be twins,' some of the guests said.

Ovedje staggered through the guests and raised his voice.

'Stop the music, stop the music,' he commanded.

'Why are you all dancing when this woman is in labour? Take her now to the hospital.'

The musicians stopped singing. Guests stopped in their tracks to see who was talking. Ovedje tied his already falling cloth firmly round his waist. Oteri was stunned. She did not understand how Ovedje knew she was in labour. Oteri's father was angry. He found it absurd for someone to act irrational during an event of such magnitude. Chief Jolomi asked the musicians to go on. Izah and some of his relatives took Ovedje away. Obruche and Oteri danced on until she complained of waist pain. He led her to her chair, but the pain did not subside. Her mother was called, and she took her to the living room to rest. Oteri let out a sharp cry, and at that moment, her mother knew she was in labour. She called in some women. Madam Najevwe wasn't a midwife, but she had good experience helping women in labour in the village. The floor, once stained with food and drinks, was cleaned and cloths were laid on the floor. Eseyoma, a neighbour who came to grace the occasion, quickly boiled water, while Isiorho assisted Madam Najevwe to deliver Oteri's baby boy after about twenty minutes of labour. The news simmered among the guests, who oblivious of the woman in labour, were enjoying the party; they now doubled their partying and asked for more wine.

Izah and Chief Jolomi looked around for Ovedje and found him in a corner struggling with a half-empty keg. Here was a mysterious drunkard who could see where clear-headed men were blind! They forcibly lifted him on their shoulders, still holding his keg of palm wine high above their heads.

★ ★ ★

The elders were assembled before the high chief. A woman, accused of being a witch, was brought before them because each of her children had died before they turned two, and she had lost a total of seven children in a row.

Izah asked her accusers if anyone saw her kill her children. They looked at themselves and then at Izah. They uttered no response because they were apparently stumped with his question. The woman's husband stood up and declared he was no longer ready to have a wife who could not bear him children. Just then, Ovedje appeared from behind them with a bottle of local gin. The elders watched him as he approached the gathering. They no longer took him for granted after the incident at the wedding ceremony.

'What is the problem, my people?' he asked, staggering to a balance.

'Eyauvie is being accused of killing all her seven children,' one of the elders elected to answer.

Ovedje opened his bottle and took out a small glass from the leather bag slung across his shoulder and poured himself some gin, swished it in his mouth, and began, 'You people accusing her, are you clean? How come you are accusing her? Why not accuse the husband? Maybe one of you wanted her for a wife, but she refused, and now you are looking for a way to get back at her . . .'

Ovedje drank some more gin and continued, 'And you elders, why sit here to judge this matter? Anyway, I'm going.'

Ovedje was tipsy. He fell over when he attempted to walk out on them. It took him another five minutes to get up. The young men who were around chuckled and laughed as Ovedje struggled with his cloth. Izah and the other elders watched. The high chief decided that the issue was more a family issue than a public one. Eyauvie was asked to go home to her family for further consultations. It was clear that Ovedje had given a clue as to how to solve the problem.

★ ★ ★

School life for Adede was an interesting one. The years went fast, and she was already in the secondary school. She was one of the best pupils, and Izah was proud of his daughter. The principal of her school invited him one day to his office to discuss the possibilities of sending her for further training to a very good university. Mr Orofua told Izah that Adede was exceptionally intelligent, and she needed all the encouragement she could get. Izah left Mr Orofua's office feeling elated. He was grateful that one of his children was in school and doing well.

He not only doubled Eruke and Adede's allowances but gave Eruke more plots of land.

Isiorho did not take this lightly, so she demanded to know why Eruke got more landed property than her.

'It is my decision, and I wish to reward her, so do not question my authority,' he warned.

THE DYING THIEF

That Eruke got even more properties afterwards aggravated the rift between her and Isiorho. She took her grievances once more to Madam Najevwe. This time, she promised to speak with Izah.

'You go home, I will speak to him,' Madam Najevwe assured her.

Isiorho was partially relieved. She was determined to ensure that there was some justice and fair play in the family. Madam Najevwe believed that the first wife should be shown more favour as an honour. She planned to talk about it in the women's meeting. She vowed to resist any attempt by Izah to relegate his first wife to the background.

Isiorho's anger was aggravated when Izah, Eruke, and Adede went to attend the award ceremony at the Oria Grammar School where Adede was a recipient of several awards. Izah invited some of his relatives and close friends. Adede received five awards. Awards were in the categories for overall best pupil and best performance in sport, mathematics, history, and literature. A party was organised to celebrate Adede's academic feat. Isiorho refused to be a part of it. She tried convincing her sons not to partake too, but they could not resist celebrating with their half-sister. Ovedje was an honourable guest there. He once again drank himself to stupor and was full of praises for the women who cooked the meals.

'You have misplaced that priority. Who deserves the praise? The women who cooked the food or the person in whose honour we are gathered here?'

Mitaye, Adede's half-brother, teased Ovedje. Although Mitaye disliked his drunken habit, he never repudiated him. Eruke became pregnant again at a very late age. The pregnancy was a surprise to the villagers who seemed to know everything that went on around her. The village midwife had told her that she had passed the age of childbearing; nevertheless, Izah and Adede were happy about the pregnancy. Adede was eighteen and almost completing her secondary school when her mother became pregnant. As a grown-up girl, she now helped her mother after school with sales of their farm produce. Isiorho offered to help, but Eruke declined, knowing that it was the tactic to take over that function having complained around to no avail.

'You don't know her motives,' she confided in her daughter.

The maize harvest was one of the busiest in Oria. Adede was on her way from the maize market when her best friend, Kate, walked up to her.

'I heard your mother is pregnant again.'

'Yes,' Adede replied.

Adede and Kate had been very good friends since their primary school days. They exchanged visits often and spent days sleeping over at each other's house. Kate was a year younger than Adede, but they got on well as friends. They shared many things in common.

'People are surprised that your mother is pregnant again.'

'Why?' Adede asked, pretending not to know the reason.

'Hmm, well, Adede, the reason is clear.'

'Kate, please don't be offended. Let us talk about something else.'

Adede was very bold and honest in nature, so with Kate she did not mince words. Kate knew that her friend wasn't at ease with that topic. Both friends walked silently along the bushy path that led to their home. Everywhere was quiet save for the shuffling of their feet as they walked over the foliage that covered the path and the chirping of the birds. Clouds began to gather above the sky, and the wind blew; Adede looked up.

'It seems it is going to rain again.'

'I think so too,' Kate said.

They quickened their steps to beat the rain. They made it.

As she drew closer to the house, she saw women gathered round on their veranda. Adede stopped at first and then slowed down. Then very gently, she walked towards the women. Her father was seated on his favourite chair, looking grim with two men by his side. Isiorho sat on the floor next to his feet, wailing and cursing.

She walked up to her father and cast a questioning look at him, as if to ask what was happening, without saying the words. Izah took her daughter by the hand and swallowed hard. He opened his mouth, but no sound came out.

'Papa, talk to me.'

Adede became hysterical; her eyes became glassy with tears. Madam Najevwe emerged from inside the house and led Adede inside. There were other women sitting in the living room.

'Sit down on that chair,' she told Adede, pointing to an empty wooden chair.

Izah had told Adede that he inherited the chair from his father.

'You are now a young girl of marriageable age. You can discern right from wrong and take a decision for yourself now.'

Adede listened, but she was impatient to hear the end, which would probably explain the mood in the air. She knew her aunt spoke in parables. But this is not time for parables.

'Every woman and everybody will pass through that stage, even your mother. Such stage brings the end of us all. Now your mother is sleeping, and no one can wake her up. She took her baby with her.'

Madam Najevwe had hardly finished when it became clear to Adede that her mother had died during childbirth. She now understood the reason why it was windy and cloudy on her way from the market. Such sign is widely believed in the village to be a bad omen. It had always been a strong belief among the people of Oria that something evil would happen when the clouds gathered and strong wind blew with little or no rain.

Life took a different turn for Adede after her mother's death. She lost interest in almost everything. Fortunately, she had passed the promotional exams already. Her principal was exceptionally happy and always used her as an example of intelligence. Kate fulfilled her obligation of friendship through frequent visits to her.

'All is not lost,' she told Adede.

Adede had confided in Kate that she thought Kate was too young to have a relationship and thought it was better that Kate finished her secondary school before getting into any serious relationship.

'There is nothing wrong with having a proposal now. Date for a while and marry later.'

Ogaga, Kate's fiancé was doing his housemanship at Eku Baptist Hospital, not far from Oria. Kate planned to settle down with him as soon as she finished her secondary school.

'I will further my education,' Adede agreed with her.

Kate and Ogaga met at Eku Baptist Hospital where she was on admission for typhoid fever. She had had a high fever and needed urgent attention. Dr Ogaga Omizu was the doctor on call when Kate was brought to the hospital. He was quick to diagnose her and followed up on her treatment. She was discharged four weeks later. Two months after, Kate and her mother paid Dr Omizu a visit to show him their appreciation for the attention he gave them. They went with a basket full of fruits. He neither expected them nor the gift of fruits. Their visit fell on one of his busy schedules. He was attending to a critically ill patient in the emergency room, and so they waited for almost an hour; later, he emerged from the room with an apologetic smile of a professional who wanted to please his guests. He invited them to the lounge where they discussed for several minutes. Elizabeth, Kate's mother, presented him with the fruits. Though puzzled, Dr Omizu accepted the basket in good faith. Elizabeth sold fruits along the Abraka–Agbor highway. She had been selling fruits on that road for many years and could tell the history of the road and the names of all the commercial drivers even in her sleep.

Dr Omizu was short of time, and so he gave his apartment key to Kate and requested her to take the fruits there. He told Kate he lived in the staff quarters within the hospital premises. Then he told her how to get there, after which he took leave of them and went back to work. He had instructed Kate to drop his key with the nurse attached to his office.

'Please feel free to visit me any time,' he had told them.

Kate started by visiting him once in a month and would stay for about an hour and go back home. Dr Omizu usually received his guests in the staff lounge; so that was his and Kate's rendezvous too. They would drink and talk casually. They talked about a variety of topics, though nothing in particular. Once, Dr Omizu had asked her what she intended to become in life. She told him she wanted to study accounting at the university if her parents supported her education. Kate continued the visit and somehow won Dr Omizu's confidence and trust. He asked her during one of the visits to help him tidy his apartment. The request was one that Kate gladly took. From then on, Kate helped him with his laundry and cooking, and her visits became an obligation rather than voluntary.

Kate thought she had settled down with her new role, but she was wrong. She had gone to drop off the keys after one of her routine visits when the nurse attached to Dr Omizu accosted her and questioned her frequency in the doctor's office. Confused and not expecting the confrontation, Kate could not answer, and the nurse declared her a nuisance and screamed at her at the top of her voice. Attracted by the shout, Dr Omizu walked out of his office into the commotion.

'Sir, this lady is a nuisance around here. Who is she, by the way? She is coming to drop off your key every now and then, or have you employed a cleaner for your apartment?' she asked without waiting for an explanation.

'And how does that become your problem? What is the nuisance in it?' Dr Omizu asked her with blazing eyes, adjusting the stethoscope hanging across his shoulder.

She was staring at the doctor, panting, with her hands to her hips.

'I'm asking you, Nurse Muesiri Eguare. Tell me her sins,' he said, glaring at her.

When the nurse could not answer, he turned to Kate who was already trembling.

'Take the key, Kate. You are welcome anytime. I have a spare key to myself. See you on Sunday,' Dr Omizu said, without looking at the nurse and returned to his office.

Muesiri gave Kate a spiteful look and quickly followed the doctor.

Kate left almost immediately. It was on her next visit that the doctor explained to her that Muesiri had had a crush on him, and even though he noticed it, he ignored her feelings and that always made her angry with any girl she thought had gained his attention. The explanation ignited a fire between them, and he asked her out formally. Although this is what Kate wanted, it came earlier than she had expected, and the suddenness of the request led her to involuntarily refuse, but she soon caved into his request.

Kate's parents did not object to the relationship and would want them to marry as soon as possible, but Ogaga would not entertain that haste.

Adede and Kate sat for their school certificate exams the same year the military staged a bloodless coup led by General Buhari. Nigerians did not bother much about the coup because they had had enough of the corrupt politicians.

Adede passed excellently, as expected of her. Kate did not pass her literature and commerce exams. Ogaga, her fiancé, looked through her result. He told her those two subjects would not prevent her from pursuing her dream profession. He enrolled her for

THE DYING THIEF

the university preparatory classes and the university entrance exams. Before she sat for the exams, Ogaga married Kate under the native law and custom. He did not feel safe leaving her a spinster for long.

'The university is full of temptations,' he had once explained. 'There may be other male admirers out there who would like to get involved with you.'

Ogaga wanted the church wedding as soon as he could.

Adede wasn't so fortunate. Tragedy struck again immediately after her exams. Her father became very ill, and a lot of money was needed for his treatment. He was unable to farm. His sons in Warri did not want to leave their families and jobs to take over the farm, and they were not wealthy enough to spare money for their father's treatment either. Isiorho was initially helpful, but as Izah's condition deteriorated, she stopped caring for him too. Adede was bewildered and wrote to Kate asking if her husband could be of any assistance to her father. Kate wrote back promising to discuss with her husband. Adede had expected another letter from her friend, but instead, she came in person in the company of her husband. Ogaga examined Izah and recommended his immediate admission to the Eku Baptist Hospital. He didn't like it that they had begun traditional treatment for him before seeking white medicine.

'Traditional medicine men usually would not know the exact diagnosis of the problem but could only associate symptoms,' he advised. Kate opened her purse and gave Adede some money, and she was thanked in return. She hugged Kate and shed tears simultaneously.

'Don't cry, my friend. All will be well. Just trust in God,' she consoled her gently, brushing her hair backwards.

Kate and Ogaga left for Eku the following day.

Izah's cousin and one of Izah's sons elected to take Izah to the Eku Baptist Hospital a few days later accompanied by Adede. On their arrival at the hospital, they were saved from the long hours of waiting for consultations, which was the characteristic of a hospital that served more crowd than its intended capacity, having had a prediagnosis with the hospital's doctor. They were ushered into the consultation room where Dr Omizu carried out a series of medical tests on him. Kate was with them throughout the process, and her presence was a great comfort to Adede. Later, they retired to her home for lunch, and they remained there until the results of the tests were ready.

Ogaga explained to Adede that her father would be transferred to a teaching hospital for advanced treatment because they lacked certain specialisations in their facility. He issued them a referral letter and Izah's complete medical report. Adede and her family were grateful for the assistance.

Isiorho was not very helpful and her many actions were deliberately made to cause disturbances in the once peaceful family. First, she took back all the plots of land Izah gave to Eruke's and Adede's welfare. Isiorho was able to convince and win her children and some of Izah's kinsmen to her side. They supported almost all her actions. Izah was incapacitated and too sick to control his home. He watched helplessly how Isiorho squandered the little money they had left. She no longer took Izah's health serious.

Further treatment was recommended for him, but there was not enough funds, and Isiorho would not part with a penny for his sake. Izah and Adede became close in his predicament.

The women's group of Oria village were about to hold their annual dance. Madam Najevwe became the leader after the death of the previous leader. She assembled all the members in order to plan the preparations for the festival. The custom was to raise funds, and every woman had to make a certain financial contribution. The town hall was the venue for the meeting. The women came in large numbers, and Isiorho was the last to come. She greeted everyone cheerfully and then took her seat. Najevwe welcomed them and reminded them of the need to make early preparations and suggested that the women from the neighbouring villages be

THE DYING THIEF

invited as well to add colour to the event. She was a good planner, and her opinions were always upheld. And so it was to this day, except by Isiorho. She took the centre of the gathering, looked round, curled her lips, and began to speak:

'Why must women who lack foresight, like Najevwe, be allowed to rule us? How can you all sit down there and listen to a debased fellow like her?'

Madam Najevwe did not anticipate any opposition. She was shocked by Isiorho's utterances, but managed to interrupt her.

'Isiorho, please mind your language,' Najevwe cautioned.

'Let me talk. I too have the right to express myself. How can you invite the women from the other village to participate in our annual dance? Has it been done before?'

There was slight murmuring. Najevwe stood up and requested Isiorho to sit down, but she insisted she must finish her speech. Some women pleaded with Madam Najevwe to allow her speak.

'Yes, as I was saying, why must we invite women from the neighbouring villages? First, it will cost us more money to host them. Next, we should remember that the people of Sanubi took part of our land and called it theirs till date. Remember too that one of our men was killed during the burial ceremony of one chief in Eku. Our high chief asked them to give account of it, but they could not. The women from those villages are not worthy of our ceremonies.'

There was more murmuring. Mamode, one of the women, stood up and said, 'I salute your courage to speak up, Isiorho. Madam Najevwe, we do not need to invite these people. I think Isiorho is right,' she said, looking around.

Madam Najevwe thanked her and then began to admonish Isiorho.

'Isiorho, you must get your facts very well before you say anything. The land dispute between Sanubi and Oria is a historical thing. Our generation cannot resolve that issue if those before us could not. Those who witnessed the dispute first-hand could not. More so, the people of Sanubi and Oria have been marrying each other. What do we do to our children who happen to have a parent from Sanubi? Then about Eku, you must be the only one who did not remember that the Eku high chief sent emissaries to our village to apologise to our own high chief. Our duty is to mend the fence and restore peace between the two communities.'

'All right, so who will bear the cost? How many women are wealthy enough to contribute towards a big festival you are trying to hold?' Isiorho snapped.

'Isiorho, do not worry. We will make it.'

'Najevwe, no, let us face the facts. How are we going to contribute? How much will be enough?'

'I will bring a basket of rice,' Atuyota, one of the members, offered.

'I will bring a gallon of oil,' voiced another.

Twenty more women made other pledges.

'You see, Isiorho. You can see that we are not as poor as you are trying to make us look,' Najevwe said.

'Najevwe, you lack foresight. Whoever made you the leader of this group?'

'Isiorho, you are becoming insolent to me and the donors. Please sit down.'

'Najevwe, listen to yourself. Can you even feed yourself?'

'Isiorho, we are not talking about that here now.'

'I will feed you and all the guests who are coming.'

'Sit down, Isiorho, and calm down. Do you want to bite the hand that fed you?'

'Just because you are my in-law does not mean I cannot tell you the truth.'

Isiorho and Madam Najevwe continued to exchange more words. Other members tried to restore peace.

Madam Najevwe became furious and slapped Isiorho across her left cheek. Isiorho retaliated. Their fisticuffs brought the meeting to an abrupt end. It took the intervention of the young men around to separate them from each other's throat.

Adede woke up early enough to prepare for her journey to Warri. She had arranged to meet with Ruke, who introduced her to the sale of second-hand clothes. She took the tough decision to earn a living since Isiorho starved the family of every fund. She had to fend for herself and support her ailing father too. There was hardly any food in the house. Isiorho was never at home. She had a client almost every day with whom she inspected the family property, or she had an event to attend. Adede was bitter from lack of food in the house and access to the family money.

She pleaded with Kate for some money to begin a small business with. Kate wished she could continue with her school but could understand Adede's desperate situation. She needed money to keep life going.

Adede met Ruke at the highway from where they boarded a bus to Warri. The bus went through Eku and Okpara towns. It made a brief stop at Osubi to refill the tank. The driver told the passengers to pay up their fares because they were approaching Effurun from where they could take an intercity bus to Warri. Adede disliked it when the passengers were dropped off at Effurun instead of Warri.

'We are being cheated,' she told Ruke.

'They won't change that soon, Adede.'

Adede and Ruke crossed over to the PTI roundabout where they boarded a bus to Effurun–Sapele Road. Ruke explained to Adede that the name of the roundabout is an abbreviation of the Petroleum Training Institute located in that area. The bus was packed full. Passengers pressed against one another. The conductor sat on a small wooden bench, squeezed between the door and the front seat. Adede saw his distress. His sitting position wasn't comfortable. There was a slight gridlock around the Effurun market. A soldier who boarded a taxi in front of their bus elected to help in controlling the flow of traffic. It was a chaotic scene with traders loading and unloading their wares right on the road. A middle-aged woman fell in an attempt to lift her basket of vegetables. She was helped up again by her fellow tradeswomen. Traffic was normal again after a quarter of an hour.

'If not for this soldier, we would have been held up here still,' Ruke told Adede.

'It is always like this on Effurun market day,' the conductor said.

The bus stopped at a makeshift bus terminal. All passengers disembarked. Adede and Ruke took a taxi to Enerhen junction, where they ran into another traffic gridlock.

'We are heading to Warri central market now,' Ruke explained to Adede, who had apparently forgotten her geography of Warri.

Ruke was not an intimate friend of Adede. They had become close only when Adede wanted information on the sales of second-hand clothing. Ruke had been in the trade since they were in the fourth grade. She settled down to continue with the business as soon as she completed her secondary school education.

Ruke told Adede of her plans to open a fashion boutique as soon as she had enough money for it. She spoke Urhobo fluently, although she was originally from Obiaruku, a neighbouring town of Abraka where Ukwani was spoken. Her father was the driver of Dr Eferhua, the dean of physical education department at the Delta State University. Dr Eferhua was from the Oria subvillage of Abraka. He had used his influence to get Mr Enebeli and his pregnant wife a house in Oria. Four months after they moved into their home, Ashiedu, Enebeli's wife, gave birth to a baby girl. The landlady named her Ruke.

Enebeli died in a tragic motor accident along with his boss, Dr Eferhua, many years later. He was driving from Asaba to Agbor after a conference when a truck lost control and ran over their car. Enebeli died on the spot while Dr Eferhua died three days later at the hospital. Ruke, her mother, and two brothers could not go back to Obiaruku. Her mother had established a small restaurant on a parcel of land that Enebeli bought from his landlady.

The taxi stopped at Enerhen junction. Both girls alighted and began to walk slowly.

'Warri begins after the Shell Club you see fifty metres from here,' Ruke lectured her.

Adede looked ahead of her expectantly. She had heard much of the bustling city of Warri and its conurbation. They walked towards the ever-busy First Marine Gate bus terminal from where they boarded another bus to the central market. It was an hour before midday when they arrived. Ruke led the way to the second-hand open market, giving Adede ample time to look around the market.

Wooden stalls dotted everywhere, with clothes hanging loosely from them. Their numbers formed a labyrinth in the section of the market they occupied. Ruke held Adede's hand, leading her carefully through the narrow and congested lanes. She gave her tips on how to find the best and cheapest deal. Ruke bought three sacks full of clothes. Adede bought two. They left the sacks in the care of an Ukwani man whom Ruke had befriended over the years to enable them get some food. Ruke seemed to know every nook and cranny of the central market. She walked past the clusters of shops along the beach. Thick billows of smoke filled the air. Ijaw women were preparing smoked fish. Adede salivated. Ruke stopped near an almond tree. Under it were two long wooden benches. A lady sat behind three medium-sized cooking pots. She wore a loose orange dress which accentuated her rotund figure. Two men were already sitting on the bench of which the colour had turned from brown to greyish.

'This is the woman I always buy food from whenever I come here.'

Madam Tasty as she is fondly called by her customers welcomed Ruke with familiarity of a businesswoman. Ruke introduced Adede to her. Madam Tasty smiled and nodded slightly at Adede. Ruke sat on the bench, while Adede remained standing.

'Why not sit down?'

Adede hesitated a while and then sat down on the edge of the bench because she could not stand the way it looked. Ruke bought some rice with cooked beans. Adede preferred rice and tomato stew with fish. Ruke ordered some drinks from the hawker who was walking past them. Ruke gulped her drink and ate ravenously. She scooped spoonfuls of rice into her mouth. Adede asked for more rice and fish. She could not resist the taste of the stew. That must have earned Madam Tasty the nickname, she thought.

Madam Tasty handed her a plate of fish and another one of steaming rice.

'Thank you,' she told her.

Madam Tasty asked Ruke about her plans to open a fashion boutique.

'I'm on it,' Ruke told her gulping some more Coke.

Adede could not finish her bottle of Fanta before they left. She was too full. Two boys loaded their sacks into two wheelbarrows. Wheelbarrows were the means of transporting buyers' wares from inside the market to the public transport parks.

Adede witnessed yet another chaotic transportation scene. She wondered how Ruke managed to make her several business trips to Warri all these years with a lot of transportation laxity in that city. They paid extra charges for the sacks of clothing. When they arrived in Oria, it was late in the evening. They had to give bribes to almost all the police they met at the checkpoints.

Isiorho was dragged to the elders by Mr Okoro, the new teacher that was transferred to Oria. She sold him a plot of land, but by the time he wanted to start his building, three hefty men accosted him and chased him away on the grounds that ownership did not belong to Isiorho, but to them, and warned him never to put his foot there again. Mr Okoro confronted Isiorho who pleaded with him that she didn't remember that the land was already sold but promised to refund the money at the end of the month. Mr Okoro looked forward impatiently to the end of the month. Isiorho never turned up when the month finally came to an end.

Okoro decided to meet Isiorho at her home after a few more days. Isiorho's niece, whom he met, told him she wasn't at home. Mr Okoro made three other visits before he met her.

She was reeking of alcohol. Mr Okoro twitched his nose.

'Isiorho, I have come for my money,' Okoro announced.

Isiorho looked at him.

'Money?' she asked absent-mindedly.

'You have to come tomorrow.'

Mr Okoro was infuriated; he stormed out of her house and went straight to an elder's house. A meeting was convened the following day. The high chief ruled after hearing both parties that Isiorho must give Mr Okoro another plot of land as she obviously had no money to pay him back. She had no option than to comply.

Izah's health wasn't improving, and Adede was saddled with his care as her stepmother, half-brothers, and other relatives had abandoned him. Only a few of his relatives came to ask about his health. None of them offered any financial help. Adede travelled quite often to Onitsha and Aba to get her father's drugs from the meagre money she made from the sales of second-hand clothes. During one of her trips to get her father's drugs, she discovered she could also buy used clothes from Aba.

'They are even cheaper there,' she once told Ruke.

Ruke wasn't keen on changing her business route. She told Adede it was too stressful travelling to Aba. Adede chose the eastern route in which she excelled. She bought clothes and food for her father each time she made a trip either to Aba or to Onitsha. One evening, Adede came home from her shop and saw that her father was weeping. She knelt before her father, wrapped her arms round him, and wiped his tears. She had never seen her father cry before.

'Papa, why are you weeping?' she asked meekly.

'Your stepmother threw away the keg of palm wine and food you had bought me. I have been so hungry. Adede, my daughter, I think I won't survive this sickness. Isiorho is giving me too much trouble.'

Adede shed a tear, and she sat up again, holding her father by the hand. 'Papa, nothing will happen to you. You will be fine. I will cook something right away. As for Isiorho, I will deal with her,' she said with much resolve.

'No, my daughter, it is not necessary,' he pleaded.

Adede walked into her mother's kitchen. She still had some yam and red palm oil with which she made a quick supper for her father.

The thought of her ailing father occupied her mind. She had promised her father that he would get well, but she didn't know exactly how. Ogaga told her it would cost lots of money to carry out the operation, but because they could not afford the bill, Ogaga kept sending her the prescription, and she had managed to buy the medicines all this while. Adede put out the lantern and went to bed after her father had eaten.

Oria witnessed changes after the village annual festival. Some preachers came from Warri on a crusade to evangelise. A huge number of villagers turned up. They heard one of the preachers could heal, wrought miracles, and solve whatever problem one has. Ruke told Adede about it, but she was reluctant to attend the crusade. She told Ruke to pass by her house when she was on her way. Ruke did look her up on her way, and they went together.

Pastor Afolabi was a charismatic and evangelical fire brand. He came with two other pastors and many assistants. His choir had also accompanied him. The choir sang like angels, at least the villagers thought so. Pastor Afolabi was a motivational speaker. By the time he mounted the pulpit to preach, people were already singing his praises. Then he called for those who had afflictions and needed prayers to come forward. About fifteen people stepped forward.

Pastor Afolabi went to them, followed by the other pastors and assistants, and laid hands on each person. What followed some of the prayer sessions was a spectacle to the people of Oria. Seven out of those people who came forward fell on the floor, one after the other. They were either possessed or under the influence of the anointing power of God.

The assistants attended to them in a secluded area for further counselling and ministration. Fear gripped the villagers when an elderly woman ran from behind the crowd, screaming at the top of her voice. She tore at her clothes as she screamed and fell on her knees before Pastor Afolabi and started confessing how she was responsible for many mysterious deaths in her family. Some young men ran forward in a bid to lynch her, but Pastor Afolabi restrained them.

'She is a new creature now,' he thundered.

More people stepped forward for prayers. Ruke went for prayers too. Adede looked around her and then at Ruke and felt the need for some spiritual reassurance, so she followed Ruke.

Ruke waited patiently as Pastor Afolabi prayed with Adede. When she was about to go, he called her back.

'The Lord will work wonders in your life in due course,' he told her.

'Amen,' Adede said.

Adede went back to her seat. Ruke was caught up in a spiritual frenzy. She had begun praying and singing, oblivious of Adede's presence. Adede glanced at her friend and then sat down on her chair. There were more dancing and singing. By the time the crusade ended, it was 1 a.m. Pastor Afolabi held his crusade on a Friday night because it was a weekend and hence convenient for most people.

Ruke sang all the way home. Adede followed her quietly, consumed by the thoughts of her problems but drew strength from the pastor's prophecy.

Adede reached the front of her house and bid Ruke farewell. Ruke joined another band of attendees that drifted towards her home.

Ruke, convinced of her new faith, sold all she had, gave up her business, and became a worker in Pastor Afolabi's church in the service of the Lord. She gave her life to Christ. This was sad news for Adede who needed Ruke's companionship in her business. Ruke, in her bid to be free, persuaded her mother to go back to Obiaruku and undertake the responsibility of her younger brother's education. Uchenna, the elder brother, became a front desk manager in a hotel operated by a Lebanese called Hassan. He relocated to Calabar.

Her mother objected to relocating to Obiaruku. There was no way she could leave a landed property they had acquired for Ruke.

Ruke gave Adede some amount of money to help her father. Adede hugged Ruke gratefully. She knew the money was from the proceeds of the shop she sold.

Pastor Afolabi came to pick up Ruke to wherever her new-found home was, against her mother's advice to stay in Oria. Her mind was made up. Pastor Afolabi's words carried weight.

'She don go,' Ashiedu told Adede in pidgin English that Ruke had gone.

She thanked Ashiedu and left. She had gone to Ruke's house at her request.

Adede felt all alone now. She walked back home, feeling strange and knowing that she had no one to confide in any more.

Isiorho was in the living room when she returned home.

'Won't you build your life? You are depressed because of Ruke, who blindly follows all these fake preachers.' Adede cast a cold look at her and, without saying a word, continued to her room.

Mr Orofua was transferred to Sapele, but he had always thought of Adede. He wasn't happy that she could not continue her education. His uncle's friend came to visit him from Agbor.

THE DYING THIEF

Mr Osaigbovo was a voluntary lecturer who would assume the responsibility to explain to those who cared that he hailed from Igbanke, and not from Benin, to as many people who thought so given his name.

'We share border with Benin and Agbor. My people speak both Bini and Agbor, but in my own area, we speak more Agbor, also known as Ika Ibo.' Mr Osaigbovo would reel out his dialectic lectures.

He was in Sapele to get a form to register his son in the technical school. He met Mr Orofua in his house though he wasn't expecting him after a very long time. They discussed at length. He confided in him that his son wasn't so brilliant, and that was why he wanted him to have vocational training instead. He explained to him that his son was bent on travelling to Europe, like many of his friends who went and came back looking for wives.

'My neighbour's son has written to his father that he is looking for a wife too. You may know him. I understand he is an Urhobo man from Ughelli, one Mr Emudiaga.'

'You mean the same person who owns Mudia Petrol Station in Agbor?'

'Exactly! He would be moving to his own house soon.'

'He is hard working.'

'I think I know a young lady that will make a good wife for your neighbour's son. She is very, very brilliant,' Mr Orofua emphasised the word 'very' to Mr Osaigbovo about Adede.

Before leaving, he promised to talk to Mr Emudiaga about Adede.

Mr Orofua accompanied Mr Emudiaga and Mr Osaigbovo to see Izah and Madam Najevwe. They formally presented the issue of Mr Emudiaga's son's intention to marry Adede. Izah was too frail to talk much, so Madam Najevwe did the talking for him. They agreed that both Edmund, Emudiaga's son, and Adede must see each other and become familiar before any further arrangement could be made.

'Let them meet each other and see if they like each other,' Izah pressed.

Edmund had arrived a week earlier from Houston, USA. He was eager to see the very brilliant and intelligent lady he had heard about. Adede was thrilled. She wrote to inform Kate and Ruke about Edmund's proposal to her. Edmund visited Adede in Oria. He told Adede he was married to an Irish American with whom he had a child, but things spun out of control before their daughter turned one.

Roxanne, his wife, had an affair with her boss. He caught them red-handed when he went to see why she did not come home early from the departmental store where she worked as a cashier. They were on the desk consumed in each other's arms.

'I divorced her immediately and lived alone for seven years till my friends advised me to get a wife once more.'

Adede could not understand why a woman could be unfaithful to her husband that way. She wrote again to Kate to tell her about what she knew of Edmund.

'Scrutinise him well,' Kate cautioned in her reply.

Edmund continued visiting Adede from Agbor. He was often in her shop.

'Adede, this sale of second-hand clothes and hardship is not good for you. You almost had an accident at Aba market the other day. Please let me take care of you. Stop punishing yourself. For two months, you have been observing me. I will take care of you. Your father could come with us. It would be very easy for him to do so since he has serious health issues,' he told her.

Adede gave Edmund a warm hug. He had succeeded in convincing her. Edmund married Adede in a grand ceremony a few months later. She discovered she was already a month pregnant by the time she married. Kate and Ruke were in attendance. Isiorho tried to be nice to Adede right from the day she heard about Edmund. Madam Najevwe knew of Adede's pregnancy. Kate advised her to stay with them in Benin till she was ready to fly.

'Your stepmother could do anything,' Kate cautioned.

Madam Najevwe and Ruke agreed with Kate.

Ogaga got a new job as a medical consultant with a United Nations' funded organisation, so they moved to Benin where the new office was. Madam Najevwe stayed with Izah till Edmund came back for him.

Adede heaved a sigh of relief.

'This is my basket of fortune.'

Ruke laid her hand on Adede's head and began to pray. She reminded her of what Pastor Afolabi said. Edmund came for Izah a week later. Isiorho ran to him, weeping.

'Please forgive me, Izah. When you get to America, send for me. Tell Adede to forgive me too,' she pleaded.

Izah looked at Isiorho blankly without a word. Madam Najevwe was happy he was going to get a better treatment for his ailment abroad. Edmund's driver reversed the car and drove off with a screech. Madam Najevwe kept waving until the car disappeared into the distance.

PART II

Life

Life . . .

Life
Is like a mountain
With great height
And craggy edges.
Getting to its summit
Is a strenuous climb.
Life
Is like a sea
With vast width
And treacherous currents.
Reaching its shore
Is a dangerous swim.

Eguono

Eguono,
Love that must be shared.
Love that is true,
Love that is selfless.
Love that is incorruptible.
Love that is everlasting.

CHOVWE INISIAGHO

Let Me Love You

Let me love you
Just the way you are.
Let me see you
Just the way you are.
Let me know you
Just the way you are.
Let me in your heart,
In its shade and hue,
In its brightness and darkness
Even into its nook and cranny
. . . let me!

Home

Home is where I find rest.
A place I live in.
My living room,
My kitchen and my bedroom.
Home is where I find peace.
A place I'm safe in.
My wife,
Daughters and sons.

I Will Not

I will not dance
Or sing
In the ceremony of my forebearers,
With ignoble steps
You've painted so wonderfully.
It is an initiation disguised in haste.
I will not eat
Or drink
In the feast of my ancestors,
With the unsavoury recipe
You've garnished so tastefully.
It is dinner cooked by Beelzebub himself.
I will not want
Or beg
In the assembly of my peers,
With the bloody incision
You've made so skilfully.
It is the cut that leads to doom.

Parish Request

I sat on a pew,
To take a view,
And meditate.
To consolidate
My spirituality,
For its reality.
I was in a parish.
Not to tarnish,
With my dark colour
And not to devour.
But to ask for water,
A fact of the matter.
I thought we were one.
For all has been done.
By Christ for us,
Son of God wondrous.
My request refused,
I'm so confused.

Circumcised

I was cut.
I bled,
I screamed,
Had laceration,
They say it's our tradition.
I was hurt.
I kicked,
I struggled,
Had bruises,
They say it's the coming of age.

CYBER LOVER

Kofi kissed Kevwe passionately, then rubbed her stomach tenderly. He placed his ear on it.

'What are you doing?' Kevwe asked.

'Trying to listen to my baby, of course,' he said.

'Ah, you know it is going to be a girl,' she told her husband.

He did not hear Kevwe. He had his ear still glued to his wife's bulging stomach. He stood up, pulled Kevwe to him, and kissed her again.

'OK, love, just take care of yourself. I have to leave now,' he said, adjusting his tie. He ran a comb through his hair very quickly and wore his coat.

He was ready to leave for work. Kevwe reached for the table where his briefcase was seated.

'Here, darling,' she said, handing the briefcase to him.

'Nice of you, my princess. See you later,' he said, hurrying out of the house.

Kevwe walked to the window. She pulled the curtains apart and opened the window. The wind was blowing softly outside. She leant on the iron bar and looked down the street. She could see the cars meandering their way through the narrow streets and people on the sidewalks, hustling along. She spotted a teenage boy and girl walking hand in hand. It reminded her of her first love and her failed marriage. Her eyes glittered with tears as memories of her past replayed in her mind's eye. The baby kicked in her stomach.

'*I should be grateful,*' she consoled herself. She had the opportunity of falling in love again.

Kevwe had always wanted to live, study, and work in Europe. Close to her graduation from the university, she met Donald during the departmental seminar. He was a lecturer at the university but was doing his doctorate degree in Germany. He gave a talk on the same topic as Kevwe's thesis. After the seminar, Kevwe asked to have his contact details so she could get more information and materials for her work. Donald obliged her. He returned to Germany two weeks later. Kevwe carried on with her academic load. She had totally forgotten about Donald. She finished her exams, which was a big relief for her as it was for every student. She had enough time to concentrate on her thesis. It was when she encountered difficulties in her literature review that she remembered Donald and the promise he had made. She grabbed her address book from her bookshelf and flipped through it slowly till she got to the page where Donald's address was written. She closed her books and shoved them to one side of the table. She took a plain sheet of paper and began writing a letter to Donald. Donald wrote back three weeks later with a lot of research materials. Kevwe and Donald continued exchanging more letters. She graduated with a lower second class. Her thesis was one of the best. Donald was glad to know he contributed to her success. Kevwe got a job with a private company after her youth service year. Working in the accounts department of Marigold Global Company was nerve-racking. Kevwe was not good with figures. She feared causing the company financial loss should she make any miscalculation. As time went on, she began to feel comfortable with her job and so decided to register for a postgraduate diploma in business studies. Somehow, the urge of travelling overseas to further her studies haunted her. She wrote to Donald, requesting him to send her application forms

THE DYING THIEF

for postgraduate studies in Germany. Donald replied with a long counselling letter shortly after. He tried to advise her about the difficulties foreigners encounter when they study in Germany. Kevwe had her mind made up. She was determined to study in Europe. Donald visited Nigeria every year. In his next visit, he delivered Kevwe's admission forms himself. It was a pleasant surprise for her to see Donald in their house. She introduced him to her parents. Mr Orode, Kevwe's father, engaged Donald in some hearty discussions. He adored education and encouraged ambitious students. His ears twitched at the mention of doctorate degree. Donald was a time-conscious man. He excused himself politely and left for his next appointment in Benin City, promising to visit Kevwe again. He had declined any form of entertainment from his hosts.

Donald kept his promise. He visited Kevwe. He had asked her to join him while he went downtown to do some shopping. Kevwe willingly obliged him. She had a quick change of clothes and joined Donald again where he was waiting.

'You look good,' Donald remarked.

'Thank you,' Kevwe smiled, revealing her evenly spaced teeth.

They climbed into Donald's Mercedes 200 E class. Donald drove cautiously through the congested streets of Ugboroke District until he came to the major road that led into the city. He told Kevwe that he wanted to eat out before he began shopping. Not long after, they arrived at a restaurant. Donald parked the car on the orange dusty park. They went into the restaurant, and Kevwe was surprised that the restaurant looked small on the outside but ran deep inside.

Donald ordered drinks and then some food. After the meal, Donald took her off balance with a marriage proposal. He was plain and straight, leaving her startled. She did not expect to hear such a statement from Donald. She had thought they were just friends and that Donald was her mentor. Kevwe looked away shyly.

'Give me some more time to think about it,' she told Donald after a short while.

Donald paid for the food and drove Kevwe back home. It was not a shopping after all.

Everything happened so fast for Kevwe. Her mother and elder sisters convinced her that she would lose nothing if she married Donald. No sooner had she accepted his proposal than the date for introduction and bride price were fixed. Donald and Kevwe had been friends for about two years, but the relationship was more formal and centred around academic issues. Donald had been secretly admiring Kevwe and had deliberately planned his visit to enable him woo her into marrying him. He did not want a lot of noise about his marriage. The ceremony was a low-profile one and was attended by their close friends and family members alone.

Donald and Kevwe had their first baby towards the beginning of spring.

Motherhood and marriage weren't easy for Kevwe. She called home regularly to ask questions and get advice on baby care from her mother. One of her sisters posted her a book on childcare and marriage. Finding time to read it was one thing, putting it into practise was another. Donald was hardly home. He was always away at the university, doing his research work. He came home late in the evenings, feeling tired and irritated. Donald was a fastidious man. He criticised almost everything he saw. At first, Kevwe trembled at his sight, but when she got used to it, she decided to put up with him. The arrival of their second baby did not bring any change. The baby was only four months old when Donald began to beat her. It took the intervention of their neighbours to stop him sometimes. On one occasion, Kazuko, a Japanese lady, who lived with her German boyfriend, came to Kevwe's rescue. Both ladies always exchanged pleasantries and occasionally visited each other. She had heard Kevwe screaming, so she raced down from her fourth-floor apartment. Kazuko forced the door open and arrived just in time to save Kevwe from Donald's grip. Donald had clenched his fist and was hitting Kevwe repeatedly, leaving her almost unconscious.

The relationship between Donald and Kevwe worsened. He would get furious at the slightest provocation. He restricted her movement to their apartment. She wasn't allowed to interact with people around her. She became a shadow of herself. They began to attend church services less frequently. They had little or no social life and very little contact with other people. Kevwe realised she was married to an abusive man. Life in Germany was terrifying to her now. Kevwe was always home with their kids. Kazuko had told her about the women's shelter and had suggested she call the police whenever Donald assaulted her or showed any sign of aggression. Kevwe knew nothing about these facilities and opportunities. She wasn't sure if she wanted to take advantage of them. The idea of reporting one's own husband to the police was strange to her. She never wanted to betray Donald even if their relationship wasn't going on well. Kazuko could not understand why Kevwe was hesitant and indecisive. She wasn't sure if it all had to do with the Nigerians' culture of not exposing a spouse's fault to authorities. She knew Kevwe was in danger if she remained with him.

Donald came in one evening with a small van. He began to move his belongings one after the other. Kevwe watched him curiously as he shoved cartons and sacks about their apartment. She wanted to ask him questions, but she refrained from doing so. She went to her children and began to cuddle them. Donald finished packing his belongings. He sighed, and in a gruff voice, he turned to Kevwe and said, 'I need my peace and concentration for my studies.'

That was the only statement Donald made. The children had begun to cry. Mena looked at her then at her father. The children did not know what was going on, but the tone of their dad's voice and the tense atmosphere made them know there was trouble.

CHOVWE INISIAGHO

Kevwe rocked Ono, their little baby, who was six months. Donald left, slamming the door hard behind him.

Ono let out a little cry. Kevwe heard the van's engine start. She rushed to the window to look. Mena, her two-year-old daughter, followed her, tugging on her skirt. Kevwe took her hand as if to reassure her that all would be well without her father. Kevwe placed Ono on the sofa in the living room. She wedged her with a small pillow so that she does not roll over. Then she placed Mena on a high chair. It was midday, and she had to prepare lunch. It was going to be lunch just for two. Being a single mother wasn't what Kevwe had hoped for. The days and weeks that followed were harrowing. Kevwe had to do the groceries alone. She would put Mena in the pushchair and strap Ono on her back. It was an art of carrying a baby that she had learnt from her mother. Having a baby on the back is a common sight in Africa, a tradition that has existed for generations.

'A woman must be cautious as she puts her baby on her back. Keep the cloth around the baby and gently fasten it from above the breast and on the abdomen,' her mother always told her.

She had heard the stories of babies falling off their mothers' back before they could be strapped.

'It is high time Nigerians did something about this issue,' she had argued with her sister.

'You think it is the government's responsibility?' queried her sister.

'They should carry out awareness programmes,' she insisted.

'How?'

'The government should hold seminars for women, especially at the grass roots level. They should give practical tips or demonstrate safe methods of placing a baby on their backs or, at the most, come out with new methods or simple carriers developed solely for strapping babies to their mothers' backs.'

Kevwe entered the supermarket. Some Germans stared at her. It was strange for them to see a baby strapped to a mother's back the way Kevwe did. She bought all she needed and left. Kazuko came to see Kevwe in the evening. Kevwe served her some tea and biscuits.

'How are you coping?'

'It is not easy, Kazuko,' Kevwe confessed.

'Listen,' she told Kevwe, pulling her chair closer to her.

She sipped her tea, took a bite from her biscuit, and began to lecture her on the rights of women and how they must learn to be independent.

'You have to be strong. If you continue like this, you will end up being a wreck,' Kazuko sipped her tea once more.

Ono began to cry. Kazuko helped change her diaper before both ladies went back to the living room with the children.

'You need to have some counselling or join a women's group. You could even join a children's play group.'

There was a knock at the door. It was Kazuko's boyfriend. He had heard Kazuko's voice. Kazuko opened the door immediately as soon as he identified himself.

'Hello, Kevwe,' he greeted, patted the kids on their heads, and then sat next to Kazuko.

Kevwe had tried to teach Rafael how to pronounce her name. He placed more emphasis on the 'V' in her name than the 'W' and 'E' as in the English word *we*. She offered him tea and biscuits too. Ono cried again, and Kevwe quickly got up to make her some food. She came back to the living room with Ono and her feeding bottle immersed in a cup of cold water. Kazuko was rocking Mena.

'Do you know where Donald moved to?' Rafael asked Kevwe.

Kazuko had told Rafael about Donald.

'No,' Kevwe answered reluctantly.

Rafael stood up and paced about the room with his cup of tea in his hand. He looked at the Nigerian flag hanging from the wall. Rafael had a comical way of doing his things. He studied arts therapy and worked with the University Clinic of Cologne.

'Kevwe,' he looked at her intently.

'You must face life strongly. Donald is abusive, and I think he won't come back again.'

Kevwe looked at Kazuko as if she needed a reassurance from her.

'I think so too,' Kazuko nodded.

Kazuko reiterated the need for her to see either a therapist or engage in something that would occupy her mind since her kids are still young. Rafael looked at the time. It was already 10 p.m.

'We must take our leave, Kevwe. I will think of how to help you,' he promised.

Kevwe thanked them. Kazuko put Mena on her bed and left with Rafael to her flat.

Kevwe told her sister on the phone no woman should pray to be a single mother. Being a single mom was taking its toll on her. Her typical day began with bathing the kids and feeding them.

She would sit with them and do house chores and shopping in-between. After lunch, she would watch television or some Nigerian films. They were mostly old ones that she had to watch over and over again. The days went so fast, and before long, it would be night-time. There would be a quiet dinner, and they would all go to bed. Kevwe would lie on the bed, alone. She would toss from one side of her bed to the other, trying hard to sleep. It was at that point that she knew she needed emotional satisfaction, which the children could not provide her. Kevwe cried herself to sleep. Someone kissed and caressed her. She moaned and cuddled up to him. There was a loud knock on the door, and then she woke up. Her pillow was in her hand. She sat up and looked around her. It was then she realised she had been dreaming. She jumped out hurriedly from her bed and looked through the peephole in her door. It was the postman who had been knocking. He gained

THE DYING THIEF

access to her flat because someone had left the main entrance to the building open.

'Ich komme.' She told the postman she was coming to open the door.

Kevwe grabbed her morning robe and dashed to the door. There was a parcel for her from London. She wasn't expecting any. She signed the delivery bill and thanked the postman. She closed the door behind her and went with the parcel back to her room. She placed it on the table and lay down again to sleep. She wished so much that she could be home with her parents and siblings. She hated marriage and Europe now. One could die of loneliness, she thought. There had been stories of people dying in their houses only to be discovered when letters were piling up in their letter boxes or when they began to decompose. The phone rang, and Ono was woken up by its sound. Kevwe was confused. She was torn between picking up the phone and soothing the crying baby. She sprang up and carried Ono, rocked her, and hurried to the living room to take the call. It was the gynaecologist's assistant. She had called to remind her of her appointment which was nearing. Kevwe forgot she was scheduled to see the doctor that day. She began to feel the day was going to be hectic; she sobbed. She did not know how to cope with the kids and many other things she had to do. And here is another appointment she had to keep: a woman in Europe could hardly afford a nanny or housemaid, she reckoned.

She remembered her friends who had maids serving them in Nigeria. Kevwe was short of time, but she was able to bathe a crying Ono, whom she calmed with a pacifier, and then dressed up. Her next target was to prepare food for her children, a task that became suddenly cumbersome for her because she was already nervous. She spilt hot water on the dining table in a bid to hasten up. She packed the baby bag full of diapers, snacks, baby food, flask with hot water, and some children's clothes. She cleaned Mena up and dressed her in something fresh. She did the same for herself.

Because there was no time to comb her rumpled hair, she wore a cap. She had just thirty more minutes to her appointment. Kevwe rushed to the tram stop, which was a five-minute walk from her flat.

The tram came as scheduled on the route planner. She alighted at Ebertplatz Station from where she took a bus to her gynaecologist's practice. Mena asked for biscuit, and the request reminded Kevwe that Mena didn't have her breakfast packed in the bag hanging on her shoulder. She looked at the time, and it was five more minutes before her appointment. The bus came to a halt midway in its journey. The mother of two was by now impatient. She was running late, and she might miss her appointment. There had been an accident at Krefelder Strasse, forcing the police to cordon off the road temporarily. Traffic was diverted to alternate routes. The driver advised all passengers to disembark. Kevwe hissed and grumbled. She knew it was a bad day from the onset. She got off the bus like every other passenger. The elderly lady sitting next to her cursed and raved.

'It is not his fault,' said another man, walking behind the old lady.

She gave Mena some more biscuits and began to walk slowly to the opposite side of the road. The road was in chaos and vehicles were reversing in all directions creating more confusion on the street. Police cars and ambulances tried earnestly to control the crazy traffic and the confused crowd. It was a multiple collision caused by a truck. Kevwe walked on, looking for the replacement bus provided by the transport company. For the first time, she saw how dirty the Nippes District could get. It was an area for the low-income earners and the middle-class. It was home to a lot of Turks.

There were some streets which could pass for slums: old houses, overflowing garbage cans, and filthy rags heaped on a mountain of rubbish. A gypsy girl ran up to her, offering her a stick of rose. Ono had finished her biscuit and had begun to whimper. She wanted to come down from the pushchair. Kevwe declined to take the rose from the gypsy. She knew it was a gimmick gypsies employed in begging for alms and picking pocket. Mena pointed at some sugar candies displayed in a kiosk. Kevwe reached into her bag and gave Mena a small packet of orange juice. Buying candies from the kiosk could be expensive. She paused to look for the bus that would take her back home. She made few enquiries, but no one seemed to know what to do. She walked to the shopping mall to look at offers on display and do a bit of window shopping.

Ono tried to come down from her pushchair again for a second time, and Kevwe made her sit down.

It was almost midday; she went into a Turkish restaurant along the road where she had lunch. She did not take breakfast before leaving home. She shared her meal with her kids. She never got to meet up with the appointment that day.

Kazuko and Rafael bought a new house on the outskirts of Cologne and moved there. They invited Kevwe and her kids for the house warming, but she was too afraid to attend.

'It is just a social gathering,' Kazuko convinced her.

She wasn't used to attending parties. She had been stereotyped by the lifestyle of Donald.

'Donald may come in anytime, and I will be in trouble,' she explained.

Kazuko was dazed by Kevwe's assertions.

'Girl, you have to live your life and enjoy it,' Kazuko hung up and sank into her sofa.

She told Rafael that they have to find ways to help her. She could not understand why Kevwe cannot break free from Donald's ghost and be independent.

'She has been too intimidated or brainwashed,' she mumbled.

Rafael decided that they would pay Kevwe a visit. They told her she needed to do some yoga and join some social groups that would enable her interact and get integrated. Rafael gave her some addresses and told her she could also get an Internet connection and take up some long-distance courses since her kids were small, but she could neither leave them to attend a school nor work.

'Be productive and useful to yourself. You cannot worship a man because he is your husband or live in fear because of him. He has even moved away from here. How are you sure he will come back? Maybe he has another woman there,' said Rafael. Kevwe broke down into tears. She was hit by reality. Kazuko walked over to her and began to pacify her.

Mena left her toys and ran to her mother as if to console her too.

'We want the best for you,' Rafael said, trying to apologise.

He felt he was too harsh. Kevwe wiped her tears, and they discussed further till late into the afternoon. She didn't let them go till they had lunch together. Rafael promised to get a second-hand computer for her and arrange for an Internet provider. He then left with Kazuko for Brühl, where their new home was. It was about 8 p.m. Kevwe heard the jingling of key turning the door lock; it was Donald. He had come after three months of unexplainable disappearance.

'I came to see my kids,' a defiant Donald said.

Mena ran to him.

'Daddy,' she screamed, embracing him.

'Where is Ono?' he asked Kevwe.

'Sleeping,' she replied.

He took Mena by the hand, and they went into the living room. He sat her on his lap, opened his bag, and gave her some biscuits and a teddy bear. He called Kevwe and invited her to a quiet discussion. She sat on the edge of the couch, next to the radiator. He told her he would be back again in six months when he was done with his doctorate and that he wanted them to relocate to Canada within two years. He suggested Mena begin nursery school the next academic year. He emphasised he would be the one to register her. She took a deep breath as if to reassure herself there was no danger with Donald's visit. She offered him dinner, but he declined. He explained that he had eaten from the student cafeteria before coming. He gave Mena a peck on the cheek, and they went together to see Ono, who was still asleep in the room. Mena tried to speak to her father, but he stopped her.

'Not too loud,' he whispered, but it was too late. Ono was stirred from her sleep by their voices. She sat up, rubbed her face, and called out to her father. Donald lifted her very gently from the bed and pecked her on the cheek. Kevwe looked on in total disbelief. She wished that could happen always, and then she tried to comfort herself that Donald's visit could be a sign of change. Donald spent another hour with his family and left for God-knows-where that he stayed.

Kevwe was a staunch Catholic but was open to Protestantism. Her mother warned her not to mix herself with different doctrines.

'I'm not a kid, Mama.' Kevwe would remind her.

She had gone for the first time to seek counselling from a pastor. She had gotten a flyer from some Christians evangelising on her street, and she thought it would be a good idea to seek their pastor's advice. She made some phone enquiries and was given an appointment at 3 p.m. She opted for that time because she felt it would be a convenient time for her and the kids. She took a tram to Neumarkt and then another one to Poll where the Ghanaian pastor had his office. She got off at the station and followed the description given to her. She looked around her as she pushed Ono in the pushchair. Mena stood on the attached board. It was a gift from Kazuko who impressed on her that it was a better way to transport both kids instead of having one strapped to her back or using a double pushchair, which could be difficult to push. Kevwe got to Ensener Strasse where the Blessed Redeemer Christian Ministry was situated. The church was located on the ground floor of a modern six-storey office complex. It was in a quiet section of

Poll. All she could hear as she entered the premises was her own footsteps. She came to number 12 and rang the bell.

Pastor Adusa opened the door. He ushered her into his office at the far right corner of the church's auditorium.

'Welcome to the Lord's house, my sister,' he greeted Kevwe warmly and offered her a chair to sit on.

He gave her children some toys to play with. Mena cheerfully took them from him and settled down to play with them. Ono stood a while but soon joined her sister. Pastor Adusa said a brief prayer and then enquired to know how he might help Kevwe. She told him about her marital problems, pouring out her heart. Pastor Adusa took a deep breath and clasped his hands. He was touched by Kevwe's problems. Like a father, he began to advise her. Pastor Adusa wanted her to simply pray and avoid Kazuko and her boyfriend because, to him, they were unbelievers. Their culture and mentality were different, he stressed.

'The pride of a woman is in her marriage,' he cautioned her.

He prayed with her again. Before she left, he gave her some gift of money.

'Feel free to come here. Next time, my wife will be here. She is also a Nigerian,' Pastor Adusa told her. Kevwe's face shone.

'That is wonderful, sir. Where about in Nigeria is she from?' she asked.

'Ibadan. We met in those days when Ghanaians flocked to Nigeria for greener pasture. I was a primary-school teacher then, while she was a final-year pupil of a secondary school near the school in which I taught. She became pregnant by me, and her parents abandoned her. Today, we are blessed with five children, and even her mother is now here with us,' Pastor Adusa was euphoric with the history of his marriage.

'Congrats, sir,' Kevwe sputtered, wondering whether it was the right thing to say.

'It is the Lord's doing, my dear.'

Kevwe left with her children and began the lonely journey back home.

Kazuko and Rafael got Net Media Company to provide Internet services for Kevwe. Everything took less than an hour to set up. When the technicians left, Kazuko laid the table with sushi and some exotic fruits which they all ate. Kazuko finished her food before every other person. She was famished. Kevwe was the last to finish because she had to constantly get up to attend to her children. Rafael played with the kids while the ladies cleared the table. When they were all settled, Kevwe told them about Donald's visit.

'Be wary of his visit,' Rafael told her. 'Men who brutalise their wives can hardly stop,' he continued.

Kazuko nodded, affirming Rafael's vantage point. Rafael showed Kevwe the basics of computer and helped her to open a Yahoo! email account. They stayed for another three hours and left. Ono began to cry, and she knew her diaper was wet. At 9 p.m., she put the kids to bed and tried the Internet herself. By the time she finished, it was 1 a.m. She put out the lights, rolled down the shutters, and went to bed. She replayed Rafael's advice and that of Pastor Adusa's in her head. She did not know whose advice to take.

Kevwe continued to fiddle and play with the Internet until she got used to the basics. First, she registered for a correspondence course in event management. She spared time for her children, her studies, and the Internet. Rafael had taught her how to use the Google search engine to find whatever she wanted. She typed every word in her vocabulary in the search engine. Out of curiosity, she thought it would be a good idea to get news about the rapidly growing Nigerian film industry. She typed in celebrate-naija.com. To her amazement, the site did exist and with variety of news items. She was excited with the headlines she saw. There were news, fashion, and gossips from home. She read one of the comments about an apparent supremacy struggle between Nigerian and Ghanaian actors. The string of comments that followed motivated her to leave her own comment. She supported the Ghanaians. She called Kazuko and Rafael and thanked them for introducing her to the Internet.

'My boredom seems to have ebbed away.'

Kazuko could hear a tinge of excitement in her voice.

'You sound happy,' Kazuko told her.

Mena pulled the fringe of her blouse, and she turned to her. She was pointing at Ono who had spilt porridge all over the sofa and the carpet. She had to cut short her conversation with Kazuko to clean up the mess. She looked forward to weekends – the days she set aside to read and comment on the articles from celebrate-naija website. She loved the comments and the arguments that ensued. Commentators tried to outdo each other with facts and wits. The weeks that followed saw frequent exchange of email addresses. People were getting more familiar with themselves.

The Internet was now her new world. Kevwe became a regular and avid reader of the site. She was becoming a popular visitor among other contributors.

Pastor Adusa called to follow up on Kevwe's welfare. Donald picked the call and passed the phone to her.

'Good day, Pastor,' she greeted nervously.

She did not want Donald to know she had involved a third party in their affairs, so she quickly told the pastor she was busy and would call back.

'You can continue calling men and addressing them as pastors,' Donald said sarcastically.

'That is a man of God you are talking about.'

'Kevwe, to hell with your pretence and pastors. Sit there and let them bamboozle you and ask you to pay tithes which they alone will enjoy. You are so naive. Don't let me see any of them near my house,' Donald warned.

She shuddered. She went to her room and closed the door behind her. Ono tried to walk to her father who supported her before she could stop. He sat her on the sofa and continued teaching Mena her alphabets. It was his second visit in a week. He had begun visiting Kevwe and his children more frequently in recent times. He went to Kevwe's room and tapped the door noisily; she opened, and he handed her two books.

'They are for Mena. She needs to learn some simple alphabets, colours, shapes, and so on. Please spare time to practise with her. I will bring a timetable with me when next I come.'

Kevwe was bewildered. She felt that a child of Mena's age needs no timetable.

'I have noticed you now have an Internet connection in the house. My only advice to you is to be careful. The Internet could be dangerous.'

His statement was like a bombshell to her.

She knew he was critical about everything and unnecessarily finicky. Donald left, refusing to eat. It was almost his habit each time he came. Throughout the two weeks he spent with them, he came home at odd hours. The next thing he would do was to launch into a barrage of complaints. The next morning, Kevwe logged on to celebrate-naija web site. There were backlogs of articles to be read. She giggled when she read some hilarious comments and gossips. She was an hour into reading articles when she remembered she was frying eggs. She rushed to the kitchen to remove the frying pan from the burner. She opened the window to allow the huge smoke that had formed to dissipate and give way to fresh air.

The smoke was choking. She left the kitchen, closing the door behind her. She leant against the door and coughed hard from the harsh air she had inhaled. Mena ran out of the room, staring at her mother who was wiping tears from her red eyes. She went into another bout of cough before hugging Mena. She carried her back to the bedroom where they lay together. Kevwe wanted to go about her morning routines quickly and return to her cyber world.

There were comments she wanted to place and respond to. She got up after another half an hour. Mena had been trying to sing some nursery rhymes she had heard on the children's TV station. Kevwe lifted Ono from the bed. She was long awake and was playing with the stuffed animals around her. An agitated Kevwe bathed her little girls in turns, after which she served them breakfast. She allowed them watch some cartoons when they were done eating. Kevwe turned to her computer and continued with the article she was reading. Before placing her own comments her cursor had frozen. Rafael had told her she should either refresh the page or shut the computer down. She thought she should seize the opportunity to rest and play with the kids. Just then, the phone rang. It was Kevwe's mother from Nigeria who was at the other end. They spoke at length. Kevwe updated her on Donald.

'Always pray the rosary,' her mother reminded her. 'Our mother Mary will always intercede for you.'

Sometimes, she questioned why the Catholics prayed to Mary and Jesus at the same time. Kevwe had stopped saying her rosary long ago. She said ordinary prayers instead. Her childhood friends and many of her fellow Catholics had told her praying the rosary and asking mother Mary to intercede started with the marriage feast in the Bible, where Mary asked her son, Jesus, to help the celebrant with more wine, and Jesus turned water into wine.

'Obeying her mother does not mean we were asked to pray to Mary,' Kevwe had told Onyeka.

'Why do Catholics interpret certain verses of the Bible differently? "My son, help them", which Mary said is not the same as pray in my name.'

'What about Elizabeth? Did she not show respect to Mary in Luke 1: 49?' Onyeka contended.

'Leave that thing. I am not a diehard Catholic like you,' Onyeka sighed. 'God help you, Kevwe.'

Kevwe burst out laughing. She pitied her friend whom she felt misunderstood some basic biblical teaching. She laughed because she did not want to go into further arguments with Onyeka.

She finished her conversation with her mother and hung up. It was 2 p.m. She had to make lunch and take a short walk with the kids.

Kazuko told her it was important she tried playing in the park with her kids at least once in a week. Emphasis is placed on childcare and development in Germany. She packed a bag for the kids and went out with them to the park close to her house.

Snow had begun falling again. Kevwe hated to go out in the snow. It was particularly difficult doing shopping when it snowed. The roads could be slippery and pushing a pram could be a difficult task. It did not make sense to shop when there was heavy snow falling. She saw another opportunity to stay back home and browse the Internet. Her whole world revolved around the Internet and her children. She dressed Mena and Ono in warm clothing before serving them sausage with a dollop of ketchup and a slice of bread each. She thought it was good to give them warm milk, but Mena insisted on chocolate drink.

'You could be so choosy, my little girl. We ate whatever my mum gave us,' Kevwe shook her head.

She knew she was just chasing the wind because Mena was too young to understand that. Ono drank only milk. She left her sausage and bread untouched. Kevwe served Mena her chocolate drink. She wiped Ono's mouth and put her in the playpen. Kazuko had helped her create it a week before. Kevwe needed to prepare for some tests. Her course on event management was going well, and she was enjoying every bit of it. Kazuko was pleased.

'You have to build yourself and get on with your life,' she told her.

Just as Kevwe settled down to study, the phone rang. She had thought she disconnected the telephone cable to enable her to concentrate. She picked the call. It was Pastor Adusa.

'Just to ask after your welfare. My wife and I would be having the silver jubilee anniversary of our marriage in about two weeks. You can come with your kids if you have time.'

That sounded nice to Kevwe. It was another opportunity to socialise and mix with people.

'We are fine, sir. I will surely be there, sir.' Kevwe was excited.

'My wife is here. Speak with her,' Pastor Adusa said, passing the phone to his wife. She spoke briefly with Kevwe and told her to do all she could to keep her marriage. She rang off and went back to study with the plan of browsing later in the night. Kevwe looked out of the window again.

The streets were still white with snow. The rooftops of most cars were covered with snow. There were snow ploughers clearing snow from the roads and workmen spreading salt on the walkways. She went back to her study and vowed to make good results.

It was 10 p.m. Kevwe had put her kids to bed. She logged on to celebrate-naija.com and began reading the articles and comments on it. She noticed a certain male by name Kofi had left her a message. After going over the message, Kevwe replied. That would be the beginning of her friendship with a fellow commentator. They exchanged email addresses and kept in constant touch outside the website. He studied public relations at the University of Ghana in Legon and worked with a telecommunication company. He loved Nigerian movies and had a library of their films. Though young, he was very versatile and well versed in current affairs. Kofi was endeared to Kevwe because of her writing skills and her support for Ghana. He told Kevwe he had lived in Nigeria with his father for three years when his father worked with a football club. Kevwe was amazed with his knowledge of Nigerian sport. Kofi was the second son of a family of seven. Kevwe felt safe to tell him all about herself and her marriage. He was of the opinion that Rafael gave a more practical approach to her problems and that many pastors followed the Bible blindly.

'It is time African women stood up to their men. They are no punching bags. Kevwe, you are not a punching bag for your husband. You are there in Europe where women's right is at its peak. Report any abuse to the police. Do you want to be killed?' He wrote back to her in one of his emails.

Donald returned from his seminar. He had gone to Nigeria for five weeks without informing Kevwe. He arrived home and began ringing the bell without any response. He rang the bell for another ten minutes still without response. It was cold outside. Donald had forgotten his hand gloves and cap. He began to shiver. He walked to the open window of their flat and called out to Kevwe. Kevwe looked through the window and saw Donald standing there. She quickly pressed the doorbell intercom to enable Donald push the door open. Donald stomped up the stairs, got in, and demanded to know what kept Kevwe from hearing the doorbell.

'You think I am a fool for being a student and in between travelling to Nigeria to solve problems?'

'You mean you went to Nigeria and did not bother to let me know?' Kevwe asked.

'Must I tell you everything?' Donald snarled.

'If you say I'm your wife, then you should.'

'Don't you ever talk back at me,' Donald scowled down at her.

'Donald, now tell me. What would you do if I talked back at you?'

Kevwe did not know from where she got the courage of standing up to Donald's threats. Donald was irked. He slapped Kevwe hard and moved to punch her. Kevwe ducked and screamed. She grabbed the phone and ran as fast as she could to her room. Donald ran after her, but she locked the door before he could get to her.

'Open that door at once. You have grown wings. You think I'm not aware of your Internet flirting?' Kevwe was awestruck.

CHOVWE INISIAGHO

Since she began using the Internet, she had also begun to visit some chat rooms. Hot tears flowed down her cheeks. She did not know whether to call the police or Pastor Adusa. Kevwe decided to call one of Donald's friends, an elderly man from Sierra Leone. By now the children were crying in the living room. Her home was in chaos. Pa Grant promised to drive by when his visitors had gone. Kevwe thanked him and hung up. Donald kept banging on the door, but Kevwe refused to open.

'Come out at once and feed the kids,' Donald yelled at her.

He was infuriated by her adamance.

'Feed them yourself,' Kevwe hit back.

Donald tried to calm the already frightened children, and in that instance, the doorbell rang.

Donald opened the door and was startled at Pa Grant's sight, showing his elderly gentle smile. He climbed up to Donald's flat.

'Don't be surprised to see me. I know what is going on.'

Kevwe came out when she heard Pa Grant's voice. He pleaded with both of them to sit. He took his time to appeal for calmness.

'Donald, you shouldn't beat a woman. I did not know that all these have been happening.'

Donald looked away and then to the ground. He was mortified.

'Uncle, please tell him to go. If you leave him here, he will beat me again when you have gone.'

Pa Grant appealed again to Donald to follow him. He offered to take him home. He reluctantly left, promising to be back again to discuss issues about the children with Kevwe.

'Say it over the phone,' she screamed.

'You don't have to be angry when you know your husband is angry. Two people cannot be angry at the same time,' Pa Grant advised.

He left and joined Donald who was already waiting for him downstairs. Rafael and Kazuko were sad to know Donald beat

Kevwe again, but they were happy she was also able to express herself and seek assistance.

'Call the police next time. Not just anybody,' Kazuko said, rubbing Kevwe gently on her back.

She suggested again that Kevwe join a female group where she could share her experience with members, but Kevwe thought it would be like letting people into her private life. Rafael offered to take all of them out for dinner; it was something Donald never did with them before.

She told Rafael she needed to dress up, so she left for her room while Kazuko helped dress Mena and Ono. They drove through Neumarkt and then to Breite Strasse to a Korean restaurant where buffet was served. It was Kevwe's first time there in her seven years of living in Cologne.

Kazuko taught her how to use the chopsticks which she kept twisting between her fingers clumsily. It was a complicated task for her. Kazuko laughed lightly. She gave up and opted to use the fork. She was astonished at the ease with which Rafael used the chopsticks. She was glad her children were served kids' menu and were not bothered with any complicated cutlery. Kazuko suggested that they could also visit the cinema after they had eaten. They chose a date spontaneously, a date that coincided with Pastor Adusa's wedding anniversary. Kevwe called Kazuko to make a change of date. Kazuko told her she would return her call to arrange a definite date because she had planned a visit to Japan. Kevwe hung up, turned to her computer, and emailed.

Donald did not come home for almost three months. He was told to wait till Mena was about three years or more before she could be admitted into the nursery school. He sent the notification letter to Kevwe after translating it into English. He emphasised the need to make sure Mena learnt her alphabets and numbers and included a learning timetable. Kevwe laughed and once again wondered what a child of less than three needed a timetable for. She knew Donald was overambitious. She wondered how he knew all her activities on the Internet. One thing she promised herself was to improve her worth and would never allow Donald to beat her. She felt Rafael and Kazuko's perception about her problems were right. Kofi had told her this earlier. She was determined to make Donald know she wasn't a punching bag. She stood before a mirror. She saw the reflection of a charming and elegant lady.

'I will make it,' she screamed.

'Mummy,' Mena called.

Ono let out a soft cry.

She had frightened her kids. She was oblivious of their presence when she shouted.

Kevwe arrived at Pastor Adusa's church for the Sunday service held in honour of the wedding anniversary of Pastor Adusa and his wife. Kevwe was used to the Pentecostal mode of worship; after all, Catholic Charismatic Renewal Movement was almost the same thing. Welcomed by the ushers, she settled into a seat reserved for her. At 2 p.m., Pastor Adusa mounted the pulpit in his finely ironed brown suit and cream tie. His appearance was greeted with a hallelujah song from the choir and carried above the roof by the congregation with dancing, jumping, and loud clapping. Kevwe was lifted above her worries temporarily. Before the song came to an end, Pastor Adusa, with a large microphone, echoed into the song a long 'hallelujah' and the congregation matched it with longer 'amen'. Then the music stopped, everyone hushed, and holy handkerchiefs draped on the drooping heads. Pastor Adusa raised his left hand and closed his eyes.

'Today is the day the Lord has made, and we, his people, must rejoice and give him thanks.'

Some shouted, 'Praise the Lord'; some, 'Hallelujah'; and others, you couldn't understand. God will understand prayer after prayer without end. When Kevwe thought it was the end, it was actually the beginning. Her mind flew back to her computer, and the pastor

THE DYING THIEF

with his congregation was once more without the newcomer though she was seated right there in front of him. As the 'amen' began to decline, Kevwe knew the end was near and kept hope until the auditorium became silent and calm. The congregation was seated, and the pastor asked the new members and visitors to stand up. Every first-timer introduced oneself and drooped their head before the pastor and a long prayer was said. When it was Kevwe's turn, she drooped her head before the pastor and a deacon. Mena and Ono were peeping from behind her and staring up at the pastor who was praying and nodding his head strangely to them and constantly wiping his face with his 'holy' handkerchief. It was the moment Kevwe yearned for – unity with God! The pastor and the deacon were also united in her unity too.

The sermon was followed by the sound of the loudspeaker for almost an hour. As the sermon progressed, the interjected choruses from the choir, often accompanied by rigorous dance, sometimes scared Kevwe's kids.

When it was calm again, Mrs Adusa mounted the pulpit and gave a long cry of praises. She could not outdo the congregation. They came back with a stronger cry, and the roof shook. Mena shivered and held on to her mum's clothes; Ono cringed and held her mum's neck, whimpering.

The offertory was done, and testimonies were called for. A lady spoke about a strange dream she had, and another lady talked about her ordeal with her runaway husband and how after five years her husband just appeared from nowhere with his friend and claimed he was charmed away by another woman he once knew but refused to marry. The church went into a rapturous praise. 'The Lord is good,' echoed from every corner. Just as the angels praised the Lord above, so did this church below. Kevwe wondered if Donald was charmed too.

The benediction was said and the congregation was dismissed.

The congregation proceeded to the refreshment.

Mrs Adusa asked Kevwe to serve herself after which she should come to her. Kevwe gave some biscuits to her children and took a slice of cake for herself and proceeded to meet Mrs Adusa who led her into a small room.

'I just want us to pray in private for your marriage and see what the Lord can do. There is nothing God cannot do.'

Kevwe told her about her last encounter with Donald. Mrs Adusa wasn't happy that Donald beat her again.

'Keep on praying, and do not lose hope. Feel free to come to us at any time.'

Mrs Adusa carried Ono and led them back to the basement, which served as cafeteria on Sundays. Pastor Adusa went over to where Kevwe sat to have brief chat with her. He was glad Kevwe was able to celebrate with them.

Donald's absence from the house afforded Kevwe the opportunity to explore new ideas.

She completed her event management course, and Rafael advised her to get it accredited with the Ministry of Education. He knew certificates from other countries needed recognition, so she promised Rafael she would consider it. Kevwe was still very much involved in the entertainment website. She spent the evenings reading articles and placing comments. Contributors developed a strong bond among themselves, enabling some to go beyond just placing comment on the site. They were like their brother's keeper. The harmony and oneness were soon disrupted when an uncontrollable disagreement in opinions turned vulgar and insulting. It was a cyber warfare and cyber vendetta. Kevwe was one of the targets. She was accused of showing off and supporting Ghanaians. The whole forum became chaotic, giving rise to two factions. Contributors accused and suspected each other. Impersonation was rife. Oge, one of Kevwe's online friends, told her she had changed her username in order to insult her. Kevwe tried to absolve herself, but Oge would not hear her out. The life on that website was a world of its own. She needed to separate cyber life from real life. Kofi called Kevwe briefly and advised her to stay away from the site until it was calm again.

Kevwe heeded his advice. Kofi promised to give her a call over the weekend. She was drawn to him. Her knowledge of how the Internet mailing system works was broadened when she received strange and junk mails in her email account inbox and was left perplexed with the mail from a man who described her writing skill as resonating intelligence. The man introduced himself as Richard and gave his location as Bochum; it was just a few hours' drive from Cologne, where she lived. She wondered how those emails got to her and how Richard got hold of her email address. It began to dawn on her that what seemed a hobby by posting comments on a website had far-reaching effects. People all over the world read her comments, but she did not know. That's the impact of Internet. She read Richard's email over and over again and could not tell if he was a mere scammer or someone serious. The mail looked harmless to her, so she replied to him. The following day Richard replied, and before long, they were into constant email correspondence.

He was the second male friend she had made online. Richard's mother was a Yoruba and his father an Urhobo, the same ethnic group as Kevwe. He explained to her that he knew her ethnicity from her name. He was an asylum seeker in Germany. His friends who lived in Germany had sent him letters, persuading him to come over. He managed to get a visa which expired after three months. He was advised to seek asylum, which he did. He later married a German woman in order to get his permanent residency. The marriage lasted for three years without the expected result. Kevwe could only encourage him. She had things bothering her mind now. She responded to other emails and then put her kids to bed. She spent the rest of the evening watching movies. Richard sent Kevwe an email two weeks later, confessing that he loved her.

CHOVWE INISIAGHO

Kevwe was startled. She replied, explaining that she was married but would keep him in her prayers.

Donald appeared again after another long absence from their house. He had tried to call Kevwe to send her his registration card for the second semester. He opened the door almost forcefully in his usual arrogant mien. Kevwe was on the phone when he got in. She waved him a welcome which he ignored; instead, he went to their children who were inside their playpen. They stood up and leant against the bars when they saw their father.

'Daddy, where have you been?' Mena asked innocently.

'You will understand when you grow up,' Donald told her.

Ono touched his moustache and smiled. Kevwe, done with her call, queried Donald of his whereabouts.

'It is not your business to know,' he countered.

He demanded to know with whom she had held that long conversation over the phone. She ignored his question in a bid to avoid any argument with him. He walked behind her, insisting he needed an explanation, but she implored him to calm down.

She was now applying Mrs Adusa's strategy.

'Well,' Donald began. 'There are a few things I would like to show you.'

He pulled out some sheet of papers from his jeans' jacket pocket.

'You have been flirting on the net. These are transcripts of some of the conversations you had with people – Richard, Ade, etc.'

Kevwe was flummoxed.

'You think you can hide anything on the Internet from me? You got an Internet connection with no security. You forgot to close your chatting websites. You do not know how to log out after sending mails. These mistakes enable others, especially hackers, to gain access to your activities on the Net. And, of course, I have been able to access your email account because you foolishly gave out your email and real name in that public forum where you became a local champion. You ridicule yourself and our marriage . . .'

'You caused it, Donald. You left me by myself, and I had to occupy myself. I turned to the Internet for comfort,' Kevwe snapped.

'And you think a man in his right senses will marry a whore like you?'

'Donald, how dare you call me a whore?'

'Yes, Kevwe, you are a bitch.'

'You are referring to your sisters, not me.'

Donald was piqued by Kevwe's vituperation. Mena and Ono, who were already terrified, began to cry. Donald charged towards Kevwe and slapped her hard. As if he wasn't done, he hit her on the head. Kevwe managed to extricate herself from his grip. She ran to the kitchen, opened the balcony door, and jumped down. She was fortunate that they lived on the first floor. She rang the doorbell of her neighbour, an old lady who had lost her husband many years ago. She begged to use her phone to call the police after narrating her ordeal to her. It did not take long before the police arrived.

Kevwe formally lodged a complaint about her husband to them. They asked to know what flat she lived in, and she readily took them there. Donald was speechless when he saw the police. They demanded that he leave the house immediately after taking statements from him. Kevwe was advised to see a doctor, but she insisted she would take some pain relief and see the doctor the following day.

Kevwe finally decided to end her marriage with Donald. It was obvious that her life was endangered by him, and her future looked bleak with Donald assaulting her every now and then. Theirs was no marriage but horror. She was thirty-five and was determined to forge ahead in life without a man. Her main focus was to have a successful career and raise her children. Kazuko and Rafael hailed her decision. Rafael knew violent men could hardly give up the habit of battering their wives. She had been in an abusive relationship for ten years. Kevwe called Kofi to break the news of her divorce. He was glad it happened at long last.

After the divorce, she relocated to London with her children and maintained a constant contact with Kofi.

She sent several emails to Richard without response. Settling down in London wasn't a problem. Kevwe had visited London a few times. She spent the first month with her childhood friend before the local council lodged her in a hotel. Her German citizenry made her settling in London much easier. Mena started nursery school, and Ono was kept in the crèche while she did voluntary work with a charity organisation, after which she got a permanent job. Experience mattered a lot in order for one to get a job in the UK. She and Kofi grew to become great email friends.

At one point, his company sent him on a three-month management course to London; he instantly seized the opportunity to see Kevwe.

'It would be nice to see my online friend,' she enthused when Kofi broke the news to her.

It was indeed a great idea for Kevwe to pick him up from the airport when he arrived in London.

As scheduled, Kofi arrived in London early morning. It wasn't difficult for them to recognise each other. They had exchanged photos sometime back.

'You do not look twenty-seven,' Kevwe exclaimed.

'And you look sexy. No one will believe you are above thirty,' Kofi told an already blushing Kevwe.

They went to her car, and she started the ignition and drove off.

'So how are you settling down?'

'It's been fine. I just got a job with Sainsbury Supermarket as an assistant manager.'

'That sounds good. Congrats. How are the kids?'

'They are with my friend. We slept over in her house so that I will have someone to look after them while I come for you.'

'That was thoughtful of you,' Kofi told her.

He looked at the city for a while, admiring the finely paved streets and neatly mowed lawns. Kevwe needed to drive about an hour from Stansted Airport to the centre of London. He reclined in the chair and yawned.

'Tired?'

'Yes.'

Kevwe glanced at him and drove on. They came to Radisson Hotel in Westminster, where he was to lodge. Kevwe turned right and parked her car in the parking lot. Kofi climbed down from the car and took his luggage from the trunk. He met the receptionist who cross-checked his details and checked him in. She went with him to his room where they discussed issues that have become their common boundary over the Internet briefly, and she took her leave to pick up her kids.

He visited Kevwe two weeks later; he boarded a bus to Victoria from where he took a train to London Bridge where Kevwe resided. She lived in an apartment which was part of a blockhouse. The walkway was full of weeds. Four garbage containers stood conspicuously in front of the entrance. He climbed up to the third floor and found Kevwe's apartment. He could hear Kevwe and her children singing. He placed a finger on the doorbell lightly and let it ring.

'Hold on,' came Kevwe's soft voice.

He looked over the balcony and then back at the door and then came the jingling of keys. Kevwe clicked the door open.

'You kept to time. Come in, come in.'

Kevwe led the way while he followed. Her flat was cosy. Mena and Ono ran out to see who it was.

'These are my kids. Come on, children, say hello to uncle.'

CHOVWE INISIAGHO

Ono peered at Kofi from behind her mother. Mena greeted shyly.

'You are welcome.'

'Thank you.'

He sat down with obvious admiration of her flat. Kevwe came back with a tray of juice and water.

'Make your choice.'

Kofi took some water.

'I will drink the juice later,' he said.

She took her children to their room where she kept them busy with some children's programme showing on TV. It was almost a routine, especially when she had much to do. Kevwe went back to the living room and sat with Kofi.

'So how do you find London?' she asked with a smile of a professional.

'It's developed of course and also ancient. Before I forget, here are a few things for you and your kids.' Kofi handed Kevwe a small plastic bag.

She looked curiously inside it and was happy to find plaques and toys. She wasn't expecting anything from Kofi.

'Thank you,' she said, holding out one of the plaques.

It was an artwork.

'This is beautiful,' she said excitedly.

She showed the toys to Mena and Ono. 'Come, say thank you to uncle.'

Mena and Ono were glued to the TV. They did not want to leave their cartoon.

'Do not bother them,' he told her.

It was past midday. Kevwe had cooked palm-nut sauce and rice for lunch. She loved traditional food, and because she was conscious of balancing her diet, she prepared vegetable mixed with plenty of shrimps. After laying the table, she invited Kofi to lunch.

'I'm already salivating,' he teased.

'The table is set and all yours, Kofi,' Kevwe said, helping herself to some vegetables.

Ono smacked her lips.

'You should eat it like this, Ono,' Kevwe told her daughter Ono who was chewing a piece of shrimp clumsily.

Lunch was over, and Kevwe cleared the table. Just then, the phone rang. It was Kazuko at the other end. She informed Kevwe she was coming to London and would see her briefly. Kofi left Kevwe's flat about 5 p.m. Kevwe wanted to walk him down to the entrance, but he declined.

'Be with the kids,' he insisted.

He continued to spend much of his spare time with Kevwe and her kids. He helped her out with shopping and some repair works that he could handle. They were just like a family now.

Mena and Ono always looked forward to seeing him every time. They would ask about him the day he did not come.

When he completed his training programme and finally departed to Ghana, Kevwe felt empty and so lonely.

'You can also visit me in Accra,' he suggested during his solemn departure at the airport.

'That would be interesting,' she replied, trying hard not to betray her emotions.

He arrived in Ghana after a six-hour flight to meet his waiting family at the airport. He was driven back home by his younger brother, and he tried his best to answer all their questions about London.

He was partially attentive and impatient. All he wanted to do was to be home fast and call Kevwe.

'You are a bit restless,' his cousin Abena observed.

'Just a bit tired,' he lied.

Kofi and his small entourage arrived home shortly to a rousing welcome from his other relatives and neighbours. They were anxious to know about London. His mother was overjoyed to see him again.

'Your father is proud of you even from the grave,' she said, smiling exuberantly.

He excused himself from his family and guests, hurried to his room, took out his mobile phone, and dialled Kevwe who greeted him with screams of joy. He informed her he had arrived safely; it was brief, and he hung up to join his guests.

'Where did you go?' his mother asked.

'Just to put a quick call to a friend.'

More guests came in. His uncle Kodjo sent for more drinks, and his mother, with the help of her sisters, quickly made some fried yam. Music erupted and a spontaneous merriment followed. He was careful not to open his luggage till the guests left. He smiled and yawned intermittently.

He whispered to his uncle that he was tired and needed some rest. His uncle explained to him that it would be impolite to ask the guests to go away. He longed so much to have some rest and speak with his family alone. He got up to help himself with some fried fish and chilli sauce. His cousin, Abena, asked how London looked like, but instead, he avoided the question and called her to the kitchen.

'I just want all these people to go, then we can all talk.'

'That is true.'

The last guest departed at about 11 p.m., after which Kofi called his family together and gave each of them what he brought.

The thoughts of Kevwe occupied his mind. They called each other at least once in a week.

He kept long hours of conversation in the nights and spent less time in his hobby, football. His brother Paul observed that he was unusually indoors, so he asked to know why. He smiled and then opened up to Paul. He told his brother that he had fallen in love with a lady and gave every detail of Kevwe.

THE DYING THIEF

'Are you sure you can cope with her age and can she still bear children?'

'Paul, age is just a number.'

Paul looked at his brother intently and shrugged his shoulder.

'If it makes you happy, do it.'

He could not hold himself any longer. He called up Kevwe one evening when he knew the children must have gone to bed.

'Kevwe,' he could hear himself say.

'I have a confession to make.'

'Yes, what could you have done wrong?'

'I love you, and I want you to be my wife.'

There was an uneasy silence for a few seconds. He was already feeling embarrassed.

'Are you there, Kevwe?' he managed to ask again.

'I'm here. Here for you now and always.'

The response was impulsive. Kevwe had a crush on Kofi from the first day he visited her in London. He blew her a kiss over the phone.

'I thought you would turn me down because of my age.'

'No, I won't do that to you. I have thought about it, and I know it does not matter. But what will your people say?'

'Once it is what I want, there is nothing they can do,' he said, assuring her.

Kevwe's family was not happy to know she was marrying a younger man and a Ghanaian at that.

'Well, Mama, you and Papa encouraged me to marry Donald, who was fifteen years older than I was. What came out of it?' She had told her mother over the phone on one occasion. Her mother had objected to her marriage with Kofi.

The question hit them hard. Kevwe's father could not say anything. He overheard what she told her mother.

'I love him, and I will be happy with him,' Kevwe added.

Kofi and his family went to Nigeria and began the marriage process. Kevwe and Kofi picked a wedding date after their families had concluded the traditional marriage rites. Kazuko and Rafael were present during the wedding ceremony. It was a good opportunity for them to visit an African country. Pastor Adusa and his wife wrote to wish them well. After the wedding, Kofi and Kevwe left for Ghana with her kids, where they had their honeymoon. Kevwe returned to England and planned for Kofi to join her soon after.

★ ★ ★

'Oh, my darling, you have been crying,' he asked.

Kevwe was jolted back to life. She had been reminiscing and did not know when Kofi entered.

'Oh, sweetheart, I did not even know when you came in. I was looking back . . .'

'You don't really need that.'

He knelt down and kissed her bulging stomach again.

'How's my baby?'

'It's fine.'

'I received an email today,' he told Kevwe, taking off his tie.

'From whom?' she asked, puzzled.

'From the owner of celebrate-naija.com. He congratulated us on our wedding.'

'You told him about us?' She was astounded.

'He will publish our story,' Kofi mused.

'Oh no!' Kevwe exclaimed.

'Yes, my love, let people say what they want. It is an Internet dating success story.'

RAPED!

Grace was a staunch Catholic. She observed all holy days of obligation and had completed the necessary sacraments available to a Catholic lay faithful. She wanted her daughter Cecilia and her three relatives living with her to follow her faith. As soon as the alarm went off, she woke up the members of her household, except her husband who had told her emphatically that he does not want to be a part of her religiousness. Natomah and his wife were opposite individuals.

Cecilia got up and tied a scarf round her head. Covering the hair during prayers is another thing her mother had taught her. Tony, Ufuoma, and Ejiro woke up next. All four gathered in the living room and said some short prayers and morning devotion followed by the holy rosary – this was the routine. Cecilia had wished her mother would allow her to sleep till about 6 a.m. before calling them up, but it never happened. Cecilia believed in going to church but did not like her mother's method. Her mother, to her, was overdoing everything. Grace woke up 4 a.m. She would take her bath, dress up, and wake others at 5 a.m. They prayed for another one hour before she left for morning mass which began at 7 a.m. every day except Saturdays.

Tony was the grandson of Grace's great-aunt. Grace offered to take care of his education. Ufuoma and Ejiro were the twins of Grace's uncle. Her uncle, Akpoyibo, was a peasant farmer who could barely fend for his family. Grace approached him with the promise of getting them educated. It was a great relief for Akpoyibo. Grace went back to her village much later to take Ufuoma and Ejiro. Their mother, Titi, prepared for Grace a big sack of garri.

'This is too much,' Grace pleaded with her.

'If you give me all these, what will you take to the market?' Grace asked.

Titi was insistent. She told Grace that training her children was like lifting a big burden off their shoulders and that the garri was a token of appreciation. Grace reluctantly accepted the sack. Grace turned to her driver and instructed him to lift the sack of garri and load it into the boot of the car. Before Johnson, her driver, put the car in motion, Grace climbed out again. She walked towards her uncle and embraced his frail frame. She held his left hand, took his thin arm, and pressed her right arm into his. Grace quickly released her grip from him. Akpoyibo opened his arms, and he let out a cry of joy. Grace had rolled some crispy naira notes into his palm. Grace hurried back into her car, leaving Akpoyibo and his wife gaping.

Grace was a very considerate and compassionate woman. She knew Akpoyibo and his wife did not have much. She cleverly gave them gifts of money when occasion presented itself. Titi was amazed when she counted the money; it was 3,000 naira. They would not get much money even if they sold vegetables for months. Titi broke into a dance, singing praises of Grace.

Akpoyibo, on the other hand, was a very cautious man. He knew it could be dangerous to show off what one has. He did not want anyone to know they had much money. Much for a village! He sneaked into the house with his wife, not minding her neighbours who were already running out to stare at them.

Grace gave Tony and the girls their pocket money before leaving for church. Tony was the next to leave. He was enrolled into the Nigerian Navy Engineering College. He refused to take breakfast. He was not used to it.

'Hurry up with your food,' Ejiro told Cecilia and Ufuoma.

Cecilia and Ufuoma hurried over their meals and left for school shortly after.

Cecilia was almost more Catholic than the Pope. Her mother's making. Her mother always insisted that all must be baptised and attend catechism classes in preparation for the sacrament of confirmation. Grace registered all the children in her house late for this class. She wasn't aware of when the classes would begin. The children had barely a week to the day of confirmation. Mr Idogho, the catechist, had advised Grace to allow them to wait till the following year, but she would not take such advice. Mr Idogho allowed Cecilia and her cousins in the class. It was an intensive learning week for them. There were about thirty children in the class. Mr Idogho had the huge task of preparing them for the confirmation which would take place the following Sunday. Cecilia and her cousins had to memorise most part of the last fifty pages of the catechism book before Friday, which was the day all catechumens would be examined on how much they knew of the Church's teaching. They had to learn the fifty questions they would be asked by heart just an hour before going to bed each day, and before they knew it, it was Friday. The catechumens had assembled in the Saint Joseph Catholic Church hall. Reverend Father Steven Erhabor, the parish priest, and his assistant, Father Edward Nwakpa, were to test them. Mr Idogho, the catechist, paired them to save time. Cecilia was paired with a young boy who passed for a Fulani.

They sat down on the pew, waiting for their turn. Cecilia wasn't comfortable sitting next to the young man. Her mother had taught her not to be close to boys, else she would be pregnant. She gently shifted away, ensuring there was a marked distance between them but was sure the boy will not decode. Tony and Cecilia's

CHOVWE INISIAGHO

school friend, Abosede, were partners. They were to be tested before Cecilia and her partner.

Cecilia watched as both of them were spoken to. It was brief. She wondered what it was. Tony and Abosede came back smiling. Then it was Cecilia's and the Fulani boy's turn to go in. Cecilia was nervous. She had never prepared for a test within a short period of time before. Jovi, her partner, held her by the hand.

'Don't be afraid. It should be easy.'

Cecilia had never been touched by a boy in this manner. She pulled her hand from him very rudely, giving him a stern look. Jovi absorbed his shock and looked straight ahead of him.

Cecilia was tested by Father Erhabor. He asked her only three questions. Cecilia could not believe she passed the test. Jovi also passed. He congratulated Cecilia and left. Cecilia was all smiles. She went to Tony and sat next to him. They had to wait for Ejiro and Ufuoma. Both girls came back beaming with joy. Cecilia and Tony knew at once that they passed their tests. Grace was glad that all four children in her house passed the tests despite the very short time left for the preparation.

Grace arranged for their white clothes immediately. Chief Natomah was elated to know that all the children in his house would be confirmed. He promised to give them a good surprise.

On the day of the confirmation, there were about a hundred of them to receive the sacrament. Most of them couldn't bring a godparent. The bishop organised an elderly man and his wife to stand for all the catechumens. This decision was a bit strange and was a blow to those catechumens and their parents who had arranged for their own godparents. Cecilia had requested her mathematics teacher, Mrs Nwokolo, to be her godmother. She was a well-known member of St. Joseph Church.

'Catholic Church is too full of dogmas,' Chief Natomah complained bitterly to Grace. 'If I sit at home and say my prayers, I will still make it to heaven,' he continued.

THE DYING THIEF

Grace had to placate her already angry husband. He believed in God but not in attending church. At first, it was strange for Grace, but after a few years of arguments and family intervention, she decided to let him be. The catechumens sat on the pew, listening with rapt attention to Bishop George's sermon. He was an Irishman who was the administrator of the Warri Diocese to which Sapele belonged. He came to Nigeria on the orders of the Pope when there was a fight between the Urhobo congregation and the then Ibo bishop. The Urhobos felt marginalised in the affairs of the dioceses. They claimed that Urhobo priests were under-represented in the seminary because the bishop deliberately did not give the Urhobo youths the opportunity to enter the seminary. Cecilia looked behind her. There was homogeneity of white colours among the catechumens. It was disrupted by a young man sitting on the third row of the pew, next to the side entrance of the church. It was Jovi. He was wearing a brown trouser and a cream-coloured shirt. Their eyes met. Jovi smiled coyly at Cecilia who quickly looked away.

The ceremony lasted for about one and a half hours. Chief Natomah, his family, the children's sponsors, and their friends went home thereafter to celebrate the rebirth of their children. Cecilia and her cousins were surprised to see that a party was being held in their honour. She was surprised too at the quantity of food and drinks that awaited them on three tables. She wondered how her parents were able to organise all the food within a short time without her having a clue that it was happening. Some of the guests gave Cecilia and her cousins gifts of cash. It was something they were not expecting. It meant an increase in their pocket money. Before they went to bed, Grace called them and reminded them of what it meant to be conferred the sacrament of confirmation in the Catholic Church.

Grace had high hopes for her daughter. She wanted her to become a nun. She had told her daughter to avoid every evil and sinfulness. She also told her there was nothing good in attending discos and that, above all, she should avoid any male company. Avoiding a male companion had become monotonous. Akpoyibo had told Grace emphatically that he wanted his girls to get married. Grace did not involve them in religious activities like Cecilia. Cecilia was a member of the Legion of Mary and Children's Blue Army. Cecilia's weekends were always very busy. She wasn't very open with her husband about what she planned for Cecilia. She knew he would kick against it, so she employed a tactful method by ensuring Cecilia engaged in a lot of religious activities. During the Easter holidays, she sent Cecilia to the convent. Reverend Sister Regina received her. She was a nun with the Religious of Jesus and Mary. Cecilia was to spend the whole of her Easter holidays there. Cecilia wished she could decide where to be. Her cousins had all gone to the village to see their parents. Grace bid Cecilia goodbye. She knew her daughter was in safe hands. Sister Regina took her to her room. Cecilia looked around. There was a neatly made six-spring bed near the window and a wardrobe for her to arrange her clothes in.

'Have a change of clothes and meet me up in the common room. I will tell you about the timetable here.' Sister Regina left.

Cecilia arranged her few clothes carefully on the first layer of the wardrobe. She put her toilet bag on the window parapet and then went to meet Sister Regina. She gave her a brief orientation of the house. They were to wake up at 5 a.m., have morning devotion, clean up, attend Holy Mass at 7 a.m., and have breakfast thereafter. Every Thursday was adoration of the Blessed Sacrament. Cecilia did not hear the other things that she said. She drifted into deep thought. She was imagining the life of a nun. She wasn't sure if she could cope with the stringent rules and the entire vocation itself. She was divided between pleasing her mother and making her choice. Cecilia went to her room. At 7 p.m., Sister Regina called her for dinner.

'Once it's 7 p.m., it's supper time, so try to be here.'

The table bell rang; all the nuns were standing behind their chairs around the two long rectangular tables joined together, head to head.

The mother superior picked up a small square book. 'Bless us, O Lord, and this thy gift which we are about to receive from thy bounty through Christ our Lord.'

'Amen,' they all chorused.

Another nun at the opposite end of the table reverently held the missal in her two hands and read the gospel of the following.

'This is the gospel of the Lord.'

'Praise be to you, Lord Jesus Christ.'

Rice and fried plantain were served. Each nun took turns to serve herself. Cecilia served herself enough rice and fried plantain. She felt awkward using just fork and knife to eat rice. There was no meat, and she wondered if they don't eat meat. Was it because it was a Friday?

Sister Regina noticed Cecilia's little fight with her cutlery. She went up to her.

'This is how you do it, my dear,' she told an already embarrassed Cecilia by demonstrating it.

'Don't be shy. We are all here to learn.'

Slightly consoled, Cecilia ate quietly looking up at intervals to catch a glimpse of the nuns who were busy chatting and laughing loudly. It was the first time she heard them talking with their full voices. Other times, they talked in hushed tones, and you have to strain your ear to hear them, at least for a visitor like Cecilia.

There was something new to learn each day. Their days were programmed such that no day actually repeated itself; there was no replay.

During Holy Mass, they occupied the front row of the pews. It was their humble reserve, and the lay faithful sat there with the church wardens always posted to sieve the sitters.

CHOVWE INISIAGHO

The table bell rang again, and she was woken from her deep thought, though the fork never missed her mouth. Supper was over.

She looked at Sister Regina, and in return, Sister Regina asked her to wait behind when others had gone.

They stood and pushed their chairs under the long tables once more.

Sister Regina picked a small missal, but did not look inside it.

'We give Thee thanks for all Thy benefits, O Almighty God, who liveth and reigneth world without end.'

'Amen,' all the nuns said in unison.

'May the souls of all the faithful departed, through the mercy of God, rest in peace.'

'Amen,' they chorused again.

Cecilia remained standing by her chair while others drifted away to the chapel. Her finger traced a line on the table, but she did not know what line it was. She noticed only two young nuns were left behind to wash the plates; supererogatorily, she joined them.

It was 8 p.m.; the nuns went into their rooms to read and prepare and to retire to bed. The next two weeks that followed were very boring for Cecilia. She was glad when her mother came back for her.

Ejiro did not come back from the Easter holiday. Tony and Ufuoma told Cecilia that a young man from Lagos came to seek her hand in marriage in absentia.

'The young man promised to sponsor her studies,' Tony told Cecilia.

Grace knew Akpoyibo had always wanted his girls to get married, so she wasn't surprised.

She only hoped the young man would truly send Ejiro back to school. Ufuoma did not have any proposal. She told Cecilia she too wanted to marry. Tony hoped to further his education.

Grace impressed on Cecilia that it was important for her to keep her virginity and must see herself as a living sacrifice to God.

THE DYING THIEF

'Our body is the temple of God. It is written clearly in the Bible. Flee all sexual immorality, my dear daughter,' Grace would counsel and preach to Cecilia.

Cecilia heard similar advice from her mother all the time. She was determined not to let her mother down. She would always thank her mother and go to her room.

Cecilia turned fifteen in May. It was a very busy month for her as she took part in almost all the activities in her school to mark the Children's Day celebration. She was also neck-deep in activities of the Children's Blue Army and the Legion of Mary in the church. Cecilia was a member of the drama group in her school and was chosen by their sports teacher to join the school march past team. They were to present a drama at Orerokpe town hall and a debate in Benin. The St Joseph harvest was drawing near. The Children's Blue Army was to present a cultural dance. The Legion of Mary was scheduled to visit the prison and the old people's home. Cecilia had a lot of meetings and rehearsals. She was hardly seen at home. Her father became worried and thought it right to speak with his wife. Chief Natomah loved his daughter. She was the only child they had. Grace had suffered many miscarriages in the early stages of their marriage. Chief Natomah and Grace had given up hope of ever having children. During those moments, Chief Natomah came under pressure from his kinsmen to consider taking another wife. He loved Grace and could not imagine himself with another woman. It was repugnant to him. He could not understand why his relatives wanted him to take another wife simply because his wife was unable to bear him more children.

'This is a woman who was with me when I had nothing. She is a woman who abandoned her comfort in London to be with me. You all know Grace is from a wealthy home. She was working as a nurse in London. I was there for a short course. I was there on the courtesy of the Ministry of Labour for which I worked, a ministry that dumped me when I was sick. I only proposed to this woman while in London. I made it clear to her I could not live in London because of its cold weather. She resigned from her job even when her British grandmother objected. Mrs Eleanor Walter is a wealthy woman. Her daughter died in a way that caused a lot of doubts and debates. Grace came to be with me. Her grandmother bequeathed nothing to her because of me. Because she believed in love, she came back with all her salary. And when I lost my job, she was there for me, advising me to invest in properties. You all know the story too well.'

Chief Natomah ended their love history speech and heaved a sigh of relief. His kinsmen were dumbfounded. They had no option than to stop asking him to remarry. He did not bother to call them as they got up one after the other, filing past him and then through the door. He got up and locked his door behind them and peeked at them through the window. It was a difficult moment.

Chief Natomah saw his wife in the kitchen. She was preparing their dinner. Grace enjoyed cooking a lot. She always made sure she prepared her husband's food herself and was grateful to her mother, who, despite her Jamaican and British ancestries, was able to expose her to the African tradition. Her mother joined the Urhobo meeting. She had told her that her father was an Urhobo man from Nigeria. He was a student who was purported to have left for home and never returned again.

Laurencia, her mother, sent her often to her Urhobo friends to learn the language and the culture.

People hardly believed that Grace was a Briton because her skin was glossy dark. Laurencia's father was an African-Jamaican and Briton married to a British lady, Eleanor. He died after a prolonged illness. It was rumoured that he had cancer of the lungs. After six months of mourning, Eleanor remarried a British millionaire. When Grace came to Nigeria, she fully embraced the Urhobo culture. She had spent ten years in Nigeria when her mother wrote to her that her father had resurfaced. They had a brief meeting during which, James, her father, introduced her to his family in the village. Since then, she kept in touch with her paternal family. She was really broken-hearted when her father and mother had a misunderstanding. Trouble began when her father, who had worked for a very long time in Equatorial Guinea and married an Equatorial Guinean and had two sons by her, returned to her mother in London. At that time, the government in Equatorial Guinea became hostile to the Nigerians and demanded that all Nigerians must leave. James had to leave for London without his wife and two sons. Laurencia was furious when she found out that James had a family in Equatorial Guinea. She threw James out and did not listen to his pleas.

They separated for a second time.

James returned to Nigeria and got a job with a bottling company. He died in a car crash just four months into his new job. Laurencia continued to live in London, alone. She died two years after James's death. She had kidney failure.

Chief Natomah walked up to his wife. He took a piece of meat and some onions from a plate she had kept on the dining table.

'My dear wife, don't you think Cecilia should slow down on her numerous activities?'

Grace stopped what she was doing and looked askance at her husband. She wiped her face with the edge of her apron.

'She is equal to the task, I guess.'

Chief Natomah left his wife. He knew it would be futile discussing further with her. Cecilia was at Sapele sports ground for the march past. She joined other selected pupils to represent her school. There were twenty schools that took part in the march past. All pupils and guests arrived at 10 a.m. The chairman of the local government gave his welcome address. The atmosphere became magical when the Nigerian Police band rolled out some melodious music. Sapele Girls College was the last to carry out the march past.

When the results were announced, they took the first position in the senior category.

There was murmuring and widespread discontentment among all the pupils that were present. They argued that Sapele Girls College had won the trophy for five consecutive years and that there was a foul play somewhere. Mrs Kelechi, the physical education teacher, allowed her team to take refreshments and stroll around the sports ground.

Cecilia was relieved that they could buy something to eat. She walked towards the car park where a lady sold soft drinks and pastries. She ordered a bottle of Coke and toasted sandwich. Just as she was about to pay, she heard someone calling her name. She looked back, and to her surprise, it was Jovi, the Fulani boy, her pair on the day of her confirmation examination. He was the last person Cecilia expected to see again – here or anywhere.

'How are you?' he greeted her with such familiarity.

'I'm fine. Thank you,' Cecilia replied blandly.

He offered to pay for her drink and the pastries.

'Let me take care of that, Cecilia. Madam, how much is your bill?'

Cecilia was surprised by Jovi's magnanimity.

'Thank you,' Cecilia said nervously.

Jovi and Cecilia walked back together. She tried hard to maintain a distance from him. Jovi told her he was there to cheer up his friends who took part in the march past. He told Cecilia he only loved table tennis but was more into his books. Cecilia thanked him again as they got close to the school bus of Sapele Girls College. She did not want Mrs Kelechi to see her in the company of this strange boy. She waved to Jovi and hurried away.

Cecilia came across Jovi frequently on her way to the Legion of Mary. They would wave at each other and continue on their way. Things took a different turn when Jovi walked up to Cecilia one day on her way from prayer meeting and asked to speak to her.

'Cecilia, I would like to speak with you,' Jovi began.

'About what, Jovi?' Cecilia asked, clutching her Bible and prayer book to her chest as if her life depended on them. She stood, obliging Jovi's request, and was curious to know what Jovi was about to say.

'So, my dear, where are you coming from? We always pass each other around this school.'

'My dear' echoed in her ears as if it's a strange pronouncement.

'Jovi, is this all you stopped me for?'

'My dear, we are friends, aren't we? The question is part of it.'

'Anyway, I'm coming from the Legion of Mary prayer meeting.'

'You are a very religious person. I only attend Mass on Sundays, and after our catechism classes, I did not join any other group.'

'Well, I am thinking of becoming a nun, so being a member of the group like Legion of Mary is very important to discern my vocation.'

Jovi cast a quick gaze at Cecilia and let out a soft smile. He shifted in his position.

'You mean you want to be a nun?'

'Yes.'

'How did you arrive at that decision?'

Cecilia was hesitant. She wasn't prepared for the question. No. She wasn't ready for any conversation with Jovi or with any other boy.

'Are you sure you want to be a reverend sister?' He wanted to be sure.

'My mother wants me to, and I don't want to disappoint her.'

He laughed.

'Hmm! Listen, Cecilia, from the way you responded, I know it is not your wish to be one. It's not a life you can live for someone but for yourself. Well, Cecilia, I've wanted to let you know something. You are a very beautiful young girl and very cultured. You stole my heart the very first time I set my eyes on you at that church. Since then, I have been thinking of how I can tell you about what I feel for you. Please let us go beyond just walking past each other.'

Cecilia was thrown off balance. She looked away shyly and blinked rapidly. Jovi was a handsome young man whose looks were captivating. Jovi took her prayer books from her. She reluctantly let them go. Her heart was racing faster now.

'Come, Cecilia, let us go near one of those classrooms. I do not want people to stare at us standing here.'

Cecilia followed Jovi like a servant following the master's order. They leant against the wall of an open classroom.

'So, Cecilia, are you ready for us to go beyond this level?'

She was mute. She did not know whether to protect her mother's interest or succumb to the emotion building inside her now. The emotion that has shut her mouth up against this boy but of which she had wasted no time to tell off in the recent past. She remembered her mother's caution about decency and sexual immorality.

'No, Jovi. It's a sin. It is a sin to date,' she said, stammering.

Jovi laughed once again.

'Cecilia, I know you are not being sincere. I won't hurt you. Going beyond this level won't take you to hell.'

'OK then, let me think about it.'

'Forget about that thinking stuff, Cecilia. We are friends, but I'm not just a friend. I want to make you my queen and my wife.'

Cecilia was bemused. She knew she felt something for Jovi. She did not turn down his love overtures. Jovi held Cecilia's hand and began to walk silently with her. He knew the direction she was headed. Her nerves were electrified, and it ran down her spine. She knew she had fallen in love now and maybe before too.

Cecilia kept longer hours at her church meetings and came home late. Her mother was the first to notice these changes. She asked Cecilia about it, but Cecilia told her there were additional

THE DYING THIEF

discussions for the old members after the usual meeting. She wasn't pleased with herself after giving her mother that explanation. It was a lie. She was not supposed to lie to her mother.

She continued to hang out with Jovi. She knew her parents would be totally against her having a boyfriend. It would be suicidal for her mother who wished for her to become a nun. Cecilia kept her relationship with Jovi a guarded secret but revealed it to her cousin Ufuoma whom she trusted so much. Ufuoma hugged her and promised her support. She also thought that becoming a nun would not be good for Cecilia. Ufuoma confided in Cecilia that she would marry as soon as she found the right man for her. Cecilia did not want to hurt Ufuoma and did not know how to tell her she should be focused on her education first; after all, she was a culprit now. Ufuoma had just a year to write her final secondary school examinations and seek higher education. She remembered Tony, who successfully completed his engineering training school. He was a very intelligent young man.

He told Cecilia his desire to go higher in his educational pursuit. He wrote the university entrance examinations thereafter and got a place to study mechanical engineering at the Obafemi Awolowo University, Ile-Ife. Grace and her husband were happy for him. They knew training Tony was one of the best decisions they ever took. With Jovi in her life, Cecilia thought it would be better for her to become a teacher in the secondary school so that she would have time for Jovi and their children when they came.

'I would like to go into the teaching profession, Ufuoma.'

'Why teaching?' Ufuoma asked, searching her eyes for an answer.

'It will give me more time for a family life.'

'Well, my dear cousin, there is still time to decide.'

'I have decided. I know Jovi, and I will get married to him. I love him. He has all I need in a man.'

'You sure know what you want, Cecilia,' Ufuoma said, hugging Cecilia.

Grace was devastated to know her daughter had been dating a boy for three years without her knowledge. It was when she reminded Cecilia about entering the Daughters of Charity nunnery that she told her mother she would prefer to get married. Everything was happening in time for Cecilia. She had finished her secondary education and had got a place to study Home Economics at the University of Benin where Jovi was studying Economics. Chief Natomah was relieved to know Cecilia had changed her mind about this nun thing. He had told his wife to allow Cecilia to decide if she wanted to be a nun or not. Nun for her mother! Not a nun for him! He was happy to know that Cecilia already had a proposal from a young man she loved. He walked up to his wife and daughter, knowing his wife had been putting Cecilia under pressure to become a nun.

'Grace, just let our daughter do what she wants. It is not the end of the world.' He was careful not be too hard on Grace. She could only stare at Cecilia who sat on the dining chair looking undaunted.

Before she resumed school, Jovi visited her parents at the instance of Chief Natomah. It was like an initiation into the Natomah family. She promised herself to make her relationship work.

Ufuoma helped Cecilia put her luggage in the car when she was ready to leave for campus. She wanted to accompany Cecilia to the University of Benin and never stopped telling her about being fortunate to have Jovi. Ufuoma would then launch into a tirade of complaints of being the only girl in town without a boyfriend. Her twin sister Ejiro was married and had two children already. Her husband sent her to learn sewing, and she is doing well in the trade.

'Your time will come,' Cecilia would tell her.

They arrived at Ekewan campus of the University of Benin and drove straight to the hostel where Cecilia would be living throughout her first year. Jovi was already waiting for her arrival. Edward, their new driver, pulled up the car in front of the hostel entrance. Jovi helped Cecilia bring her belongings from the car into the hostel. Edward waited in the car. Cecilia and her cousin also took a few of her other things. They went into the hostel with Cecilia. Jovi placed Cecilia's luggage on her bed. He wanted to get some soft drinks for them all, but Ufuoma told him that it wasn't necessary. She needed to be back with Edward to Sapele. Chief Natomah had instructed Edward to return in good time. Cecilia took her handbag where she kept her money. She left with Jovi and Ufuoma to the car. Ufuoma gave her a hug before climbing into the car.

She waved at her as the car screeched away.

'Edward is a rough driver,' Jovi remarked.

'Yes,' Cecilia said sadly.

'He does not seem to realise it's dangerous,' Cecilia added.

When they got back to Cecilia's room, Esohe, Cecilia's roommate was already sleeping.

Jovi gave her a little orientation and told her to be careful with arranging her things so that they do not wake Esohe up. One by one, they unpacked the two cartons and two suitcases. Cecilia arranged her clothes in her own corner of the wardrobe and brought out a plunging dress.

'This is what I shall be wearing for the matriculation,' she told Jovi excitedly.

'Hmm! Beautiful! You are going to be the toast of the campus that day. Someone will have to ward off intruders.'

Cecilia laughed heartily but stopped again when she remembered Esohe was asleep.

Jovi took Cecilia to Ugbowo campus where he studied, and they spent almost the rest of the day in his room. In the evening, they went to have some barbeque opposite the school gate. They checked into a hotel that night when it became too late for them to return to Ekewan campus. Jovi did not want Cecilia to spend the night in his room even though his roommates brought in their girlfriends to spend the night with them. He was a maverick. He had an unusual way of doing his own things.

He bought two toothbrushes and toothpaste from a nearby pharmacy. Cecilia was the first to lie on the bed. She was worn out and needed to sleep so badly. Jovi lay next to her, pulled her close to himself, and put an arm on her shoulder. She clasped her hand round his arm and yawned and whispered a goodnight. Jovi gently released his hand from Cecilia's grip and began to stroke her shoulder softly. He reached for her lips and kissed her tenderly. She gasped for breath as her lips were taken in. It was her first, their first.

Cecilia thought Jovi was going beyond the limit so she cautioned herself. She wriggled away from him.

'Come on, Cecilia, this is our third year together, and your family knows too well that we are dating. You are mine for good.'

Jovi told Cecilia under his panting breath. He kissed her again, this time more aggressively. He moved up his hand towards her chest and found her hardened breast. He squeezed and pressed it. She shivered and lost her breath. He moved down his hand between her thighs and found her supple slippery flesh and fingered it gently. She moved her hand behind him and held his hardened manhood pressed tightly against her back. She left it quickly and started undressing. They turned to each other and kissed more passionately. The last thing she remembered that night was her own scream as Jovi pounded her.

They woke up halfway into the thick night, lying naked beside each other with the yellowish-glowing room light. Jovi smiled and told her the towel would become a treasure for both of them. He had spread one of the hotel towels on the bed sheet. He kissed her passionately again. He took her to the bathroom and helped her clean up. She was shy and nervous. Jovi stared at her nude figure. He took the shower handle from her and splashed her with water. She laughed and did the same to him. The experience she had with Jovi was something she wanted to keep to herself forever.

A new vice chancellor was appointed by Governor Oyegun. There had been series of strikes and demonstrations at the University of Benin. Cecilia and Jovi constantly exchanged visits because they were not on the same campus. Cecilia and Esohe, her roommate, became close friends.

She was already married before entering the university. Marriage was a big deal among the female students on campus. Esohe was glad that Cecilia had a steady relationship. She would advise her on courtship. It was Esohe who opened her eyes to the treacherous campus life. Cecilia was told by one of her coursemates that Jovi was dating the commissioner of health's daughter. Many students had been seeing them together at odd spots around. She went numb. Jovi was in his final year. Cecilia had two more years to go, and it was their fourth year together. After her lectures in the evening, she went straight to see Esohe in her hostel. Esohe, too, was in her final year. She was writing part of her thesis when Cecilia entered. As soon as she got into Esohe's room, she burst into tears. Esohe dropped her pen. She had never seen Cecilia weep. She was confused. She held Cecilia by the hand and rubbed her shoulders gently.

'What happened?' she enquired.

Cecilia sniffed, and between tears, she narrated all she heard about her boyfriend to Esohe. It was then she opened up to her that Jovi had deflowered her. Esohe embraced her like a mother.

'Wipe your tears. It may be a rumour. You know people could spread rumour just to make you sad.'

Esohe advised her to ask Jovi as calmly as possible if really he was having an affair. She persuaded her to spend the rest of the day with her, but Cecilia begged to leave because she had a lecture at 8 a.m. the following day. Esohe understood her plight.

Cecilia paid an impromptu visit to Jovi at his hostel. His room was littered with clothes and empty bottles of beer.

'Have you been partying, Jovi?' Cecilia asked in utter disgust.

She had never seen his room so untidy.

'Yeah, some friends were here all night, and we had some drinks,' Jovi told her, trying to put the room in order.

'Anyway, just be careful.'

They exchanged some more pleasantries. She made lunch, and they ate together. Then Cecilia confronted him with the issue of his affair with the commissioner's daughter. Before she could finish, she broke into tears. Jovi knelt down in front of her. He kissed her forehead and took her hand.

'Darling, it is all a rumour. People are trying to come between us. We have come a long way, you know?'

Jovi gave her a long French kiss and then made love to her. Cecilia slept off like a baby in the end. Esohe was glad to know the result of Cecilia's discussion with Jovi.

'I told you it is all rumour.'

'Yes, you did.'

They were wrong. Not long afterwards, one evening, Cecilia ran into Jovi smooching a female student on her way home from lectures. She was nauseated. She screamed Jovi's name and ran off as fast as her legs could carry her. He ran after her, but he could not catch up.

She broke up with Jovi. She felt cheated. She did not accept Jovi's pleas and emissaries.

Esohe was by her side in this time of travail. Cecilia was absent during Jovi's graduation. It was an obvious vacuum. Esohe advised her to stay off men and to take her time before entering into any new relationship. She knew a part of her was missing when she realised Esohe was leaving the school finally. Her husband and two children came to help her pack.

Chief Natomah sent for Cecilia. Her mother was involved in an accident. She wept bitterly when Edward and her uncle broke the news to her. She followed them to Sapele where her father and some relatives were waiting for her. Grace was knocked down by a hit-and-run driver on her way to Holy Mass. Witnesses claimed there was so much fog that morning that the driver could not see the person crossing the road. Cecilia was informed a week after the incident. Jovi also heard about the accident. He thought he too should commiserate with Cecilia. He paid her a visit at a time he knew there won't be so much visitors in their house.

Tony saw him first. They exchanged greetings. Chief Natomah was away at the hospital, attending to his wife. Tony asked Jovi to wait while he announced his presence to Cecilia. Her countenance changed as soon as she learnt Jovi was in their house. Memories of her break up with Jovi flashed through her mind. It was a year since they parted, and they never saw each other thereafter. Ufuoma gave her a long look.

'Let him in, Cecilia. At least for your mum's sake.'

Cecilia was hesitant. She wanted to blot Jovi out of her life. Tony also lent his voice to the appeal. Very reluctantly, she turned to Tony and asked him to let Jovi in. The first thing Jovi did was to beg Cecilia. It did not matter to him whether her cousins were there.

'Forgive me, Cecilia. Let's reconcile for good. You are mine.'

He pleaded with her, kneeling. Ufuoma and Tony stole a quick glance at each other. They left knowing it was proper to allow the two lovebirds some privacy.

Cecilia was always emotional. Jovi had hardly finished before she broke down into tears.

They reconciled. Ufuoma was glad that they made up again. Tony hugged Jovi. It was one blissful moment for Cecilia. Chief

Natomah came back from the hospital. He was surprised to see Jovi around. He told them that Grace had to be flown to London for further treatment because she was near paralysis. Chief Natomah and Tony swung into action almost immediately. He left with his wife to London a few weeks later. Grace was British and so her husband was one by marriage. Grace had not been to England in many years. Her aged grandmother sent one of Grace's cousins to wait for them at the airport. It took a lot of persuasion to get her involved in Grace's medical treatment. Davies, Grace's cousin, in conjunction with the airline arranged for an ambulance that would transfer her to the hospital. Chief Natomah was able to recognise Davies from the picture he sent by courier along with some documents. Both men sat in the ambulance with Grace.

Chief Natomah was glad that there was progress due to her treatment. He was told his wife needed a long time to recuperate. He told the doctors all he wanted was his wife's recovery. He spent a month in England before returning to Nigeria. Davies and his wife took over the care of Grace. Chief Natomah would be visiting his wife from time to time.

Cecilia returned from school to meet her father. He gave her the full update of her mother's condition. Then very calmly, she told her father that Jovi and herself had decided to get married. Her father was happy. He wished her mother was there to be a part of it. Chief Natomah was an understanding father. He suggested that they discuss this issue over the weekend. Cecilia thanked her father. Ufuoma was glad Cecilia and Jovi would be getting married. She lamented at her inability to find a suitor. Her complaints were words Cecilia wished to avoid but had no choice than to put up with them and comfort her.

Jovi's family came to officially discuss their son's marriage with Chief Natomah's daughter. He had informed some of his kinsmen well ahead of time.

The bride price and date were fixed. It was a quiet ceremony. Chief Natomah wanted the wedding when his wife fully recovered. Thus began the marital life of Cecilia. She was married in her final year to her childhood sweetheart.

★ ★ ★

Cecilia arrived in a taxi with all her belongings. Her father and aunt were sitting on the veranda, relaxing. They were shocked to see her. Mariaye, her aunt, was the first to break for the shock.

'Cecilia, what happened?' she asked, rising up from her chair.

Cecilia ignored her question. She concentrated on offloading her small luggage from the taxi. She paid the taxi driver and began carrying some of her things into the house, walking past her aunt.

'My daughter, is everything all right?' her father inquired.

'Papa, Jovi sent me packing. He said I should leave immediately.'

'Only that?'

'Yes, Papa that's all.'

Cecilia went to her room to keep the suitcases she was carrying. She still maintained a room in her father's house despite the fact that she was married. She looked around for some of her cousins to help her bring in the rest of her luggage.

'Cecilia, you mean your husband sent you packing?' her aunt asked curiously.

'Aunty Mariaye, I do not mean to be rude, but you heard what I just told my father.'

Mariaye had been like a mother to Cecilia since her mother became incapacitated due to the accident. Grace was never the same again in spite of the treatment. Her spinal cord was affected, and she was bedridden. Chief Natomah decided she should live in England because she would have access to special and better medical care there. He could not relocate to England because of his chain of businesses but visited regularly. Mariaye and her family moved in to occupy one of the flats in her brother's house. Her husband lost his job, so life became difficult for them. They could no longer pay their house rent. She had to convince her husband that they should live in her brother's house. Natomah, her brother, was a big time business mogul. He owned a lot of housing estates in Warri and Sapele. Mariaye preferred to stay close to her brother so that she could offer him and his daughter some support in their times of difficulty. Ufuoma had since left the house. She got a job in Ogun State. It was a welcome idea for Natomah. He did not need to bother about house chores. Mariaye did for Cecilia all a mother ought to do.

Cecilia came out again to the veranda and sat next to her father.

'Welcome, my daughter,' her father greeted her again.

'Thank you, Father.'

'So what really happened?'

'Papa, Jovi said I cannot bear him children and that a marriage without children is no marriage.'

Cecilia told her father how she was beaten up by Jovi and how he brought in his mistress who was already three months pregnant by him.

'He is heartless,' Mariaye said, with the bitterness of a mother.

'My daughter, calm down and let's sleep over it. I will think about what to do.'

Natomah invited Jovi and his family for discussions. Jovi did not honour the invitation, but his father, an uncle, and one of his cousins were there. It was a long deliberation in which it was agreed that Jovi should have the final say and that if he doesn't want the marriage any more, the bride price should be returned.

Cecilia remained with her father, hoping Jovi would change his mind and send for her. She had dreamt of a perfect and a happy marriage, but it seemed now that all was a mirage. She remembered how they met and the first time she knew Jovi was having another affair. If someone had told her Jovi was a flirt, she would have fought with that person. He continued dating other women even after their marriage. She spent most of the times indoors. She did not want to interact with people for fear of being ridiculed.

Her father had persuaded her to go out to visit friends or take walks. Cecilia refused to listen to her father. Her young cousins came from school for holidays. They were studying at the university. There were lots to tell and catch up with. They were sad to hear about Cecilia's marriage. Ese, the eldest of her cousins, always tried to cheer her up. She was ten years younger than Cecilia. It all made no sense to Cecilia who already felt like a failure. It wasn't long before she fell sick from extreme depression. She was hospitalised.

The rumour went round the neighbourhood that Cecilia had been sent away from her marital home. She spent six weeks at the hospital. The doctors advised her to remain calm and eat well so that she does not have nervous breakdown and become hypertensive. Ese did her best to make Cecilia happy. They were often seen together.

Tragedy struck one night when everyone in Chief Natomah's house was asleep. There was a robbery attack, and the robbers stole a lot of money and other valuables from the Chief. They went from room to room searching for what to take. They asked everyone to go into the living room. Cecilia could not move so fast. The leader of the bandit, Spaco, was infuriated. He felt someone was flouting his orders. He instructed Cecilia to remain in her room, otherwise she risked being shot. Cecilia froze and trembled. Spaco moved closer to her. He pushed her violently on to her bed and began raping her. She screamed. Spaco warned her to be quiet for the last time. Her father could hear Cecilia's quivering voice and pleas.

'Please don't kill her!' He managed to plead with Spaco from where he was forced to sit on.

When Spaco was satisfied, he left Cecilia to join his gang members. They left after eating the food in Chief Natomah's kitchen.

In the morning, neighbours came to sympathise with Chief Natomah. The news spread fast that Cecilia was gang-raped. It was another blow for Cecilia. She was traumatised. Her aunt Mariaye was at hand to comfort her. She planned to send Cecilia to another city.

Two months after the robbery, Cecilia complained to her aunt of stomach ache and not seeing her monthly period. Mariaye stared at Cecilia.

'You are pregnant,' she told Cecilia excitedly.

'By that armed robber, Aunty?' Cecilia was disenchanted.

'Well, yes, but you have been married for years without a child too.'

'What do I do, Aunty?'

'What do you want to do, Cecilia? Tell me.'

Cecilia cast a long stare at Mariaye. Mariaye understood her plight and fears. Both ladies tacitly locked themselves in embrace. Cecilia had begun to sob quietly.

'Keep the baby,' her aunt whispered softly to her.

Cecilia felt miserable. She saw herself in a vicious circle of misfortune but decided to heed her aunt's advice. Her eyes glittered with tears which soon flowed freely. Mariaye used the back of her right palm to wipe her face. Cecilia spent the rest of her prenatal period with her aunt's friend in Kaduna. Mariaye had arranged with her to allow Cecilia live with her until she had her baby. Cecilia's pregnancy had caused a lot of gossip in Sapele. Her aunt thought it wise to send her somewhere else, where it would be more conducive for her to be and rest.

Cecilia gave birth to a baby boy when she was due. Her father was overjoyed when he heard the news of the arrival of his grandson. He wanted his daughter back almost immediately. He had a grand welcome party in her honour. Mariaye and her daughter Ese were at hand to give her all the support she needed. Natomah's neighbours were held spellbound at the amount of food and takeaway gifts Natomah gave out that day. No one dared to talk about how Cecilia had her son.

Jovi heard of Cecilia's child. He quickly decided to reconcile with her. Cecilia least expected him again. Jovi pleaded for forgiveness and asked her to go back home with him. Cecilia refused.

'Jovi, after five years and four girls with your new wife, you want me back? No, Jovi!'

Cecilia remained with her father and aunt. She wanted to take care of her son and think carefully of what next to do. She wasn't in a hurry to get married any longer.

BITTER EXPERIENCE

The passing out ceremony of the German Red Cross voluntary year was brief and eventful. Onome and Masasi, her Kenyan boyfriend, were happy to have participated in the ceremony of the organisation which had enhanced her skill and experience as a social worker after graduation from the Catholic University in Münster and after having spent some years in pursuit of her dream profession.

Onome and Masasi met during the African Students Seminar held at the university auditorium. The encounter, though short, ushered them into an instant friendship. Masasi was impressed with Onome's astute knowledge of African unity when the question was put to her. She had opined during the round table discussion with the organisers and other speakers that there ought to be both a standing African Student Union and a branch of the African Union in Germany.

She was also sympathetic to the idea of having the union's student representative in Addis Ababa. Her arguments and suggestions won her a standing ovation among her listeners. Impressed by her logic and argument, Masasi was compelled to ask if she had studied law.

'Social work,' Onome had told him.

Masasi introduced himself briefly. He told her he was studying African studies at the University of Bonn. They exchanged email contacts before the close of the seminar. Masasi was the first to initiate the litanies of emails that would take them to a world yet unknown but known at last. Although the email somehow found its nest among the other junk mails, Onome recognised it was Masasi's email and cautiously opened it and was a bit anxious when the headline humbly announced 'African seminar'. She was surprised to receive the email from him, knowing that many people met that way, exchanged addresses, and never heard from each other any more, so Onome never hesitated to hang the label on Masasi.

Onome expressed her gratitude in her reply and gave a short update about herself in the email.

The weeks that followed saw them exchanging emails more frequently until Masasi paid Onome a visit.

Onome told him she was born in Germany and that her parents lived in Nigeria. Onome's father had retired, and because of the burning urge to help the poor of his country, he had returned home with her mother.

'My brothers are in London, working. I prefer here. There are three of us, and I'm the only girl,' she had explained.

He told her he came to do his masters and would love to pursue his doctorate thereafter.

He lost his father at the tender age of ten. He was the third of five children – three girls and two boys. Onome had told Masasi of her plans to go to Nigeria for some months to help in the troubled Niger-Delta region.

'I want to contribute my quota by helping my people. I am inspired by both my father and the plight of the people there.'

Onome had joined the German Red Cross as a volunteer to gain experience for her humanitarian venture ahead. Masasi admired Onome's idea and passion.

She was informed by her father of the fight between the Urhobo and Itsekiri ethnic groups. Her father lived in Ugborikoko, a district in Effurun. The incessant fight between the two ethnic groups had led to a wanton destruction of lives and properties in the region. There has been an age-old acrimony between the two ethnic groups. It worsened a few years back when the Ijaw ethnic group laid claim to the city of Warri, which the Itsekiris moved to prevent. The number of people killed in the clash was the highest in the history of ethnic violence in Warri. A huge number of residents fled to neighbouring towns and villages. Ugborikoko experienced an influx of displaced people. Dr Eserovwe had to accommodate friends and relatives. He was elated to know Onome would be home to help the children affected in the crises.

Two weeks after the passing out ceremony, Onome and Masasi flew to Nigeria. They travelled during the harmattan season. Their plane touched down at Murtala Mohammed Airport at 6 p.m. Masasi was happy to be in Nigeria for the first time.

'I may run into one of your Nollywood stars like Jim Iyke,' Masasi teased Onome.

'Hmm, you think it's that easy?' Onome laughed.

Onome's father and two of her cousins were at the airport to welcome them. Onome rushed into her father's arms. They had not seen each other for two years. She greeted her cousins warmly and quickly introduced Masasi to them all.

'Welcome to Nigeria,' Dr Eserovwe told Masasi.

Augustine and Augustina, Onome's twin cousins, helped them with their luggages. Augustine drove them in his Toyota Camry to his flat in Surulere. The drive took another one hour because of the traffic jam. Dr Eserovwe explained any significant structure and landmark they passed to Masasi. They passed the national theatre, Iganmu. Masasi was impressed with the massive architectural design. He liked the giant billboards that lined the roads. He was amazed by the multitude of people that filled the streets.

He opened the buttons of his shirt when they had to stay in the hold-up for more than thirty minutes. Onome requested for cold drinks from hawkers who walked past almost every car. Augustina bought four bottles of Sprite. Masasi finished his in no time.

'Water would have been better,' he said regrettably.

'I think we can still get that. The hawkers stock everything you can imagine,' Augustina said.

'I know where this intense thirst comes from. Change of weather,' Dr Eserovwe said, patting his daughter.

'Dad, it is really hot here.'

'Is it still snowing when you left?'

'No, Dad, autumn is just beginning.'

'Ah! It's true. I mix up the seasons quite often. It is October.'

Just before Augustine could negotiate a bend that would lead him from Ojuelegba Street into Alhaji Masha Street, three police van flashed their sirens. Motorists scrambled to make space for them in the already narrow and congested road. Augustine quickly parked his car behind a stationary truck. It was difficult to see cars coming from the opposite direction. One of the vans stopped. A poorly uniformed policeman jumped out of the back seat and was screaming at the top of his voice. He shot indiscriminately into the air. There was a loud cry from passers-by who began to scamper to safety.

'What is the matter, Dad?' Onome asked her father in disbelief.

'They are always like this,' her father said, shaking his head.

'This is a routine,' Augustine added.

A taxi driver was unlucky. He did not move his car fast enough for the police to drive past.

He was ordered by another police to disembark from his car. As soon as he did, the policeman slapped him.

'You are very stupid,' he yelled at the taxi driver.

'We have our boss inside the car, and we need to get to the barracks without delay.'

'Sir, but I was trying to make way,' the poor taxi driver tried to explain, rubbing his cheek.

The policemen got into their vans again and drove off.

'There is police brutality everywhere. Even in Kenya,' Masasi remarked.

'When will Africa grow?' Augustine asked, starting the ignition again.

They finally arrived at Augustine's flat at about 10 p.m. Augustine lived in a three-bedroom flat.

It was erected on the premises of a two-storey building with a very high fence and barbed wires. There were four flats in all. The premises had concrete flooring. There was hardly any space around the building. The landlord had been very economical with his plot of land. Bad plumbing was a common problem in the area where Augustine lived. There had been cases where the slab of the sewers cracked. The decomposing waste became obvious causing some pungent smell. Augustine was grateful that it had never happened where he lived, but the adjoining compound to his house had such problems twice. Augustine heaved a sigh and climbed up with Onome's suitcase. Masasi followed behind. He insisted he would carry his suitcase alone. Veronica, Augustine's wife, came out to welcome them. She embraced Onome, taking her holdall from her.

'Welcome, Uncle Frank,' Veronica greeted her in-law.

Dr Eserovwe smiled. People had always wanted to know why he smiled especially when he was greeted.

'It is already a part of me. Smiling and laughter relax the nerves,' he would tell them.

Onome and Masasi sat in the living room. Masasi took off his trainers and his socks. He requested for some cold water to drink. Onome thought she should eat some food even though it was late. Dr Eserovwe went straight to the bathroom to take his bath. He was feeling sticky all over. Augustine took the suitcases of his guests to one of the rooms.

'I prepared some pounded yam and *egusi* soup,' Veronica told an already hungry Onome.

'This night?' Augustina wondered.

'Well, my husband told me the flight was arriving 5 p.m., so I thought you people would be back home by 7 p.m.,' Veronica told her.

'It is the usual delay in picking up luggage from the arrivals and the traffic hold-ups.'

'What is *egusi* soup?' Masasi asked.

'It is melon soup. Sauce made from melon seed.'

'Hmm! I am curious. I'd like to taste it,' he told Onome.

'You can have a taste, but is that not going to be a heavy meal for you this night?' Augustina asked.

She served Masasi some cold water. Veronica laid the table. An art she had perfected after watching series of hospitality tutorials from the Internet. Dr Eserovwe came out of the bathroom wearing a T-shirt and a pair of shorts. He was a very simple man. His elder brother, Augustine's father, died years ago. He had to take over the responsibility of training the twins his brother left behind. Augustine and Augustina were hard working. They worked hard in school and never misused the funds their uncle Dr Frank Eserovwe sent. Both twins studied sociology at the Lagos State University. Augustine came out with an upper second class. Augustina came out with a lower second class. Augustine was retained in the bank where he did his national youth service. It wasn't long before he met Veronica who was a regular customer of the bank. She had studied zoology, but somehow she went into information technology.

Veronica called everyone to the table. Dr Eserovwe blessed the food. He was very meticulous and strict with his Christian faith. Augustine served Masasi and showed him how to eat the sauce. Masasi was a good pupil; he watched carefully how Augustine took some pounded yam and moulded it into a small morsel with his fingers before dipping it into the *egusi* soup. Masasi swallowed it with a slow gulp.

'It is delicious. This is not too different from our own *sukrumawiki*. The sauce is spicier than ours, though,' Masasi remarked.

'Africa is almost the same,' Dr Eserovwe told him.

Masasi told them between mouthfuls what *Sukrumawiki* is. Onome ate quietly.

She served herself some small portion of pounded yam and soup. She was cautious of her weight. She knew beyond 8 p.m., carbohydrate like those found in pounded yam would need time to digest. Veronica and Augustina cleared the table after everyone was done eating. Augustine insisted that Onome was a guest and must not take part in any work for that day.

Onome and her father spent another day in Lagos. Dr Eserovwe wanted his daughter and her boyfriend to rest properly before embarking on the journey to Warri. Augustine and his sister took them to Yaba Motor Park where Dr Eserovwe chartered an interstate taxi to Warri. The other commuters were amazed that someone was paying so much for a taxi.

Onome asked her father why he did that. He explained to her he wanted them to be very comfortable; besides, Onome and Masasi needed a lot of space for some of the gadgets and equipments they brought with them.

'I want you to see the Nigerian landscape, Masasi. If we took a flight, you would not see much of how Nigeria is.'

'O! Dad,' Onome exclaimed.

She knew her father loved nature and would do anything to be closer to it. The journey from Lagos to Warri took seven hours. Masasi took snapshots of almost all he saw.

Dr Eserovwe, in his usual manner, explained any striking landform and landscape they passed to Masasi. He had a good knowledge of Nigerian geography. He was a voracious and eclectic reader. The taxi stopped at Ore for the driver to refuel. It was also a short break for him and his passengers. Ore was a nodal town.

Many commercial and private vehicles stopped over to eat in many of the restaurants there. Onome and Masasi climbed down from the taxi. Dr Eserovwe went with them into one of the modern restaurants that were springing up in Ore. Masasi asked to eat something typical of Ore. The medical doctor told him *amala*, a meal made from plantain, yam, or cassava flour was the staple food of Ore people and the larger Yoruba ethnic group. Onome opted for some rice.

Dr Eserovwe ordered *amala* and *ewedu* soup for himself and Masasi. The waitress served the three of them their meals. Masasi gave up eating *amala* after two attempts.

'It does not really have taste, and one has to battle with the constant slippery nature of this sauce.'

The lady who sat at the table next to theirs laughed.

'Are you not a Nigerian?' she queried.

Dr Eserovwe and his daughter exchanged glances. Masasi quietly asked to be served rice.

'Are you all right with that?'

'Yes,' Masasi told Onome, smacking his lips.

Masasi finished eating. Dr Eserovwe paid the bills. They returned to the car to meet the driver sleeping. Onome tapped him gently on the shoulder.

'Oh, you are back!'

He sat upright and stretched his hands comically.

'Why is he not fastening his seat belt?' Masasi asked Onome in German.

'They are used to it,' she whispered to him.

The driver started the ignition and drove again into the highway. He turned on his radio from where a gospel song was playing. He sang and whistled along.

'It is only God that saves,' he said aloud, almost unconsciously.

Dr Eserovwe nodded in agreement. He did not want to embarrass the driver by asking why he had to speak so loud. Onome slept off. Her father and Masasi continued their discussion about the various communities they saw. It was 5 p.m. when they arrived in Benin. The driver stopped to buy some water. Masasi asked if he could snap some photos in front of a statue across the road.

'You can't be so fast,' the driver cautioned.

'Don't bother. Just make a photo of the statue,' Dr Eserovwe advised him.

Masasi zoomed in his camera lens and took a snapshot of the statue of what looked like a Benin chief. Masasi went back to the car. The driver continued his journey again and never stopped till he got to Warri.

Dr Eserovwe and his small entourage were taken straight to his house on the outskirts of Warri. He had a massive duplex, which stood on a large expanse of land. He lived in Germany for almost thirty years. He had saved up enough money in order to set himself up back in Nigeria. His hospital was not far from his residence. His security guard threw the gate open. His wife and cook came out to welcome them. It wasn't quite ten minutes before other relatives, who were living on his premises since the Warri crises, trooped out to welcome him. Among them were little children for whom Onome had great passion. She reached for her hand luggage and gave them some candies. She was glad she bought some.

There was rainfall throughout the first week that Onome arrived in Nigeria. Behind the fence of her father's house was a streamlet which flowed with a steady and swift current with the downpour. Onome leant against the window from where she admired the alluring streamlet. Masasi went over to her.

'What are you looking at actually?'

'At the future. You and I.'

Masasi laughed, stroking Onome's hair gently. Masasi was a tall and slender man. He had the physique of a typical Kenyan. His complexion was dark and his skin supple.

Just like the Kenyan athletes, Masasi could run many kilometres at a steady speed without pausing. He jogged every Sunday morning. He had tried to introduce Onome into his morning sport regime, but Onome was too lazy to wake up in the morning.

'I wish I could do some jogging here.'

'I wish I could swim. Masasi, you human deer, do something else,' Onome teased him.

Masasi went closer to Onome. He drew her close to himself and kissed her delicately. Onome loved moments like that. She cherished every moment they had spent in their four years of dating. She could hear Masasi's heartbeat. He held her close like he never did before.

'Onome, promise me you will always love me.'

'Masasi, come on. You know I'm all yours. We have fixed our wedding for next year.'

'Yes, that is true. I can't wait.'

'Lest I forget, my dad would be taking us to Abraka. He wants us to do some sightseeing before we start our project.'

Onome and Masasi broke away from their embrace and began to get set for their visit to Abraka. Onome wore a pair of shorts and a tight-fitting T-shirt. Masasi dressed up casually with his khaki shorts and shirt.

'Hmm, you look like one of those interpreters from colonial times.'

'You think so, my dear?'

'Sure, darling Masasi.'

Onome's parents were waiting for them in the dining room.

'Good morning, Mum and Dad,' Masasi greeted his would-be in-laws, beaming.

'Morning, Masasi. Did you sleep well?'

'Yes, sir.'

'Morning, Mum. Morning, Dad,' Onome's voice rang through the living room.

'Morning,' Dr Eserovwe greeted his daughter.

'You are full of energy, Onome,' her mother remarked.

'Well, Mum, I'm sure it is because I'm happy. What is for breakfast?'

'Come on, dear. Discover it for yourself. Come closer,' her mother said invitingly.

Onome sat next to Masasi. He adjusted his chair and whispered into Onome's ear. She laughed helplessly.

'Mummy, he is asking how to say the food smells good in Urhobo.'

'Ha ha, Masasi, you want to learn Urhobo. Never mind. I will introduce you to my cousin. He will do that.'

Dr Eserovwe blessed the food. He took Onome's plate and served her. He did the same for Masasi and his wife.

'Guten appetit.' He told them to enjoy their meal in German.

Breakfast was boiled yam and plantain with shrimp gravy moderately peppered.

'This is delicious,' Masasi said.

He had learnt how to compliment food from his elder brother, who was a hotel manager in Nairobi.

'Thank you,' Mrs Eserovwe told him. 'I'm glad you like the food.'

'Are there yams and plantains too in Kenya?' Onome's father asked.

'Not quite. There are plantains and more of potatoes. We are more into bread, tea, and the Indian-style pancake, chapati, for breakfast. We learnt a lot from the Indians and colonial masters.'

'So what about James Ngugi or Ngũgĩ wa Thiong'o. Your mention of colonial days reminded me of his book, *Weep Not, Child*, a typical colonial times' novel.'

'Yes, he is one of our great academia. He tried to return home, but problems made him stay back in the USA.'

'He is one of the seasoned and veteran literary backbones of Africa.'

'Yes.'

'They should come back home. If I want a change, I'll always try to make myself an example. This is why I came back after over twenty years of service in Germany. I wanted to help contribute to Africa's growth.'

Frank Eserovwe was a pragmatist and an Africanist of some sort. They continued their meal with intermittent discussions on Africa. Mrs Eserovwe and her daughter ate silently, not making any contribution. There was a momentary change of topic when John, Dr Eserovwe's driver, entered. He had come to take his boss's suitcase and documents to the car. Onome was greatly opposed to this aspect of John's duty and did not fail to emphasise this to her father. She insisted the documents and briefcase were too personal for an outsider to handle. Dr Eserovwe looked thoughtfully at his daughter when she finished speaking.

They left for Abraka after breakfast. The medical-doctor-turned-tourist guide did not fail to lecture Masasi on landforms and communities. Onome tried to listen but was distracted by her mother when she began to intimate her about her plans to begin a poultry farm and was defrauded by a land speculator. Onome made a fist, wishing she was there to teach him a lesson. They made a stopover at Oha, where Mrs Eserovwe gave some gifts of foodstuff to members of her family. Edith Eserovwe had been an orphan since she was twelve. Her great-aunt raised her and her siblings. She made sure she gave her aunt and some members of her extended family gifts at regular intervals. She had met her husband during the village annual concert. He was then a young teacher. They married and moved to Isiokolo, a small administrative town not far from Oha. He later left to study in Germany after a year. His wife and their first son joined him as soon as he got a part time job. Edith was a housewife for a long time, raising their first two kids till she trained as a nursery assistant. It was a job she did till she left Germany. She assisted her husband as an administrator in his hospital. John swerved the car to the right when they almost got to Abraka. Mrs Eserovwe shrieked. John managed to avert an accident. A car had stopped abruptly in front of them.

Dr Eserovwe shook his head. He held his wife and meditated quietly. They got to Abraka River Resort Hotel. John drove slowly through the entrance and looked for a parking space. Onome was feeling tired after that breakfast. She managed to climb out of the car. They were going to spend a week at the hotel, while her father met some business associates. They checked into their rooms. John had a room to himself. He wished he had his girlfriend with him. John was a young man of thirty-five. He had tried to study at the Auchi Polytechnic, but he was not very intelligent. He married a lady from Akoko-Edo, but the marriage did not work out. Bunmi, his ex-wife, was of the Jehovah Witness denomination. She refused to celebrate Christmas, terming it a taboo. John had prepared some food one Christmas. Bunmi returned home and threw away all that John laboured to prepare for the celebration. After several quarrels and family interventions, Bunmi said she would not convert to Catholicism for her husband's sake, so she moved out of their matrimonial home. Since then, John never set eyes on her again. Onome and Masasi could only sympathise with him. By 2 p.m., they were all out on the beach behind the hotel. John was an incredible swimmer. He swam like a fish. He would disappear into the river only to emerge at the other end. Masasi soon emerged from the river to buy some barbeque and orange squash. He beckoned to Onome and John to join him. He ravished his barbeque hungrily.

'I love barbeque,' he enthused.

Later that evening, John took Onome and Masasi for a walk to the campus. He told them the university was once a college of education, solely for training teachers. John did not know much of the history of the town, but he told them it was a small town sharing borders with the Ukwanis and Binis. They walked into the campus. It was about 6 p.m. when they got in there. John did not have any specific place he would take them to, so they looked at the library which had a dome-shaped roof and then they left again for the hotel. By the time they got there, Onome was famished. Her mother had already ordered *oghwo evwri*, the traditional red palm oil soup, and *usi*, cassava starch meal.

Dr Eserovwe was still attending the meeting with his business associates, so he could not join them. John taught Masasi how to eat starch. It was another eating lesson for him. He had told John that it reminded him of his attempt to eat *ewedu* soup at Ore. He also gave up eating the starch after several attempts. Onome rested an arm on Masasi's lap. She gave him a stare, wondering what he would eat. Masasi took Onome's hand in his, trying to reassure her. He got up and announced that he would eat some more barbeque with bread. There were petty traders across the hotel gate who sold far into the night. John offered to get him a loaf of bread from them. After relishing his late-night meal, Masasi told Onome that Nigeria has an array of food. Onome smiled appreciatively. Still wanting to keep themselves busy, they watched some Nigerian movies on Onome's laptop before going to bed. John came to wake them up at 9 a.m. Dr Eserovwe had an impromptu invitation from a friend for them to attend his daughter's traditional marriage ceremony. Onome had wished to sleep a little longer because they went to bed late.

She was still drowsy when John knocked on their door. Masasi agreed with Dr Eserovwe that it was another opportunity for him to see more of the Nigerian culture. They took their bath and ate breakfast in the restaurant. Masasi relished the simple breakfast but soon requested for water because the egg omelette was too peppery for him. In the afternoon, John drove Dr Eserovwe and his family to Obinomba, his friend's village, where the traditional marriage ceremony was to take place. Masasi did not fail to take snapshots of the landscape and vegetation. John turned left and drove through a narrow dusty road. There were corn farms at both sides of the road. The road looked deserted but for a few villagers that they drove past. Quite often, they stood to catch a glimpse of the occupants of the car. Dr Eserovwe asked John to stop. He rolled down the window to speak to a boy dressed smartly in his school uniform.

'Young man, please where is Chief Okagbue's house?'

'Good afternoon, sir, Chief Okagbue's house is not far from the secondary school over there. About five houses away,' the young man told him, pointing at the direction.

'Thank you very much,' Dr Eserovwe greeted him.

John continued driving but not too fast because he knew from the conversation his boss had with the boy that they were close to their destination. As the car drove past the secondary school, they could hear the sound of loud music. Dr Eserovwe knew they were in the right place. John reversed the car and parked inside the open field where many cars were already parked. Dr Eserovwe and his family climbed down from the car. John locked up and followed his boss. Dr Eserovwe treated John well. He allowed him to attend occasions with him. Chief Okagbue sighted Dr Eserovwe. He rose from his chair to welcome him. There was a sizeable number of elegantly dressed guests sitting under two canopies in Chief Okagbue's compound.

'Welcome,' he greeted him warmly with a handshake.

'My wife, daughter, her fiancé, and staff,' he smiled, introducing the members of his entourage.

Chief Okagbue shook hands with each of them while ushering them in at the same time.

'We are just about to begin. Would you please sit down that way?' he told Onome, Masasi, and John, pointing them in the direction of the music stand.

'Doctor, meet my wife Chinyere,' Chief Okagbue continued.

THE DYING THIEF

Chinyere Okagbue greeted Dr Eserovwe gracefully and then hugged his wife. She was dressed in the native *akwa-ocha*, an attire common to the people of Aniocha in Delta State. Chief Okagbue hailed from Obinomba while his wife was from Ogwashi-Ukwu. The small district to which Chief Okagbue belonged was abuzz with the ceremony. The villagers loitered around, not only to get a chance to witness the event but to see if they could get some food to eat from a benevolent usher. There was brisk business already forming near the car park. Some enterprising youths seized the opportunity to sell confectionaries and cigarettes. Young girls were delicately made up, trying to impress intending lovers. Some guests were seen discussing in hushed tones, and some others were engaged in hearty discussions. A young man dressed gaily in *akwa-ocha* with a red fez hat seated on his head marched in.

He blew the traditional flute and began dancing. He seemed to have captured everyone's attention. No sooner had he entered than everybody became quiet. He began to sing the praises of Chief Okagbue. The guests watched intently. Dr Eserovwe could understand the Ibo dialect of Obinomba fairly well, because as a teenager, he had learnt how to speak Ibo while he was living with a relative who once worked in Asaba, where Ibo is widely spoken. He became an instant interpreter to his wife, Onome, and Masasi. John went out briefly to check on the car and came back again. Some elders in Chief Okagbue's family stood up and began the traditional marriage rites. Chief Okagbue's in-laws made their request and presented their gifts.

'I like this,' Masasi told Onome.

'You will do almost the same thing for me.'

Masasi laughed and gave Onome a gentle peck on the cheek. The ceremony came to a climax when the bride was led in. There was a rapturous applause and encomiums as soon as she stepped in. Chief Okagbue's daughter, Chioma, was marrying a business tycoon from Enugu.

Other traditional rites followed briefly and then the couple went outside to dance. Guests stepped forward to give them gifts of cash. It was not long before the whole place was full of people dancing. Masasi observed that almost all the money doled out by the guests were either dollars or pounds.

'This is fantastic. You Nigerians are very colourful and innovative in all you do, but why the waste of all these dollar bills and much money?'

Onome wished she had an explanation. Chioma and her husband stopped dancing. They were led by some women to sit down on two chairs specially prepared for them.

Refreshment was already being served by stewards hired by Chief Okagbue. There was more music from the band. They took a break to enable the *Atilogu* dancers perform. It was the traditional near dance drama of the Ibo-speaking nation of Nigeria. They came in with their colourful traditional attires made of knee-level skirts and sleeveless tops. A member of the troupe ran in. He began performing some acrobatics following the rhythm that came from the flutes and drums. This was followed by the entrance of other troupe members. Their hypnotic and skilfull dance steps held the guests spellbound. It was spectacular. Masasi had his camera handy. Dr Eserovwe left as soon as the *Atilogu* dance was over.

They arrived in Abraka feeling very exhausted. They woke up late in the afternoon the next day, which was a Sunday morning and their fourth day in Abraka. Dr Eserovwe had planned a week's holiday, but during lunch, he announced to his family that they had to return the next day because his attention was needed at his hospital.

Onome set off to work on her humanitarian project. She went to one of the emergency camps used for the displaced people. Her father had already told the organisers of the camp about Onome's willingness to support and help the affected. Onome had applied for funds from some organisations. A week before she went to

THE DYING THIEF

the camp, her shipped toys and relief materials arrived in Tin Can Island Port, Lagos. She employed the services of the clearing agent recommended by her father to get them. The camp was organised by a Christian group. The officials were appreciative of Onome's initiative and were glad to receive the aids and donations. The first thing she did after meeting with the organisers was to conduct a workshop which lasted a day. She addressed the affected on social care issues. She encouraged them not to see their plights as a hindrance to their dreams. This was followed by distribution of toys and candies to the children. Masasi was at hand as her cameraman and photographer. Onome held counselling sessions for young girls and women on different days. She devoted a separate day to playing and counselling traumatised children. Onome and Masasi's world revolved round the camp for the next few weeks. Their typical day began at 9 a.m. and ended at 4 p.m. Each time they wanted to leave, the children and women would plead with them to stay on. They had never seen so much warmth and affection. There was always enough food, giveaways, and activities to keep the women and children busy. Onome was touched by the story of a young boy who was just eleven years old. He had lost his parents and five siblings. His father was a manager with the Nigerian National Petroleum Corporation. Their house was set ablaze by an angry mob. He was able to run out fast enough, but his parents and siblings were not very lucky. The roof of their house imploded, and the whole house was engulfed in fire. He could still remember the cries of his parents and siblings. Peter, as he was called, roamed the streets for days until a Good Samaritan found him. It was a young man who had always seen him in the company of his parents and siblings. He passed Peter's family house on his way to and from work. He took him in and handed him to the Miracle Christian Church days later. Onome hugged Peter tenderly. She and her boyfriend took special interest in him. They spent enough time with him whenever they were in the camp. Masasi could not get his mind off him.

'We must help him, Onome.'

'Yes, I think so too but how?'

'Getting some German families to adopt him perhaps. He talks intelligently.'

There was thunderbolt. The rain began to fall like it did weeks ago. Onome cuddled next to Masasi.

There were more sporadic fights again among the three ethnic groups in Warri. News that some aid workers from Germany were going from camp to camp to help displaced people went round. Some militants felt short-changed. They felt they had to be consulted first or at least given some benefits before the aid workers began operation. They began to attack any camp they saw. They arrived in large numbers late one evening at the camp where Onome was. Onome heard their chant. The camp organisers least expected their centre to be invaded. The officials tried to plead with the militants to calm down. Instead of listening, they fired into the air. There was stampede and commotion.

'We are not here for peace,' their leader shouted.

Onome ran to where Masasi was playing chess with Peter, waving hysterically at them.

'Come, let's take cover, the militants are here.'

Masasi and Peter sprang to their feet and began to run towards one of the buildings with Onome trailing behind them. She overheard one of militants saying in her native language.

'There they are. The doctor's daughter and her boyfriend.'

Masasi was hit by a bullet in the chest. Onome looked back. Masasi was lying lifeless on the ground. Onome bent over his body and screamed. And in a split second, it dawned on her that the militants were assassins and were after their lives.

'Run, or we'll shoot you too, idiot.' Onome left Masasi's body and ran blindly. She did not know how she managed to get into the camp director's office.

The next morning, Dr Eserovwe and some Christian workers came to retrieve the body of Masasi. Onome was in agony. The people she came to help had betrayed her.

THE ESCAPE

The bus drove from Ekpoma through Iruekpen to Ehor on its way to Benin City. Ochuko would take another bus from Ramat Park to Sapele Road where she would board another vehicle to Warri. The university was on strike again; students began to leave the campus to their various destinations. She woke up as early as 6 a.m. to enable her catch an early bus to Benin.

Whenever there was a strike, the highway would be besieged with a large crowd of students. It was wise to get a vehicle early because of the demand and the uncertainty of catching a bus later on such occasion. She wanted to avoid the rush and the problem of not getting a vehicle in time or not at all.

After about ten minutes of waiting, a Mitsubishi minibus pulled up near her. The conductor asked if she was travelling to Benin. She nodded and joined the league of eight other passengers already seated inside the bus, waiting for their journey to begin. A male student who had been standing on the other side of the road joined them too. Ochuko sat next to a fair-complexioned lady who requested to know if she was a student of the Edo State University.

'Is it true that your school is on strike again?' she asked in a familiar tone.

'Yes, just terrible. We the final year students are the most affected.'

'Very terrible indeed, my neighbour's son is a student of your university too. He was home since yesterday.'

'That's smart of him to have been home since Saturday.'

'If it were in Europe, this would never happen. I had to remove my children from Lagos State University to Belgium.'

'Really?'

The conversation snowballed into another topic. The lady lashed out at the government as she placed life in Nigeria and Europe side by side. She spoke with so much authority, revealing the ills in the educational system as well as the drawback of the Nigerian economy and the state as a whole. She was full of praise and admiration for Europe and the Belgian government. She spoke of the social security system and the foresightedness of the Europeans.

'Everything works, not like here,' she added, fuming.

Ochuko was astounded. She tried to visualise life in Europe where everything was well thought out and planned and where students' academic lives went uninterrupted.

'I arranged with my cousin to get admissions for my kids. I really don't like these incessant strikes.'

'Madam, it is very terrible. I would like to do my master's abroad too, going by the way things are now in the country,' Ochuko said with some air of confidence.

'My dear, Nigeria is just a hopeless place. If you can, please leave. Even if you want me to help you, I will.'

The sound of 'if you want me to help you, I will' echoed through her ears like a mistaken shout, but she composed herself.

'Hmm, that will be great,' she told her, almost admiringly.

The bus made a sudden stopover at Ehor. The driver told them the engine was overheating and needed to cool down. Some passengers began to query the driver's preparedness for the journey.

'Na make the bus break down una want?' The driver said in pidgin English.

He demanded to know if the passengers preferred the bus be damaged first. He opened the boot, got a container of water, and poured it into the radiator. Thick steam billowed into the air. The driver stepped back to prevent a direct heat going into his eyes. He informed the passengers that they needed to wait awhile before continuing the journey. It was just a few minutes before eight o'clock in the morning. The grass was wet from dew, making it impossible to sit on. Some passengers had begun shuffling from one foot to another. Others just squatted because it was strenuous standing. Ochuko and the lady walked towards an orange tree and leant there. They seemed to have found a common interest in each other. She told Ochuko to call her Bridget instead of madam.

'We Nigerians should break free from this unnecessary officialdom of calling people sir or madam. It even makes me feel very old,' she said, rolling her eyes.

Ochuko managed a smile.

Bridget opened her bag, took a piece of paper, and scribbled her address on it.

'Here is my address, in case you need any assistance from me.'

Ochuko was appreciative of her gesture. She was beginning to feel hungry. She told Bridget she wanted to buy some biscuits across the road where a bright yellow-coloured kiosk stood with its doors open.

'Be fast about that. We may be leaving soon.'

Ochuko barely crossed the road when the driver asked all passengers to board the bus again. Bridget informed him a passenger had gone to buy snacks across the road. The driver hissed and cursed. Bridget pleaded with him to be patient while Ochuko returned with her biscuits and oranges clasped against her chest.

'You nor fit even say sorry for keeping us waiting,' the conductor tutored her in his best manner.

'Ah, I did not know we were moving soon. Why asking me to apologise?'

'How you go know?' the driver snarled, expecting Ochuko to have stayed back.

'It is too early to start arguing, my people,' an elderly man attempted to ameliorate the situation.

Bridget patted Ochuko on the back, whispering something into her ears. Ochuko nodded, trying to sit down at the same time. Bridget had told her both men were too crude to be argued with. The trip from Ehor to Ramat Park in Benin City was smooth. All passengers disembarked. Bridget gave Ochuko a motherly embrace, and they bid each other goodbye. Ochuko was glad to be in Benin City just before 9 a.m. There wasn't much traffic on the road, and most shops were just beginning to open for the day. The usual hustle and bustle in Ramat Park was gradually building up. Ochuko joined a bus going to Sapele Road, from where she boarded an intercity taxi to Warri. She heaved a sigh of relief and closed her eyes to have a short rest. She was exhausted because she rose early in the morning. She only realised she had been sleeping when the taxi arrived at Okorighrwe, a commercial district of Sapele, where hawkers visibly hawked their wares. As soon as a car arrived, the hawkers rushed towards them like swarms of flies. The local government had tried to curtail the menace of street hawkers but did not succeed. The hawkers endangered both their lives and that of other traffic users. There had been cases of cars crushing hawkers to death. The driver drove cautiously through the potholes; it was a sign of a failed and corrupt government, Ochuko thought. The politicians would promise better infrastructure in their manifestos but refused to fulfil them once they are in office. The dusty red sand of Okorighwre often found its way on the uncovered fried meats and the edible worms sold by the roadside food vendors and hawkers. Edible worms were a delicacy among the people of the Niger Delta. Ochuko relished them a lot and was tempted to buy some, but she refrained from doing so because of the unhygienic handling and preparations. The taxi meandered its way through the crowd of hawkers and potholes. Ochuko thought their presence constituted a nuisance on the roads. She could not really say if their art of selling their wares was foolhardiness or that they were simply daring. Some ran in and out of the potholes to catch up with moving vehicles. A lady travelling in a car on the opposite side of the road bought sausage rolls. When she stretched out her hand to pay the hawker a bill of 10-naira note, the driver sped off, and the lady held out her hand through the window, the bill flapping as it fought through the wind. The hawker ran after the car until the lady squeezed the money into a small ball and threw it down by the side of the road; the panting hawker bent over to pick it from the ground and headed back to his mobile store.

'This is dangerous,' Ochuko's cab driver remarked.

Almost all the passengers seemed to agree as they chorused their resentment for the hawker's action. They arrived in Effurun at about 11 a.m. Ochuko hailed a cab which took her directly to her abode. When the cab arrived in front of the black-gated house with low fence, she paid the driver and went off with her luggage.

Ochuko arrived into the warm embrace of her parents and siblings. It was a mixed celebration – the joy of seeing her again and the sorrows of an upsetting strike.

'There is strike again,' her father said, walking back into the living room with a newspaper half-opened in his hand. Chief Nesieama always wanted to be abreast with current affairs. He had two large shelves of newspapers and magazines.

'How was your journey?' her mother inquired after a while.

'Papa, the strike won't ever stop. Mama, the journey was good, only that I'm so tired. I have been up very early to catch a vehicle in time. So many students wanted to travel today too.'

'We thank God you came home safe and sound,' Chief Nesieama added.

Ochuko opened her bag and brought out the biscuits she had bought for her younger siblings. She insisted the loaves of bread be kept for breakfast the next morning. Ochuko thought she could sleep, but the excitement of being home again keyed her up.

'Go eat something,' her mother told her.

She walked to the kitchen where the househelp was pounding yam. It was past midday, and Mrs Nesieama had asked the househelp to prepare pounded yam and vegetable soup for lunch. Both ladies exchanged greetings.

'How is your study?' she asked, suspending the pestle in the air.

'School ought to be fine, but I'm home again a third time this year. How sad!'

'Things go better,' she encouraged her in pidgin English.

'I pray so, because I'm really frustrated right now.'

Ochuko opened the fridge to see what was available. There were parboiled paste tomatoes, precooked chicken, eggs, butter, and bread.

'Will the food be ready anytime soon?' she asked.

'Make I say in one hour. I still dey pound the yam and I never cut the okra.'

'That will take longer than one hour then. I'm very hungry . . .'

Ochuko reluctantly cut some chicken wings and broke some eggs she snatched from the fridge and prepared a quick sauce and boiled yam for lunch. She enjoyed cutting her yams into thin slices and eating them with fried eggs.

She pleaded with Fejiri, her younger brother, to tidy up the table while she went back into the living room to join her mother who was pedicuring her father's feet. She loved the close bond between her parents.

They met in their youthful days when her father was twenty-four and her mother, sixteen. They married two years later. This explains why they had grown-up children who were already married. Ochuko asked to relieve her mother, but she insisted that she had just finished eating and must have a rest. She sat next to her father and watched her mother cut his fingernails.

'So what are your plans while the strike lasts?'

'I would like to learn sewing.'

'Can you cope?' her mother asked, not expecting that from her.

'Of course, Mother,' she said, calming her doubt.

She began her sewing classes after the third week of staying at home. Getting a place proved to be a daunting task. No tailor was willing to sign Ochuko as an apprentice. She made the mistake of introducing herself as an undergraduate student to the intimidation of those less educated, sometimes only till primary school, women who would train and boss her. And just when she was finally accepted by one, news came that the strike had been called off. It was still a rumour, and she wasn't sure if it was real or a speculation, but in any case, she was determined to go to the school and find out herself.

Her parents asked their driver, Goddey, to take her back to school. They wished her success in her final exams. Goddey drove the Peugeot 306 station wagon gently through the oxblood gate and on to the road.

He adamantly chose the long and lonely Abraka route against Ochuko's preference for taking the Benin route. One thing she liked about Goddey was his adventurous spirit and his willingness to cover up some driving mischief when she sometimes stole a drive. Her parents didn't like their children driving the car. They had the feeling that they would damage the car, but nonetheless, the driver would violate his bosses' rule and let Ochuko have some shots at driving whenever they were alone.

When they got to Umunede, he allowed her sneak behind the steering wheel.

They arrived in Ekpoma at about 2 p.m., and Goddey helped transfer her luggage from the car to her flat and soon the neighbours swarmed in to welcome her as is the custom among the community of students. Some came to see what she had brought and what they could get. She had done her homework well and had shopped for both co-tenants and some of the indigenes in the neighbourhood. She decided, as a matter of personal policy, to help the needy, but her close friend, Gina, saw it differently. She had sternly advised Ochuko to put a limit on her kindness.

'People are wicked. They could even harm you for your kind gestures,' the usually superstitious Gina said.

She read spiritual meanings into anything, and she had imbibed the typical customs and tradition of the Ishan ethnic group, and that made her very cautious when interacting with other people. She complained about how the landlord got pissed when his visitors were not greeted and other self-made taboos that bother most of the landlords. For her, it all has some spiritual implications, even the exorbitant rent charged off the student.

Ochuko was mesmerised by Gina's superstitious stance. She stood momentarily with her gaze fixed at Gina, and a very tragic incident replayed through her mind.

She remembered one of her elective classes in sociology and especially the lecturer who taught the subject. He was a young man who graduated from the university in 1979. He would always talk of the oil boom days of Nigeria. He told his students that there were student rates in transportation and courier services. He told them of subsidised social services for students.

'There were meal tickets with which we could go to eat in the cafeteria. We were served a choice of foods and assorted drinks. We had bursaries. But imagine how landlords here milk money out of you students. Very pathetic.'

Ochuko saw Mr Ehi as a very simple and an exemplary man. He would ride his bicycle to school while his colleagues drove cars. He had an awkward taste and lifestyle. Nobody believed he had his masters from Holland. He told his students he was aware of people's perception of him. Then he would tell them he learnt the art of bicycle riding from Holland where it was compulsory for everyone to know how to ride one.

'It is a form of exercise also. Life expectancy in Holland is higher than what we have here. So if people like, they can laugh at me for all I care.'

The students were shocked to know Mr Ehi died in a car accident the following month on his way from his cousin's wedding in Auchi – the man who never drove a car was killed by a car.

The student union president described him as meek and a fighter of injustice in his eulogy. He had held a meeting with the landlords in Ekpoma, accusing them of being unfair to the students. Gina told Ochuko she was sure the natives worked Mr Ehi to his death. Many of them felt threatened with his claims.

Goddey finished offloading the remaining luggage and climbed into the car. Ochuko walked towards him and handed him a small brown envelope with some money inside.

'For your wife and kids,' she said.

Goddey smiled, thanked her, and drove away.

The final exams were over. Ochuko threw up her pen as soon as she came out of the examination hall. For the first time, she tried to savour the freshness of the air around her. Then she went to the most expensive restaurant on campus to give herself a good treat. She ordered fish in batter, Spanish tart, and bitter lemon. She finished eating and paid her bills and asked the waitress to keep the change. The waitress was forced to ask what she was celebrating.

'I just graduated,' was her response.

The waitress appreciated the unexpected tip. Before she could offer a thank you, Ochuko had left. She got back to her rented room and fell on her bed with a great bounce.

'Free!' she screamed.

She wasn't satisfied with just lying down on the bed. She got up again and inserted a cassette into her cassette player, turning up the volume very high. She did not hear the knock on her door. It was Gina.

Gina had to go to the window from where she called out her name as loud as she could. It was then Ochuko realised that someone had been knocking at her door. She sprang up from the bed and opened the door.

'The music is too loud, my dear. Don't forget these natives are not happy with us students.'

She opened the door for Gina before turning down the volume of the music. Gina embraced her warmly.

'Congrats,' she told her friend.

Gina brought with her some self-made chin-chin. Ochuko had two bottles of Coca-Cola left in the fridge. She brought them out and placed them carefully on the mahogany table.

'So you are now a graduate?' Gina teased.

'That is how it is, my dear.'

'We thank God,' Gina said, pouring herself some drink.

'So what next?' I think I will skip youth service and go straight for my master's.

'You think it is possible?'

'I'm thinking of doing it abroad.'

Ochuko recounted the many strikes which delayed her graduation.

'Hmm, that sounds good. Well, we will pray for our country,' Gina said, wondering if her friend had made the right decision.

Both friends discussed far into the night and went to bed in the early hours of the morning. Ochuko woke up and hurried through her morning routine. She had to report back to school to sign and return a few documents. By midday, Goddey had come to take her back to Warri. He came in the company of her brother Tony and their gardener Migu. The three men helped her with the removal of her belongings. Gina got sadder as the room emptied out. Ochuko could only give her a long hug. She took her hand and led her to a corner where some of her properties were packed.

'Here, Gina, these are for you.'

Ochuko had given her friend her television, refrigerator, cupboards, all her cooking utensils, and some foodstuff. Gina was transfixed. She was overwhelmed with her magnanimity.

'Thank you, Ochuko. Thank you so much,' Gina stuttered.

Ochuko paid a brief visit to the landlord whose house was behind her flat. She pulled out some crispy naira bills from her purse and handed them over to him.

'Papa, it is small. Just take it and buy some kola nuts.'

Gina caught sight of the money she gave to Pa Osagie; Ochuko looked back and saw the objectionable look written clearly on her friend's face, pale from anger. She knew at once that Gina was not pleased.

'Be careful,' she muttered when Ochuko left the landlord to join her again.

'Don't worry, Gina, it'll be all right,' she whispered.

Ochuko walked through the controversial Okere District of Warri. She had gone to shop for some periwinkle and ingredients with which to try out a new recipe. She was oblivious of the traders and noise around her now as she concentrated on her supplies and preoccupied with the urge to travel overseas for further studies.

'You are giving me a 100 naira instead of 20 naira,' the trader said, alarmed.

Ochuko was jolted. She put back the excess money in her purse and handed the trader a 20-naira note. She muttered a thank you, which left the trader bewildered. She hurried back home barely paying attention to traffic. She dropped the ingredients in the kitchen and begged the househelp to help her prepare the periwinkle. She immediately left for her room to strategise an idea she had developed on her way from the market. She brought out some plain sheets and began to write some letters. She wrote to the Norwegian Embassy for information on studies in Norway. It was then she remembered Bridget who had promised to help her travel to Europe if ever she wanted.

As if propelled by an unknown force, Ochuko dashed to her wardrobe and began to check all her handbags for Bridget's address. She was not sure in which bag she had put it, but because she was determined to find the address, she did not relent. She was disappointed that she could not find the address after searching all her bags thoroughly. She felt she was losing the surest hope of studying in Europe. She went back again to the table and fondled with the letters she had already written. Her mind drifted again to finding Bridget's address. Her greatest weakness was being impatient to plan out her actions. She got up once more and went through a few books she remembered were in her bag the day she met Bridget. She painstakingly went through them one after the other. She heaved a sigh when she finally saw a small piece of paper with Bridget's writing warped up somewhere at the back. *Sometimes my impatience pays,* she thought. The address was still there intact. She got up again from her kneeling position and several hours of going through so many books on her shelf. She stretched herself but felt slight pains round her neck, waist, and knees.

She thought it would be faster to get help from Bridget rather than going through the embassies. She wrote out the address once more in her address book and went back to the kitchen only to discover it was 10 p.m. She had spent a long time in her room, so she forgot about cooking. She opened the pots on the cooker to see what the househelp had cooked. She took the ladle from the cutlery rack and served herself some yam porridge. She ate slowly, and when she was done, she went back to her room. Without discussing with any member of her family, she left for Benin City the next morning. She arrived in Benin at 10 a.m. and chartered a taxi to Bridget's home. She was not ready to go through the rigours of trying to locate the address Bridget gave her. She simply showed the address to a taxi driver who agreed that he knew the exact location. It was in a quiet area of the government reserved area, with history from colonial times. The taxi dropped Ochuko off in front of a huge iron-gated house which had the inscription 'Be Good to Your People'. She paid the cab driver and walked to the gate. The gate was rather huge and intimidating. Ochuko knocked but got no response. She tried again, and it was still the same result. Then she shook the iron gate, which rattled noisily. The pedestrian gate threw open. A heavily built man emerged from inside.

'Good day,' the sound escaped her mouth without meaning it.

The sight of the man almost made her tremble.

'Please, I'm looking for Madam Bridget,' she heard herself say.

'Good day to you too, lady. We have no Madam Bridget in this house,' he blurted out.

'But is this not the address of this place?' she said, showing him the piece of paper with her.

He took the address from her, almost ripping it off her hand. He looked at it with much disdain, shifting his gaze from the paper to Ochuko.

'Yes, the address is correct, but the person you mentioned does not live here. You must have been tricked.'

Ochuko paused for a while and suddenly remembered Bridget had told her another name too.

'Hmm, sorry, sir,' she spluttered. 'What about Mama Ayo?' she managed to ask the already angry-looking man.

'It is now you are asking for the right person. She is not around now. She is in Belgium at the moment visiting her kids.'

'Oh OK. When do you think she will be back?'

'End of this month.'

That would be three weeks from the time she had visited.

'All right, could you please tell her Ochuko from Warri came to see her?'

'Yes, definitely. Wait, there is a visitor's book. Let me get it so that you can write your name and address in it.'

He went inside and came out with a hard-cover notebook.

'Here, write your name and address in it.'

THE DYING THIEF

She wrote her name and address and then left.

She wished she had met Bridget.

Ochuko was posted to Imo State for her youth service. After the orientation camp, she was sent to a secondary school in Owerri for her primary assignment. She had to teach mathematics in an all-boys secondary school. The first thing she noticed was the lackadaisical attitude of the pupils towards studies. She was determined to instil discipline in them and show the pupils that she would not tolerate truancy. She punished those who failed to submit their work by the deadline. She made them stay an hour extra in the school or prevented them from observing break times. Most pupils felt she was too strict and wicked.

She got what she did not bargain for shortly before the Nigerian Independence Day celebration. Two boys were involved in examination malpractice. Ochuko sent them away from the examination. She took a step further by reporting the incident to the school principal. During the assembly, the principal, Mr Okoro, called the offenders out and stood them in front of the assembly. He dubbed them as the bad eggs of the school and as such they should be flogged. The physical education teacher was given the task to discipline them. Mr Udoh gained reputation for his grasp of the whip. He stepped forward with a thin whip in his hand and lashed them in turns; they went away with five strokes each. The punishment did not go down well with Emeka, one of the recipients of the punishment. He felt embarrassed and hatched plans with his friends to lay siege for Ochuko in town.

They knew her apartment, but they did not go there; instead, they intercepted her on her way to the church one early Sunday morning. Emeka hit her first, followed by his two companions. Ochuko screamed, but the boys disappeared before help could come. A young man on his way to church helped her up. It was a black Sunday for Ochuko, a day she wouldn't forget. She was taken to the hospital where she remained for some days on the springy stubborn brown leather hospital bed. News of the incident went round the school. Emeka was summoned to the principal's office, but he denied ever being involved in the brutal act. It was all a cover-up. The school could not do anything further because of lack of evidence, and Ochuko had no witness. She became traumatised and sought to be reposted to her state of origin on security and health grounds. Mr Okoro had hoped Ochuko would finish her youth service with them but appreciated her method of discipline instead.

'She would have helped boost the image of this school,' he said of Ochuko.

Other female youth service members serving in that school no longer felt secure. They opted to be posted somewhere else in protest. Safety was scarce. Ochuko wanted to serve in a government ministry but was turned down wherever she went. In the end, she had to continue her primary assignment in a secondary school. This time, she was careful not to be too strict with the pupils. She had learnt a lot from Owerri. The youth service year was, to Ochuko, not very eventful, and it passed so fast. The passing-out parade was devoid of fanfare as instructed by the director general of the programme. He wanted it to be a sober affair in memory of the death of some members who lost their lives in a fatal motor accident. The National Youth Service programme had come under attack from members of the public, parents, and non-governmental organisations. They believed the programme had outlived its usefulness because the members were no longer safe. If they were not involved in accidents, they were either victims of rape, religious attacks, kidnapping, or murder by ritualists. There were also the problems of underpayment and serving in remote villages with no basic amenities or infrastructures. Ochuko got news of a young man with whom she served in Owerri. He was missing for two days, save for his headless body that was found at the gate of a primary school some days later. She wept bitterly when she heard the news.

She remembered him vividly. His name was Benjamin, an indigene of Benue State. His death was a shock to Ochuko. She had barely finished breaking the news of Benjamin to her brother when one of her sisters informed her that a lady was there to see her. Ochuko walked with her to the living room and was surprised to see her visitor was Bridget.

'Bridget!' she cried.

'Ochuko, long time! You have a big scar on your knee, what happened to you?'

Bridget asked, reeling off all the questions at once.

'Oh! Welcome, Bridget. Good to see you again.'

'Thank you,' Bridget said, still shifting her gaze from Ochuko's face to her knee.

'I got injured in Owerri,' Ochuko quickly explained.

She knew Bridget was waiting for answers. Ochuko related briefly to Bridget her experience in Owerri. Bridget hissed and consoled her.

'Some pupils could be very terrible,' she concluded.

'Anyway, I know you are surprised to see me here. I came for a wedding in Aladja, so I thought I should check on you. I wasn't really sure I will meet you.'

'I was at your place in Benin City,' Ochuko cut in, leading her to the living room of their second-floor flat. She asked one of her cousins to get Bridget something to drink.

'No,' Bridget interrupted her, 'I am so full. You know am just coming from a wedding party. I left before it ended.'

Ochuko's cousin, Joshua, took leave of them.

'Yes, I was told you came to see me,' Bridget continued.

'When did you actually return to the country?'

'Last week. I had to compulsorily come to this wedding because the lady whose son is marrying is one my business associates. Her son has been living here for the past fifteen years.'

'That is great. I thank God you met me.'

'It was a gamble.'

Ochuko began the issue of her desire to study abroad. She asked Bridget to help her secure admission in Belgium. Bridget told her it was better if she studied in Germany because there was little or no tuition fee.

'My children have already started and are far into their studies before I knew. Anyway, I will ask my friend's husband who works in one of the German companies to help you secure a visa. When you get there, you can apply straight away to study in a school. It should be faster that way. You can come to Benin City with your passport next week.'

'Why don't I give it to you right away?'

'If you say so, then bring it.'

Ochuko went to her room and came back with her passport, which she handed over to her.

Before Bridget left, she introduced her to her parents. Bridget was a very affable lady. She knew how to worm her way into people's hearts. She spoke and greeted Ochuko's parents as if they had met before. Ochuko dropped Bridget off at the motor park and ensured the taxi drove off before she left.

Akpesiri, Ochuko's uncle, was angry to know that she gave her passport out to a complete stranger to go away with.

'Do you know her?' he asked the silent and staring Ochuko. The enormity of giving away her passport out to Bridget hit her. She had her head bowed and fumbled with her fingers. A sudden fear gripped her. She wasn't sure if Bridget wanted her passport for an ulterior motive or not. Ochuko was engrossed in thoughts and did not hear her uncle's next question.

'I'm asking you,' Akpesiri said, tapping Ochuko lightly on the shoulder.

She jerked. She wanted to start an argument with her uncle but did not find her voice. She wished the ground would open and swallow her. Ochuko was crestfallen. It was five weeks since Bridget left with her passport and had not returned it.

'You just have to go to the police station and declare that the passport of yours is missing. Why were you so naive as to giving your passport to a total stranger? You have not acted like a graduate that you are. You have carried on as if you are not aware of impersonation and human trafficking.'

'We just have to go to the police,' Ochuko's father echoed his brother's words.

They left for the police station almost immediately. Upon arrival, Akpesiri told the police constable that his niece's passport had been taken away by an unknown person for over five weeks and had not been returned. The constable peered at Akpesiri, who, in turn, glanced at his brother. The constable had some tribal marks on his cheek which gave his ethnicity away. It wasn't difficult to know he was a Yoruba man.

'You want to make a complaint about a missing passport?' he asked them.

Chief Nesieama nodded.

'What did you say happened?'

'But I already told you all about it just now.' Akpesiri was getting impatient.

'Do you want to answer me or not?' the constable roared.

Ochuko's father sensed trouble. He knew his brother was hot-tempered, so he took over the talking. He explained to the police constable all that happened.

'You people will have to go to the people trafficking agency in Benin.'

'This ought to be your job,' Akpesiri interrupted.

'Do you want to argue with me?' the constable asked the already-angry Akpesiri.

He tried to suppress his anger and restrained himself from speaking further. He knew if he spoke again, there could be trouble.

He stormed out of the police station. Chief Nesieama was left alone with the constable. He pleaded with the him for help. After a long persuasion, the police agreed they would investigate the matter but that he would be responsible for fuelling their patrol van. He gave Ochuko's father a list of all they needed for the investigation. Ochuko's father thanked him and left. Akpesiri was bitter. He was already fuming when his brother walked up to him. He berated the police force for their corrupt practices.

'Can you imagine his reaction and him telling us to pay for the transportation cost? What is this country turning into?' Chief Nesieama said, corroborating his brother's claims.

He was short of words.

'Well, let us try another police station.'

'They are all the same.'

Both brothers drove to another police station. Chief Nesieama pleaded with Akpesiri to allow him file the complaint this time. He greeted the police officer and gave his complaints. The officer brought out a big notebook and placed it on the counter. It was an old notebook with a cover held loosely by thin threads. Akpesiri looked at it disdainfully.

'Write your statement here. Give the name and address of the suspect.'

The officer flipped through the notebook and pointed at the page on which Chief Nesieama was to write. He confidently took the notebook from the officer and began to write but stopped when he remembered he did not ask Ochuko about Bridget's details. He told the police officer he had forgotten to ask his daughter about the suspect.

'You can't be serious,' the police officer lashed out at him.

'You came here to lodge a criminal complaint, and you do not know the suspect's name. I could arrest you for false allegation or take you as a suspect,' he threatened.

Erhieguke Nesieama was embarrassed. He was a very meticulous man and could never have made such a grievous mistake.

'Officer, let me go back home and get all the details,' he pleaded with the stern-looking policeman and left.

Akpesiri was already getting upset, but he did not utter any word. He had promised his brother he would not say anything when they get to the police station. Erhieguke left the police station with his brother. He regretted not having the name and address of Bridget handy. He kept on blaming himself till they got home. Akpesiri only told him to concentrate on his driving. Ochuko rushed to open the door as soon as she saw her father and uncle through the window. Her uncle wore a long face. Chief Nesieama walked to his favourite spot in the living room, the white sofa close to the bookshelf. From there, he could reach the books with ease.

'Get me some water,' he told Ochuko.

She served her father and uncle some water. Chief Nesieama drank slowly. His brother left his glass untouched. Mercy, her mother, came in shortly after. She had left office earlier because of the ongoing repair works.

'How did it go?' she asked her husband.

'We will go back another day. I forgot to ask Ochuko about her so-called friend's details. I mean, name, address, and so on. I could not make any statement. It escaped my memory totally to ask for those details. So unlike me.' Chief Nesieama was quick to accept his fault.

'Dear, let Ochuko and one of her elder brothers do that. You left your business today just for this problem. Let the children go about it themselves.'

Ochuko and her mother left for the kitchen.

'Those policemen are not civilised,' Akpesiri said, not wanting to hide his resentment.

He was always very critical of the government. Lunch was served. They went to the dining table where they ate quietly. Ochuko returned to her room after lunch. She wished she never gave her passport to Bridget.

She hoped the police could help her recover her passport. They had promised to swing into action.

A loud noise rocked the door and stunned her to life; she rushed to the door and threw it open. It was the househelp, Sisi.

'One woman, dey ask of you, Ochuko,' she informed her. 'She say she be Bridget,' she continued.

Ochuko sprang to her feet at the mention of Bridget and headed straight to the living room, with Sisi following behind.

'Oh! Ochuko, I know you must have been panicking. Mr Helmut, the German man, was on leave, so I had to wait for him to return,' she said without waiting for Ochuko to say anything.

'Thank God, you came in the nick of time. I had given up ever seeing you again.'

'Well, I won't blame you, but I want you to trust me always.' She said handing Ochuko her passport. Ochuko flipped through and stared at the page with the German visa.

She held it close to her chest and twirled slightly.

'Come and sit down. It is a pity my parents are not home. I would have taken you to them straight away with the passport.'

Everything appeared to be in her favour. She got a letter of appointment from a transport agency, and she would be going to Germany to study. Ochuko insisted that Bridget stayed with them and have lunch and celebrate her German visa.

'Ochuko, you really don't have to worry. I have to be in Benin City. Business is waiting for me there.'

Ochuko laughed.

'You are too busy, Bridget. Relax a bit, at least, with me.'

Ochuko was a very hospitable person. She was able to talk Bridget into taking lunch. She dashed to the kitchen to make some quick meal. Bridget could not believe the speed with which the food was cooked. She ate, relishing every morsel of pounded yam and every bite of fish she took.

'You Delta people are true specialists of this white melon soup with okra,' Bridget said, helping herself to some more fish.

'I'm glad you are enjoying the meal.'

Bridget felt lazy after eating but managed to leave before it was 3 p.m. Ochuko was bouncing off the walls because of her German visa. She dreamt of how life would be in Germany. There was a three-month visa in her passport.

'My dream is gradually coming true,' she muttered to herself.

She could not wait to break the news to her family. Her uncle Akpesiri was bewildered that Bridget showed up after a long time. He kept on looking at Ochuko's passport, not believing it was true.

'Wonderful!' he exclaimed, handing the passport back to Ochuko.

It was like an impromptu family meeting in which Ochuko's uncle Akpesiri presided over. While he spoke, Ochuko's passport went round. Her siblings looked at the visa one after the other. Akpesiri suggested they inform the police immediately so that the case could be closed.

Ochuko did not withdraw the case in good time. A team of police from the human trafficking prevention unit arrived in Bridget's home, and all pleas and convictions that the passport had been returned to the owner with a visa fell on hard rock; she was bundled up to their station for further investigation. It took the combined effort of her lawyer and the presence of Ochuko for the force to believe and release her. But the damage had been done, and Bridget was displeased.

A rift developed between Ochuko and Bridget when Ochuko's explanation did too little to allay Bridget's disappointment. Ochuko's family tried to resolve the conflict, but Bridget felt betrayed that she was not briefed when she came to hand over the passport.

Ochuko's travel to Germany was delayed for about a month. Bridget made arrangements for her cousin to receive Ochuko at the airport.

'He will help you with the issue of master's and residency.'

Ochuko left for Germany with the blessing of her parents. Her uncle Akpesiri and one of her siblings saw her to the Murtala Mohammed Airport in Lagos, from where she boarded the KLM flight to Germany. Matthew, the supposed cousin of Bridget, was on hand to pick Ochuko from the airport. He held a cardboard bearing Ochuko's name. Ochuko matched his face with the photo Bridget gave to her. She walked towards him.

'Welcome to Germany.'

'Thank you.'

Ochuko smiled timidly.

Matthew helped her with her suitcase. Bridget had told her not to take too much load, but because Ochuko was a fashion freak, she took with her a lot of trousers and dresses. She had bags to match any shoe she wore. Matthew led the way out of the arrival lounge.

'Hope you enjoyed your flight?' Matthew asked her.

'Yes,' Ochuko replied.

'You must be a shy person,' Matthew remarked.

Ochuko smiled again.

'So you want to study here?'

'Yes.'

'Hmm, German language is very difficult, but we'll see how it goes.'

Matthew got to his car and put Ochuko's suitcase in the boot. He opened the door for her, and she climbed in. She sat down jet-lagged and yawning. She wished she was in bed so badly. Matthew started the ignition and drove off. Matthew was a very lively man. He told Ochuko about his first few years in Germany and how much he missed home. Ochuko smiled weakly. She could not say much. Matthew soon pulled up in front of a four-storey building.

'So I'm taking you to Bridget's friend Aunty Stella. She will help you settle down for a few weeks while I help you sort out your admission,' he informed her.

They disembarked from the car. Matthew helped her again with her suitcase. He led the way as usual, and she followed behind. He pressed a bell beside the door. As soon as he pushed the door open, they both climbed up the stairs till they got to the second floor. Matthew stopped in front of a flat.

'Come in, come in,' came a persuasive voice from an older lady.

'Aunty, good morning,' Ochuko greeted her host.

'My dear, welcome,' she greeted Ochuko warmly in return.

'Bridget gave a perfect description of you.' Ochuko managed a smile.

She longed for a good sleep.

'Sit down, sit down. You do not need to stand there, my dear.'

'Matthew, take her luggage to the guest room.'

Aunty Stella spoke with so much authority. Ochuko thought she must be an assertive person. She went into the kitchen and came back with a tray of biscuits and juice.

'You are fortunate that someone like Bridget helped you. It would have been difficult for you to secure a German visa. What is that your name again?' she asked rather sarcastically.

Ochuko felt embarrassed but did not show it.

'Ochuko.'

'No English name?'

Ochuko was perplexed by the question. She had wanted to ignore her, but because she was Ochuko's host, she decided against it.

'No, madam. I don't have one.'

'OK, let me shorten your name. How about Ochuks or Chukky?'

Ochuko laughed.

'Not bad, madam,' she said.

'So, Ochuks, how was your flight? Don't be shy. Take some juice and that biscuit.'

'Madam, if it is possible, please give me some solid food, like rice or fried egg and bread.'

'I like that. I like people who are honest and straightforward.'

Ochuko saw the motherly side of Aunty Stella. Matthew hailed Aunty Stella as she danced into the kitchen, flaunting her skills. She microwaved some rice and grilled chicken for Ochuko. She laid the table meticulously, ensuring that no cutlery was missing on the exquisite glassy table.

'So, my dear, come over and eat. Matthew, you are not a visitor, so don't expect me to treat you like one.'

Ochuko went to the dining table. Matthew went into the kitchen to help himself.

'Aunty, you know I will definitely not wait for you to even say a thing.'

Aunty Stella moved Ochuko to Hürth, a small town on the outskirts of Cologne some weeks later. She showed her the other young girls who were under her care. Ochuko wasn't quite impressed with their looks and their habits. The apartment was untidy and reeked of cigarette. There was a black ashtray with heaps of cigarette stubs on the window parapet.

There were five young ladies in all. They greeted Ochuko. Aunty Stella introduced Ochuko to them.

'You will be here with them. This is your new home. I will be coming regularly to see you. The kitchen is there. Charity or any of these ladies will show you around,' Aunty Stella said flippantly, pointing at Charity.

Charity smiled revealing her cigarette-stained teeth. She wore hot pants and was having an outrageous Afro hairstyle with a ridiculous colour. As if not done with her weird fashion taste, Charity pierced a small ring through her nose and was chewing some bubblegum triumphantly. She tried to make some bubbles each time she chewed. Ochuko was irritated.

'Make sure you work well and don't get into quarrels,' Aunty Stella told her.

'What work?' Ochuko asked, startled.

The girls burst into a bout of raucous laughter. Ochuko felt foolish and looked about her. She was embarrassed.

'Chukky, you will be receiving clients. You are to work for Bridget. She paid a lot of money for your visa which you have to pay back.'

Ochuko was dazed. She had indicated to Bridget her interest to further her studies. Bridget had promised to help her realise that dream. Here was Aunty Stella singing another tune. Aunty Stella had taken her passport from her with the promise of processing her residential visa before beginning her studies.

'Work,' Ochuko repeated the word again, mystified.

'Yes. You thought she brought you here for nothing?'

'I don't understand.'

'You are to have sex with men – top clients. Make good money. Some percentage will go to Bridget, and I will keep the rest. Bridget spent a lot of money to bring you here. You need to cooperate. You will gain your freedom only when you can pay up all the money.'

She shuddered. She had been blackmailed and deceived. One by one, everything began to fall into its place. She now understood why Bridget kept her passport long after taking it. She began to doubt if Bridget actually knew a German man. All her hopes to study were dashed. Bridget had failed and betrayed her. She had been sold and cajoled into prostitution.

When she arrived in Germany, she had managed to contact her cousin in Lagos. She told him she arrived safely in Germany and would send him an address as soon as she settled. Her cousin was to pass on the message to her parents. Ochuko began to sense there will not be any contact address to forward to her cousin. She felt caged.

'Aunty Stella, please listen to me. Bridget did not tell me all this. She agreed to help me secure admission just like her daughters in Belgium.'

Aunty Stella and the five girls burst into another round of laughter.

'She told you she has daughters in Belgium?' Aunty Stella mocked.

'The girls she claims to be her daughters are all working for her. Don't be naive.'

'Aunty Stella, please get me out of here. Let me go back home instead of doing this rubbish.'

She hardly finished talking when Charity slapped her. Her palm hit her like a sting. She appeared to see a partial eclipse, save for the stars that flashed through her eyes. She turned around holding her cheek.

'You slapped me?'

'Yes. I will do it again if you do not zip your mouth. How dare you say prostitution is rubbish?' Charity retorted

'Next time you should think before you say anything, take care of yourselves, girls,' Aunty Stella said casually.

She went through the door and closed it behind her. Ochuko's cheek burnt. She knew she could not put up a fight with Charity because she looked wild and crude. Charity blew some more bubbles with her chewing gum, then ordered Ochuko to get up.

'You are still brooding over that slap? That is a lesson for you and a welcome initiation.'

Ochuko stared at her without uttering a word. She was stupefied. Charity walked round her.

'You will learn how to dress sexy.'

The other girls giggled. They were nonchalant.

'Follow me. Let me show you around,' Charity ordered.

Ochuko followed Charity about, feeling like a zombie. She was shown the kitchen, bathroom, and bedrooms. She was to share a room with one of the girls. The flat was big, and there were four rooms. It was sparsely furnished. Ochuko and Charity went back to the living room where the other girls were already sitting and chatting away. Charity introduced each girl to her one by one. She got up again and walked to a cupboard and brought out a file.

'Here are the five rules upon which we operate. We are bound by them.'

Charity tossed the file at Ochuko. She tried catching it, but it fell on the floor. She bent over and picked the file up nervously.

'Oh! My dear, that is the right position for a man to bang his woman. It is called the doggy style. The way you bent to pick the file is doggy style.'

No one needed to tell Ochuko that Charity was very vulgar. She quickly stood up, trying to hide her surprise. They all laughed at her again. One of them, Patience, walked up to her.

'Relax,' she told Ochuko, patting her on the shoulder.

'You will soon be used to it.'

Ochuko looked away. She knew she would never get used to selling her body for money.

'That reminds me. This name, you have to change it to something that these Europeans can remember. What was that name Aunty Stella called you?'

Ochuko cast a stare at her.

Charity smacked her lips and snapped her fingers, trying hard to remember it.

'Chukky or Chokky,' Anthonia, one of the girls offered.

'Yes, Chukky is the name. But I prefer Chiko or Chick.'

'Even if I do not know anything, I should be allowed to choose my name. I do not want to be called either Chick or Chiko,' Ochuko said, trying to suppress her disgust.

She left for the room. The other girls were still in the living room, watching some movies. They were wild and too loud. Ochuko could not imagine herself being a prostitute.

She remembered how she lost her virginity to a man who claimed to be interested in her and later abandoned her. Since then, she promised never to have sex with any man. She imagined how it would feel having sex again and with people who just wanted it just for fun and are out to pay for it. Ochuko turned when she heard the creaking sound of the door. It was Angelina, her roommate.

'Cheer up, Ochuko. We all have to do this work. Just try your best. You will be free as soon as you pay up your money.'

Ochuko looked at her. She told Ochuko that she studied chemistry at the College of Education, Ekiadolor in Edo State, but opted to travel abroad because she felt there were better opportunities in Europe. Ochuko was dumbfounded.

'But prostitution is not the solution.'

'Ochuko, you must not let Charity hear you say that. She is an ex-convict and very aggressive. Just play along until you pay up.'

She told her how Charity spent some months in the prison for beating up a taxi driver in Spain before relocating to Germany.

'She is like a man.'

Ochuko was gobsmacked. She knew they were being subjected to servitude.

'Ochuko, worry less. Join us in the living room. I thought I should see how you are faring.'

'That is kind of you, Angelina.'

Angelina waved at her and left.

She wished she could ask Bridget why she had to trick her into this. She pictured how prostitution could be. She could not imagine herself being a sex slave. She shuddered at the thought of becoming nude and a man climbing atop her.

Aunty Stella brought her some skimpy clothes to wear a few days later. Her movement was restricted. Some men had begun visiting them. Charity tried to get Ochuko to be friendly with them, but Ochuko could not cope. She threw up the first day she saw one of the men that came. Angelina had to help her clean up.

'She is sick,' Charity told Mr Simons, the man she wanted to connect Ochuko with.

That was the opportunity Ochuko cashed on. She pretended to be sick. Angelina covered her and made her some tea. Charity decided they leave Ochuko at home. It was 10 p.m. when they left for their business.

Ochuko waited for what seemed like an hour. When she looked at the time, it was almost midnight. She got up from the bed and wore a pair of jeans and a T-shirt. She knelt down and, from under the bed, took a pair of Nike trainers which Matthew gave her. Very quickly, she went to the kitchen to get a small knife. She was prepared to escape from the sex gallows.

She grabbed a jean jacket from the jacket stand and opened the door. She had been told that the handles of the door were made in such a way that it could be opened from inside but from outside, only with the key. She paused awhile before closing the door. She opted to take the key with her. It was dark outside. The lights from the few houses in the neighbourhood in which she lived partially illuminated the narrow road that connected their street to the major road. She passed a stretch of woods on her way. She clutched the knife to her back pocket and walked briskly towards the road.

She hated Bridget and cursed the day she met her. She looked back at every step she took.

She walked for about fifteen minutes before getting on to the major road. Not knowing where to go, she knocked at the first house she saw, but there was no response. Then she walked on, with cars zooming past her. She looked around; there was a sudden dead silence everywhere. She had been warned back in Nigeria not to take a lift, but she was tempted to.

She kept walking on. She knew from the two times she went to the supermarket with her housemates that the city was north of the direction she walked. Not before long, she came to a small hotel into which she walked. She saw the night porter and approached him.

'You speak English?'

'Just a moment,' the porter told her.

He went into the office behind his desk and fetched another man.

'Hello, how may I help you?'

Ochuko told him she was escaping from a woman who was forcing her into prostitution. The man explained to her it was only the police that could help her. She was petrified at the mention of police. She ran out, leaving the man at a loss. He did not understand why Ochuko had to run.

'The police will help you,' he tried to convince her.

Ochuko did not listen. Unknown to Ochuko, the man called the police. They caught up with her near a supermarket. The police called out to her.

'Hey, young lady, it is dangerous to walk alone this night. Follow us. We will help you.'

She looked at the direction from where the voice came. At first, she saw shadows of people cast on the ground. Then she walked slowly towards the shadow. The three men became visible to her. She recognised the man with whom she just spoke at the hotel.

'The police is your friend,' he assured Ochuko.

Ochuko broke down in tears.

'It's OK. We will help you,' the younger officer told her.

She was glad they spoke English. She was driven to the police station and was given a room to sleep for the night. The next day, she gave some statements. She was assured she would be sent back to Nigeria. She was allowed to talk to her cousin. He was glad she came to no harm.

Charity and the other girls returned to the flat and discovered that Ochuko had escaped.

Angelina was alarmed.

'Could she have been kidnapped?'

'Don't be silly. Who will kidnap her?' Charity asked in her usual rude manner.

'Don't rule that out, Charity,' Ngozi, another roommate, insisted.

'Well, let us call Aunty Stella then.'

'Whether she was kidnapped or not, you people have to leave that flat fast. I smell trouble,' Aunty Stella charged over the phone at the other end when Charity informed her about the missing Ochuko.

The police took details of Aunty Stella and Matthew. She could not tell the police where they live, but she gave the address of Bridget.

'It will be difficult for us to go to Nigeria, but we can inform our colleagues there.'

She waited while the police investigated the whole imbroglio.

AUTHOR'S NOTE

1. The story 'Unbelievable Marriage' was originally a short story written in German under the title 'Unglaubliche Flitterwochen'. It won the author the first place at the literature competition at Benedict International Business and Language School, Cologne, Germany, in 2010.
2. The poem *Parish Request* was written for the Catholic magazine *African People's Light* in Germany in 2012.

INDEX

A

Aba 81–2, 161–3
Abeda (Afghan woman) 45
Abosede (Tony and Cecilia's school friend) 120
Abraka 79, 145–7, 150
Abuja 9, 21–2
Adede (Eruke and Izah's daughter) 65–6, 68, 71–3, 75–6, 78–86
Adjoa (Edore's room-mate) 40–3
Afi (Mark's wife) 54
Africa 25, 27, 95, 140, 142, 146
Agbor 79, 84–5, 174
Ahmed (Ekua's boyfriend) 42
Akpesiri (Ochuko's uncle) 164–6, 168
Akpos (Steve Osas's close friend) 36–7
Akpoyibo (Grace's uncle) 119, 122, 124
Alena (Turkish cleaner) 33
Angelina (Ochuko's room-mate) 173–4, 176
Angelique (Steve Osas's fiancée) 36–7, 39, 43
Annabel (Kofi's lady friend) 34
Anton (ship captain) 29–31
Aschaffenburg 38–9, 43
Ashiedu (Enebeli's wife) 79, 84
asylum 36–8, 41–2, 44, 110
Atilogu dancers 150
Augustina (Onome's cousin) 139–42
Augustine (Onome's cousin) 139–42
Aunty Stella (Bridget's friend) 169–74, 176

B

Belgium 161, 164, 172
Benin 84–6, 124, 144, 152, 160, 165
Benin City 93, 152, 154, 160, 163–4, 167
Benjamin (Ochuko's acquaintance) 163
Bible 39, 103–5, 124, 127
Boris (sailing captain) 31–2
Brazil 28–30, 56
Bridget 153–4, 160–1, 163–4, 166–72, 174, 176
Bunmi (John's ex-wife) 147

C

Camara (Christian missionary) 38–9, 43
Catholic Church 61–2, 121–2
Cecilia (Grace's daughter) 119–24, 126–37
Charity (Ochuko's room-mate) 171–4, 176
Chief Natomah (Cecilia's father) 121, 124–6, 129–30, 133–6
Chief Okagbue (Dr Eserovwe's friend) 148–50
Chief Riega (Tare's father) 13, 15
Children's Blue Army 122, 124
Chioma (Chief Okagbue's daughter) 149–50

D

Davies (Grace's cousin) 134
Denis (Kayo's father) 49–54
Donald (Kevwe's first husband) 92–6, 98–103, 105–12
Dr Eserovwe (Onome's father) 139–51
Dr Weiss (physician in Germany) 32–3
Dr Eferhua (Enebeli's boss)

E

East Timor 29–30
Ebi (gardener at Tare's house) 13–14
Ebiere (Mark's fiancée) 50
Edmund (Adede's husband) 85–6
Edore (Lukas Koenig's wife) 24–48
Edward (driver of Cecilia's family) 130, 133
Effurun 78, 154
Eguare, Muesiri 75
Ehor 152–3
Ejiro (Cecilia's cousin) 119–21, 124
Ekpoma 18, 152, 156–7
Eku 76–7
Ekua (Edore's room-mate in asylum) 40–3
Eleanor (Grace's grandmother) 125
Elizabeth (Kate's mother) 74, 104
Emeka (Ochuko's student) 162
Emmanuel (thief) 8–10, 15–22
Equatorial Guinea 125
Erhabor, Steven 120–1
Eruke (Adede's mother) 65–7, 71–2, 76
Ese (Cecilia's eldest cousin) 136
Esohe (Cecilia's room-mate) 130–3
Europe 9, 25, 28, 36, 45, 84, 92–3, 97, 105, 152, 160, 174
Europeans 27, 55, 66, 152, 173
Eyauvie 70–1

F

Felicia (Tare's friend) 11, 14
Frankfurt 39, 55–6
Freitag, Inge 43–8

G

Germany 24–5, 28, 30, 34, 36–9, 41–2, 49–50, 53–4, 59, 62–3, 92–4, 110, 146–7, 168–9, 172
Ghana 105, 115, 117
Ghanaians 33, 40, 55, 101–2, 109, 117
Gina (Ochuko's best friend) 157–9
God 15, 20, 26, 35, 39, 43, 45, 47, 63, 76, 82, 102, 108, 121, 123–4
Goddey (driver of Ochuko's family) 156, 158–9

Grace (Cecilia's mother) 119–22, 124–6, 129–30, 133–5
GRA (Government Reserved Area)

H

Hajia (boss of security operatives) 60
Hamburg 30–1, 47
Hans (Mark's friend) 54–6
Hawa (John's wife) 52–3
Henry (Ochuko's brother) 168
Holland 157

I

Ibo 149
Ifeoma (Tare's friend) 10–11, 14, 22
Ijaw 35, 139
Ilesha 51
Ingrid (Hans's wife) 54–6
Isiorho (Izah's first wife) 66–7, 69–72, 75–8, 81–2, 84–6
Itsekiri 139
Izah (Adede's father) 65–73, 76, 85–6

J

Jahlid (Moroccan sailor) 32
James (Grace's father) 125–6
Jite (Mark's younger sister) 53–4
John (Denis's older brother) 52–3
John (Dr Eserovwe's driver) 146–9
Jos 52
Joshua (Ochuko's cousin) 163
Jovi (Cecilia's husband) 120–1, 126–37

K

Kate (Edore's best friend) 34–6, 39, 72–6, 78, 85

Kayo (Denis's daughter) 49–63
Kayode (Maggie's husband) 51
Kayoghene, see Kayo
Kazuko (Kevwe's Japanese friend) 94–6, 98–102, 104, 107, 112, 114, 117
Kevwe (woman who remarried) 92–118
Koenig, Lukas 24–32, 47–8
Kofi (Edore's visitor) 33–4
Kofi (Kevwe's second husband) 92, 105, 110, 112–14, 116–18

L

Lagos 19, 51, 54, 60–1, 124, 142–3, 150, 168, 172
Laurencia (Grace's mother) 125–6
Legion of Mary 122, 124, 127
London 20, 97, 112–16, 125–6, 133–4, 138

M

Madam Najevwe 67, 70–1, 73, 76–8, 85–6
Madam Tasty 80
Maggie (Kayo's aunt) 51–3
Mallam Musa 52
Mama Ayo, see Bridget
Mama Riode, see Isiorho
Mariaye (Cecilia's aunt) 134–7
Mark (Kayo's uncle) 49–54, 56
Masasi (Onome's Kenyan boyfriend) 138–51
Matthew (Bridget's cousin) 168–70, 174, 176
Mena (Kevwe's eldest child) 94–6, 98–100, 102–4, 107–15

Mitaye (Adede's half-brother) 71
Mother of the Redeemer Charity Centre 61
Moyoma (Kayo's mother) 51–2
Mr Braun (husband of Kayo's boss) 58–64
Mr Ehi (Ochuko's lecturer) 157
Mr Emudiaga (Edmund's father) 84–5
Mr Enebeli (Ruke's father) 79
Mr Idogho (catechist) 120
Mr Nwachukwu (Emmanuel's master in Lagos) 19–20
Mr Okoro (new teacher in Oria) 81
Mr Okoro (principal in Aba) 162
Mr Orofua (principal in Adede's school) 71, 84–5
Mr Osaigbovo (voluntary lecturer) 84–5
Mr Paul (asylum officer) 41, 43
Mrs Adusa (Pastor Adusa's wife) 109, 111
Mrs Aigbe (director of the Mother of the Redeemer Charity Centre) 62–3
Mrs Braun (Kayo's boss) 57–9, 63
Mrs Kelechi (Cecilia's physical education teacher) 126–7
Mueller, Johannes 25–31
Musa (night guard of Tare's family) 13

N

Nancy (housemaid of Tare's family) 15
Nesieama, Erhieguke 165–6
Neumarkt 100, 107
Nigeria 24–5, 33–4, 36, 40, 48, 50, 52, 54–5, 60–1, 105–6, 125–6, 138–9, 144, 152–3, 175–6

Nwakpa, Edward 120
Nwokocha, Angelo 62

O

Obiaruku 79, 83
Obinomba 148–9
Obruche (Isiorho's son) 67–70
Ochuko (Chief Erhieguke Nesieama's daughter) 152–64, 166–76
Offenbach 55
Oge (Kevwe's online friend) 110
Oha 147
Okagbue, Chinyere 149
Omizu, Ogaga 73–6, 82, 86
Oniovosa (Jite's cousin) 53–4
Onitsha 81–2
Ono (Kevwe's youngest child) 95–102, 104, 107–15
Onofere (Kayo's grandfather) 50, 52–4
Onome (Masasi's girlfriend) 138–51
Onyeka (Kevwe's friend) 104
Ore 143, 148
Oria 73, 77, 79, 81–2, 84–5
Osas, Steve 34–9, 43–4
Oteri (Obruche's wife) 69–70
Ovedje (Adede's granduncle) 69–71

P

Pa Grant (Donald's friend) 106–7
Park, Mungo 26
Pastor Adusa (Kevwe's pastor) 100–2, 105–9, 117
Pastor Afolabi (preacher from Warri) 82–4
Paul (Kofi's brother) 116
Peter (orphan) 150–1
Poll 100

Priscilla (Kayo's friend) 62–4

R

Rafa (Edore's room-mate) 40–3
Rafael (Kazuko's boyfriend) 96, 98–9, 101–3, 105, 107–9, 112, 117
Randersacker 43, 45
Richard (Kevwe's online friend) 110–12
Riega, Tare 8–22
Rodriguez (ship cook) 27–30
Ruke (business companion of Adede) 78–86

S

Sanubi 77
Sapele 84, 121, 130, 133, 135, 137, 154
Schweinfurt 37–9, 42, 48
Sisi (cook of Ochuko's family) 167
Sister Regina 122–3
Spaco (rapist) 136
Stella (Emmanuel's sister) 9, 17–19, 21–3
Sweden 9, 18, 20, 22

T

Tin Can Island Port 150
Titi (Ufuoma and Ejiro's mother) 119
Tony (grandson of Grace's great-aunt) 119–21, 124, 133

U

Uchedike (Steve Osas's close friend) 36
Ufuoma (Cecilia's cousin) 119–21, 124, 129–30, 133–5
Ugboroke 139

Ukwani 79–80, 147
Urhobo 35, 79, 84, 110, 121, 125, 139, 145

V

Vero (maid in Tare's house) 8–9
Veronica (Augustine's wife) 141–2
Victor (Stella's fiancé) 9, 17–19, 21–2

W

Warri 66, 68, 75, 78–82, 135, 139, 142–4, 151–2, 154, 159, 161
West Germany 49–50

Y

Yusuf (John's best friend) 52–3

Printed in Great Britain
by Amazon